THE CARRIER

THE CARRIER

Jamal Mahjoub

PHOENIX HOUSE
London

First published in Great Britain in 1998
by Phoenix House

© 1998 Jamal Mahjoub
The moral right of Jamal Mahjoub to be identified
as the author of this work has been asserted in accordance
with the Copyright, Designs and Patents Act of 1988

A CIP catalogue record for this book is available
from the British Library.

ISBN 1 861 59100 4 (cased)
ISBN 1 861 59101 2 (paperback)

Typeset by Deltatype Ltd, Birkenhead, Merseyside

Set in 11·5 pt Bembo

Printed in Great Britain by Clays Ltd, St Ives plc

Phoenix House

Weidenfeld & Nicolson
The Orion Publishing Group Ltd
Orion House
5 Upper Saint Martin's Lane
London, WC2H 9EA

ACKNOWLEDGEMENT

Many thanks to Gillon Aitken & co. for their enthusiasm and support. Thanks also to Rebecca Wilson and staff at Weidenfeld & Nicolson. A special debt is owed to Ahdaf Sovief and Aamer Hussein for friendship and guidance.

CHAPTER ONE

The legend that is Algiers awaits. Its strange and tenacious roots tangle in the imagination. It is like a mysterious, unexplored body to be unravelled layer after layer by the hands of an experienced lover. To the naked eye it sits quite simply like an old horseman's saddle upon the knobbly, twisted spine of the mountains of Kabylia. The harbour, packed with vessels arriving from every conceivable point on the globe, rings to the tune of unfamiliar tongues in the breathless, incessant chatter of humanity and the turn of the tide. A city that lives and breathes salt water and blood, perched precariously between reckless flight and the fall of utter ruin. Mankind presented in its most raw, most desperate form, such that few could resist being both enchanted and repulsed at the same time. It is the most singularly notorious harbour in the world, nothing less, and not a place to venture lightly. Here lurks the legend of Barbarossa and Euldj Ali. Here a man could become king, find his fortune or, if fate would have it, lose everything he possessed, including his life, between a single rising and setting of the sun. Anything and everything the heart might desire could be found within the tightly wound entrails of the casbah, and many had, indeed, lost their way there. A city where the privateers and the freebooters, the traders and the slave merchants, all found shelter from the sea, each of them fighting for their own little piece of the world. This was no longer the age of great empires and kings, but rather a time of petty tyrants, greedy middlemen and pompous stamp wielders. The Dey paid lip service to Istanbul, but little more, for the blue domes and the Diwan were far beyond the horizon. Just as the casbah marked the line between the rulers and the commoners in Algiers, so did the mighty Mediterranean form the boundary between the Sultan and the remote outposts of his empire on the vivid North African shores.

Whatever might have been recorded about the man known as Rashid al-Kenzy has been scattered down the passage of centuries like a fine trail; difficult, if not impossible to follow. A thin and fragile course indeed, leaving only disparate fragments in the way of clues to be pieced together; a task only to be undertaken by the mentally unsound or by the most stubbornly persistent of scholars.

It is said, however, that all of God's creations are blessed in one way or another. Sometimes one just has to look a little harder to find the gift. Also, that a man's fate is tightly bound in a thousand layers of sheer muslin which can take a lifetime to unravel.

The sound of shouting rises from the streets. It is late afternoon on an otherwise unremarkable day in the month of Muharram, in the year of the Hegira 1016, or 1609 in the Christian calendar. In a small square in the Mudajarre quarter lived the al Andaluseen, those who had fled over the years from the wrath of the Unbelievers in Spain. The crowns of the palm trees shook as people scurried across the square with their heads down and their faces shielded against the sting of sharp grains of sand. The Yani-Ceri guards had come for him under a misapprehension; not an infrequent occurrence, but in this case he was luckier than most of the innocent lambs whom the law sacrifices for its own purposes: His neck was to be saved by a curious intervention of fate. But since, of course, he had no idea of the outcome, Rashid al-Kenzy did what any man would do in such a situation – he ran. He ran faster than any man ever ran in his life. He would doubtless have run further too, than any man, except for the fact that in his confusion he had no idea where he was going – just as he had no inkling of what crime he was supposed to have committed. He was terror-stricken and so, although he was a man of reasonable intelligence and some learning, he ran like a goat, uphill, which was a mistake. It was a mistake to run at all, for the Yani-Ceri are many and they are ruthless and they will always, eventually, corner their quarry, unless one happens to possess the ability to transform oneself into a hoopoe bird and fly away over the mountains to the south. They caught him, of course, and they beat him soundly. Then they dragged him by the heels through the squares and the alleys, back through the jeering crowd where the common people spat upon his dusty, soiled form. With his arms held up to his face for protection, he bore the brunt of their hatred. Once a slave, always a slave, he thought to himself. They slashed at him with palm fronds and pelted him with pebbles and stones. The women wailed in despair, beat their faces and tore at their hair in incomprehensible fury. Youths joined in the sport, running agilely alongside, pausing only long enough to thrust the odd kick in his direction. The guards hurried on their way, for they too fell prey to this uncontrolled onslaught. They dragged him unceremoniously off through the narrow streets of the casbah and beyond, winding up through the stone arches and down the curling steps, head thumping like a water bag, into the barrack square. Here they tied him to a stone and left him lying in the sun for two days to weaken him before they unshackled him and dragged him inside.

3

CHAPTER TWO

Later, Hassan was to learn that the whole thing had been triggered off by Mercury – not the substance you find in thermometers but the heavenly body, or rather an artistic rendition of the planet created in stone by a local artist. It was he who discovered the blocks of granite lying on the hillside above the lake. They had been there for as long as anyone could remember, but no one had apparently ever thought to ask how they had managed to get there in the first place. Land surveyors, geologists, generations of farmers, telephone engineers, military advisors, no one had ever asked the question of why and how they had been brought there. Rock of this type was not natural to the region, nor indeed to the country as a whole; somebody had imported it.

It was while they were digging up the massive blocks of stone that they discovered the remains of the body.

A curious beginning, thought Hassan to himself. He was sitting in the car, on a road miles from anywhere. He was lost. He had pulled off the road and then climbed out to begin rooting through the back for a map which he had once owned. That was when it started to rain. He gave up on the map, but by the time he got back into the car, throwing himself inside, he was soaked through, water dripping from his face.

Strange beginnings, then, for this intriguing job.

'Why me?' he had asked, when Jensen told him about it.

'I'm going on holiday,' came the cheery reply, 'and besides, who else is better qualified?'

Hassan strode along the corridor trying to keep up with his senior and somewhat taller colleague.

'I'm just not sure this is a good time for me to leave.'

Jensen spun lightly to face him. Jensen was as quick as a skinny dog. The neon strip lights filtered through the long wisps of silvery hair. 'Don't be so pessimistic,' was all he said, before turning and loping away.

Hassan went home to an empty apartment and sat there in the darkness wondering what had ever possessed him to buy such a large place. Three days later he was on his way. He left Copenhagen at noon, and by four o'clock in the afternoon he was parked by the side of the road, completely lost.

'How hard can this be?' he asked himself, tapping on the wheel, water still dripping onto his clothes. He eased the car back onto the road and spent another hour driving back and forth, criss-crossing, doubling back. Then he stopped again. This time he found the map tucked down behind his seat. The kind of place a small child might have pushed it. He was, he noted, driving on a road that ran almost precisely along the parallel of 56 degrees and 17 minutes latitude.

It was not much more than a bend in the road, an intersection. He pulled onto the forecourt of an abandoned garage, with grass pushing unruly tufts up through the cracks in the concrete. The clouds flung one last virulent handful of rain his way and then scurried off westwards. Disturbed, was the only word to describe this kind of weather. High wind that made trees snap and bristle, interspersed with sudden furious bouts of rain. Already the heavy sheet of cloud had been whipped away to allow piercing sunlight through again.

He climbed from the car, feeling the blood rush back into his legs. A bird was warbling nervously somewhere nearby and water dripped from the bobbing leaves of a large oak. There was a rolling door that no longer closed properly on what must once have been a workshop, and an old petrol pump with a metal gauge that had been disconnected years ago.

He stretched and then, without thinking, he leaned his elbows on the roof of the car, feeling the water soak through his shirt. Perhaps he needed this, he was thinking. Time away from the world, away from himself.

There was a flag fluttering at the edge of the forecourt. He realized, after staring at it for a time, that the building had been turned into a shop of some kind. He went over and pushed open the door. A bell sounded. He moved between the shelves, not really looking. He picked up a newspaper, some coffee, a packet of biscuits. There was a box full of groceries in the back of the car. He didn't need anything.

'Hi.'

She was small in build. She had dark hair, cut in a practical, unremarkable fashion, and a rugged, rural complexion. She was about fifteen, he guessed. She had that awkward adolescent sense of her own presence. The smile vanished from her face and she began to shuffle newspapers and magazines on the counter. He found the piece of paper in his pocket with the address. She glanced at it for a moment, avoiding his eyes, and then turned back to the machine, a hand waving off in the direction over her shoulder. She placed a handful of coins on the counter.

'It's just down the road here, turn right at the end. The house is on the left, green with a broken gate. The old woman lives next door.' He nodded his thanks. She rested a hand on the till, her other hand on her hip, watching as he struggled with the door.

A red tractor appeared as he stood there beside the car. The driver tilted his head in greeting as he went chugging by.

The house was one of the last ones before the village gave way to a depot of farm machinery and then beyond that open fields where he could see cows grazing.

'Yes?' enquired the old woman who answered the door. She was out of breath, a minuscule but sturdy figure wearing an acrylic dress with roses that had long since faded printed on it.

'Mrs Ernst? The museum sent me.'

She peered at him for a moment or two. 'They told me you weren't arriving until Monday.'

'I'm sorry, there must have been some misunderstanding.' He found himself raising his voice, thinking that she had some trouble with her hearing. She muttered something to herself which he didn't catch. Then, reaching a coat from behind the door, she stepped firmly out into the afternoon light. She barely came up further than his waist and seemed to have something wrong with her hip which made her rock alarmingly from side to side when she walked.

'Is that your car?' she asked, pointing a finger.

'Yes,' he replied, faintly amused. 'That is my car.'

'It's a nice car,' she said before wheeling round again and rocking away. He imagined he could hear her chuckling to herself as she led the way.

The house was green, at least as far as the windows and door were concerned. The rest of the walls were simply white-washed.

'My sister and her husband lived here, but then she died and he moved away. She left the house to me. I tried to sell it but nobody wants to live here anymore. Everyone wants to live in town. All the young people move away. In the summer sometimes we get people staying for a week or so.' She talked in a breathless wheeze as he followed along from room to room, switching on lights and opening windows, cupboards, washing machines.

It was a small, unremarkable house, old-fashioned in style. The low roof had once been thatched but this had been replaced by grey tiles, now dotted with clumps of soft green moss. The back door led into the kitchen, which was gloomy, but clean and uncluttered. There was an adjoining living room with a faded sofa and a small table. The front door had been converted into a storage cupboard for brooms and an ironing board. The bedroom was up a short flight of stairs that curled up on itself beside the bathroom. A converted loft room that smelled of fresh pinewood. The walls were slanted so that the only place Hassan could stand up straight was right in the centre of the room. It was nice, he thought, comforting.

'Is everything alright?'

'Fine,' he called back down the stairs. 'It's just fine.'

'There's a girl who comes by once a week to do the cleaning and laundry.' Her voice faded away into the distance as she continued her guided tour.

'Mrs Ernst,' he called down, 'which way does this window face?'

'Pardon?'

'The window. Which direction does the window face?'

There was no reply so he came back down the stairs. She was wiping a finger along the window sill. 'East? West? Any idea?'

She looked at him blankly. 'How would I know a thing like that?'

8

They looked at one another in silence. He turned towards the door.

'You haven't seen the bathroom yet.'

'I'm sure it's perfect.' He smiled, realizing his mistake only after he had spoken. She looked him over again, as though wondering what she might have missed earlier.

'You work for the museum, you said?'

'Not this museum. I work in Copenhagen. They asked me to come over to look at something they recently found.'

'You're some kind of expert then?'

'Something like that.'

The vagueness of his response was not helping matters. She clicked her tongue and began rocking towards the door. 'Well, if you need anything you can just let me know.'

'Thank you.'

When she was gone, Hassan climbed the stairs again. He sat down on the edge of the narrow bed and looked out over the thick green of tall trees. Beyond that the land seemed to fall away and, although he could not be sure, he had a feeling that the lake was there, just out of sight. He lay back and stared at the wood above his head, listening to the silence.

He must have fallen asleep, because when he opened his eyes the room was dark. He went out and collected all his luggage from the car. Holdalls, cases, and a couple of large cardboard boxes with his papers and books. These he set on the small table in the living room, sitting down for a moment. He was thinking about the lake again, and the house. How much, he mused, had things changed in four hundred odd years?

He sat in the kitchen and listened to the silence of the small house for a short while. It was different from apartment silence, he decided, less dark than city silence but wider, as though it

9

were endless. Curiosity made him reach for the telephone. He lifted the receiver; the line was dead.

CHAPTER THREE

The qadi was stretched out full length on a long couch covered in tangerine silk. He was sound asleep and snoring evenly. Kneeling upon the cool, turquoise ocean of Andalusian tiles close to the qadi's feet was a bird-like scribe busy polishing the brass case in which he kept his pens and ink. He looked up when the guards came in and shook his head. 'Come back tomorrow,' he said dismissively, turning his attention back to his polishing.

The first guard said nothing, but merely stepped forwards and gave the couch a firm kick. The scribe protested shrilly, but too late: the qadi shuddered and woke up, licking his lips and rubbing his eyes.

'Well,' he enquired with a yawn, 'what has he done?'

'This is Rashid al-Kenzy,' the first guard muttered.

'Al-Kenzy, al-Kenzy, al-Kenzy . . .?' The qadi pulled a face. 'I give up. What did he do?'

'He killed an honoured and respected member of the community.'

The qadi winced. He pulled himself upright and swung his feet off the couch. He gazed at the floor silently for a moment. 'Did he indeed?' He spoke slowly, without raising his head, 'Who exactly?'

'Maimonides the merchant.'

He raised his eyebrows and looked at the bruised and blistered figure that was Rashid. 'The Jew? You killed the Jew?'

'Sire, I beg you . . .' he mumbled through swollen lips.

The qadi pushed his feet into his sandals, taking his time. He scratched his beard and walked over to the window which faced out onto the bay. 'Don't beg,' he sighed without turning. 'It is humiliating for those who have to witness it. Did you kill this man or not?'

The prisoner shook his head in silence. The qadi shrugged and turned to the guards. 'How did he do it?'

'Sorcery,' said the first one. The second one nodded eagerly. They both immediately began to talk at once. The qadi held up his hands. 'Please, I have two ears, it is true, but even a man as wise as myself cannot listen to two versions of the same story at once.' He examined the two men carefully and then nodded to the first one. 'You are the tallest, you start.'

So the guard began again, and when he fell silent the qadi smiled and held up his hand. 'So . . . this man was in the pay of Sidi Cherif, whose daughter he saved from a painful and premature death, yes? Then, one day he went to his room in the house where he lived and, for some unaccountable reason, he began preparing a loathsome potion with which he took the life of the honourable and respected merchant Maimonides in order to ingratiate himself further with this Sidi Cherif whom everybody knows is, or was, the man's greatest rival.' The qadi paused in his summary, looking from one guard to the other. 'This is a very serious matter,' he declared quietly. 'Who told you this nonsense?'

'Everybody.' The two guards looked at one another, as though in doubt, and then began to speak again, in unison. The qadi waved his hands in the air for silence.

'Who is everybody?'

'The whole quarter was after him.'

'We actually saved his life by arresting him.'

'Maimonides' cleric warned us it would happen.'

'And how,' smiled the qadi, 'would he have known that?'

The first guard, the tall one, stepped forwards. 'Sire, it was this cleric who came to us and informed us of the whole matter.' He shrugged his shoulders. 'How else would we have known what was happening?'

'I ask myself that very question every morning,' said the qadi. 'You know what? I ask myself why God created the Yani-Ceri guards. Why in His infinite wisdom he brought them all the way here from Anatolia to make my life complete?' The guards remained stonefaced, giving no indication that they had the faintest idea what he was talking about. The qadi looked Rashid al-Kenzy up and down and he shook his head in despair. Then he got to his feet and stretched his arms above his head. 'The only magic potion around these days is gunpowder.' He came to a halt, face to face with the first guard. 'Superstition! This is the kind of talk you hear from old grandmothers – the nonsense you might catch in those wretched quarters where the infidels fill their heads with the intoxicating aroma of wine. Let the savages fight it out amongst themselves; why bring these matters to me?'

'The people of the quarter had taken matters into their own hands.'

'They would have killed him for sure.'

The qadi took a deep breath and sighed. 'Would that they had saved us the trouble.' With a dismissive hand he turned away. 'It is not my concern.'

'But what about Maimonides the trader?'

'What about him? He was an old man. He died. Men grow old and die every day.' The qadi rubbed his eyes and sat down again. He stroked the cloth of his robe with one hand. The two guards looked at one another. The second one turned his mouth downwards, but the tall one decided to put his question anyway.

'If the Jew died a natural death, then why should they pick on him?' He nodded in the direction of their prisoner.

'It is obvious, is it not? Look at him.' He gestured at the kneeling man. 'Some men are just born that way.' He fell silent, however, then he got to his feet again and stepped closer to examine Rashid with a careful eye. 'It is curious,' he remarked, almost to himself. 'The dark hue of his skin suggests a man of lowly origins, a slave even. However, the refined manner in which he speaks the language of the Prophet tells us that he is, or once was, a man of some standing or,' he paused, thoughtfully, 'at least of some ambition. He has certainly received some kind of tuition, most likely religious training among some distant herd of fanatics.' He paused, looking Rashid al-Kenzy in the eye. 'He is in all likelihood a reckless and very dangerous man.'

The prisoner kept his eyes on the floor. The qadi clicked his tongue and turned away to pace back towards the window. Through the narrow aperture came the sound of the sea and the rackety whine of the gulls. 'Superstition has a disturbing effect on people. They tend to get nervous and agitated. I would rather put you to death for stealing.' He shrugged. 'Tell me why I shouldn't.'

The prisoner took a deep breath and bowed. 'Although I am not well known in these parts, my reputation is without reproach in the regions of Tarabullus, Cairo and on the island of Cyprus. I may be guilty of many things, Sire, but I am innocent when it comes to the matter of this merchant's untimely demise.'

The qadi held up a hand. 'Your talk convinces me of two

things: firstly, words come easily to you, regardless of whether or not what you say is true, and secondly I am certain that if you truly are not guilty of this sorcery for which you now stand accused, then you must be guilty of something else, and no doubt something equally devious.' He raised his eyebrows as if anticipating some rejection of his assessment. But there was no response forthcoming. He turned to the guards. 'There you have it, gentlemen. Take a good look at our friend here. Look at his eyes. May God be my judge, no matter where he goes I'll wager they find something to hang him for.' He addressed the two Yani-Ceri guards. 'Let this episode be a lesson to us all. The people are easily upset by such matters. An old man dies and their little heads start churning all this nonsense up. And that, my friends, is where the greatest danger to any of us lies; the foolish misguided thoughts that get into people's heads.' He looked from one guard to the other and then, turning away with a grunt of despair, he dismissed the case. 'Whoever he is, throw this man in prison for a month and we will see if we get any sense out of him after that.' Then he waved them away and, stretching himself out on the couch again, he closed his eyes.

Rashid al-Kenzy was born under an unlucky constellation, or so one might conclude from the circumstances surrounding his entrance into this world. He was the child of a slave woman, no more than a child herself at the time, who had long since given up all hope of ever setting eyes upon the village in the lands known as Nubia where she herself was born, or of ever hearing the joyful clatter of clear water gushing through the stony river cataracts from which her people took their name. Rashid's sheer physical appearance added to this sense of misfortune. No, he was not blessed with a particularly robust build, and he was also somewhat below average in height. He could not be described as handsome, and because of the weakness of his bones he had a back which was so curved as to draw comment in whatever circles he happened to show his face. But his heart was pure and, although his God-given talents remained well hidden, his eyes were bright and clear. He was born with his teeth, as they say. God, in his wisdom, gave Rashid al-Kenzy a keen mind and he would indeed need every ounce of that which was given him to find his way out of the maze into which the Almighty was about to cast him.

A sad-faced dog nosed half-heartedly over to the far corner where a deep, square hole in the ground marked the only sanitary arrangements available for the prisoners. In the yard a few figures shuffled about, chains on their feet. The wind picked up a handful of sand and brushed it across the stony ground towards the inner wall where a dark hollow ate its way into the massive rockface of the military barracks which rose up towards the sky.

It was a long, arched stone cavern filled with mournful shadows and extrapolated misery. People sat here and there on mounds of rubble. Rashid al-Kenzy picked out the harsh smell of the other prisoners before the light revealed them. He was grateful for the firm feel of the rock at his back when he closed his eyes to sleep. There was nothing else to do except wait, and he was thankful in his own way for the respite which these prison walls allowed him. If the truth be told, he had grown tired of the lies and deceit which had been his daily trade, convincing trusting people that he could perform miracles of one kind or another.

Rashid al-Kenzy slept for three months, dreaming every night about the wind in the harbour blowing in off the waves, tugging at the long indigo scarf around his head. And then, as he wakes, the wind turns the circle of the quay to leap up the tortured tangle of streets, alleyways and stone stairs, past the casbah, the high walls of the Pasha's palace and the Yani-Ceri barracks to find him huddled, shivering in a corner among the disparate collection of murderers, blind lepers, beggars, and the amputated stumps of thieves. His mind rested for a moment on the square where the palm fronds sway, deep in the Spanish quarter where the Andalusians and the dizzy mariners sip cardamom-flavoured coffee and dream their sailcloth dreams. It was here that he had played backgammon and talked away the evenings. Here, where he had leaned his elbows on the worn tables, stroked the brass cups with his fingertips and listened to the women singing their children to sleep. And it was here that his past had caught up with him, the long, righteous tail whipping down upon him, intent on tearing him limb from limb for his betrayal.

Betrayal?

He had never asked for their trust.

No, he had never asked for their trust, but then again he had never refused it. Soon after his arrival in that windy port, some two years ago, he had awoken one night to the sound of wailing and shouting coming from the street below. His hand reaching instinctively for the long bladed dagger which was always beneath his head, wherever he slept. But as he descended the steps to the torchlit crowd and the flicker of faces thronging the shadows and doorways, he slid the knife away under his clothes. The commotion was coming from the house of the old patriarch, Sidi Cherif.

She was a young child, perhaps three years old. Her heart had grown slow and silent and her tongue was turning black. There was an air of hysteria in the yard of the house where the girl lay stretched out on a thin woollen blanket. Rashid had been nudging himself forwards through the crowd to get a better idea of what was going on when suddenly a clearing opened up before him; the crowd parting like a shoal of fish changing direction in the blink of an eye. He found himself staring into the face of the dying child.

He struggled against the flow to turn and extricate himself, but the crowd had tightened around him. He drew a deep breath and surveyed the chaos before him; the men jostling one another and the women wailing.

'Water,' he muttered to the man standing next to him. 'She must have salt water.' The man did not seem to hear his words. He turned and looked at Rashid for a moment. Then he began gesturing excitedly, shaking and shouting. Rashid found himself suddenly at the centre of the light. They looked at him in expectant silence. He cupped his hands to his lips. 'Salt water,' he repeated, blankly.

It took a moment, but then they seized on this stranger's words as the last hope of salvation. The word went down the street and the water and salt came back up it. Taking the cup, Rashid forced the girl to drink, dribbling the water over her lips and finally forcing it down, holding her jaws clamped shut to make her swallow. She kicked and struggled and then gave way, lying there limply, unmoving. Then the salt seemed to awaken her throat and a shudder went through her entire body, causing it to lift up from the ground into his arms. She coughed, and then again, this time deeply as something inside her belly stirred. A spasm passed through the frail body and she retched, vomiting the contents of her stomach all over him. The women rushed in to embrace the crying child and there on the ground was the long grey worm which had almost killed her.

Rashid rose up to the jubilant embraces and kisses of the people around him. Everyone wanted to touch him, it seemed. Women reached out to brush his shoulder, or tug at his arm, to then touch their fingers to their lips in the hope that some of the blessing, the baraka, would rub off onto them. He felt himself borne aloft on their kindness and gratitude, and he felt something else too – the power which comes from the hands of people. He was swept along on the current of their warmth to the patriarch, Sidi Cherif. A stout, grey-haired man who embraced him fiercely before holding him at arm's length. 'My life is yours,' he said simply.

From that day on he was never in need. People bowed to him in the street when he passed. They begged him to come in and drink tea with them, to wander through their humble homes bestowing his blessings upon their lives just by his presence. It was as though he had become a saint. They called him 'the learned one' when he passed by; 'Good day, ya mu'alim sir!' Merchants delivered goods of every size, shape and nature to the house where he stayed without his even requesting them. Shopkeepers sent him gifts: a jar of their best honey, nuts, apricots, and once even a small herd of sheep, which he gave to his landlord and which roamed the house from that day on until the a'id al Bairam when they were sacrificed and the entire neighbourhood was invited to join in the feast. Merchants and traders invited him to sit with the proprietor and glasses of sweetened warm milk flavoured with cinnamon and almonds would arrive before him. The mothers of eligible girls took to parading them slowly in front of his house or, in the case of the most single-minded of them, to inviting themselves in on the most flimsy of pretexts. Young widows giggled and got into his way, making a show of averting their eyes when he squeezed passed them in the narrow alleyways. When he went to the mosque to pray, people would push friends and neighbours aside and invite him to stand beside them on the worn carpet. Some came to him for advice, for confidential consultations on their private lives: a business venture, an imminent marriage, illness, infertility and every other worry under the sun, all of which he was completely unqualified to comment on. Merchants and traders sent envoys to ask him for advice on the best time to sell or buy their wares. His reputation began to spread. It was said that he was trained in astrological divination and the ways of the stars, that he had studied at one of the most prestigious academies in the east, but which no one knew the exact name or location of. The answers which he was able to provide, often based on pure common sense, were often the most appropriate, but usually were a matter of deciding what people wanted to hear. His knowledge was revealed in the quotations with which he embellished his replies, the examples he gave and the manner in which he spoke. His fortunes began to take a turn for the better as his reputation grew. It seemed there was nothing which this remarkable man was not capable of. He returned to the money lender in the casbah and found the possessions which he had deposited there on his arrival ready and waiting for him, no payment necessary. He had brought a child back from the dead and this was evidence enough of his being blessed with great baraka.

For his part, Rashid al-Kenzy never resorted to untruths or deception. He did not question the whys and wherefores of this good fortune. He was an outsider here, just as he had been in other places at other times. He had learned to be grateful for the opportunities that came his way, whatever they happened to be. To their minds he resembled an unremarkable slave, hardly worthy of attention let alone reward, and this endeared him to them even more. 'This is the way of the world,' he observed to himself. 'Truly no man can fully understand the course of his life.'

Foreboding? Instinct? Whatever it was that he felt, it was

right. For a while they trusted him and then, just like those shoals of fish that circle the oceans, they twitched again and changed direction. The crowd came howling down the stone steps calling for his blood.

It did not exactly happen from one day to the next.

In fact a year went by, precisely a year. Work was finished on the new mosque, the Dey passed quietly away and a new one was found. A ship went down in winter storms on the rocky coast to the east of the city (the only survivors were three silver-tailed monkeys who floated into the harbour clinging to a piece of the wreckage) and Rashid al-Kenzy discovered a grey hair on his chin. But, apart from that – nothing.

Later he would wonder what might have happened had he not embarked on the mission that took him away from that city. What would have become of him if he had not followed that golden arc leading northwards towards the Green Sea, tracing the epicycle of his fate up through the kingdom of cross-eyed superstition, squeezing through the stony Straits of Gibraltar to be swept away north to the ends of the earth? He wondered about this, but he found no answers – what is written is written.

He was not bothered by the other prisoners. They kept their distance ever since word spread of the crime for which he stood accused. One night the captain of a Tunisian caique came to him. He stood over Rashid al-Kenzy as he lay in his corner of the cell.

'It is true you are the one?'

'Which one?' Rashid asked, looking past the man at the group who hovered at a distance awaiting the outcome of this confrontation.

'The one who killed the Jewish merchant.'

'Allah in his wisdom knows that he was an old man, his time was up.'

'Perhaps,' the leader thrust his face forwards and Rashid could not take his eyes off the swollen boil where once there had been an ear, 'you should have let God decide that.'

Rashid looked up at the faces of the men of behind him, men who held the prison in the grip of the terror which they meted out when it so pleased them. It surprised him to note that they were wary of him.

'They say you carry the curse of the devil inside you.'

'To each man his own god,' replied Rashid, carefully. 'I only set eyes upon the man in question once.'

'Then what they say is true? That you cast a spell which brought the most horrible and painful death upon him, using sorcery?'

'I am a simple man of only meagre learning.'

The men were edging forwards to get a better view of the curious figure seated among the dust and rubble of their prison. The captain impatiently waved them away.

'You maintain that you did not do this thing?'

Rashid nodded. The captain turned and signalled to a man who stood in the crowd. He turned back to Rashid. 'You would submit this claim to a challenge?'

'God is the judge of all men.'

'That's all well and good, my black brother, but I have another judge to assist me.' Saying this, he turned and motioned for another man to step forward, a very thin man with a hollow face and bulging eyes.

'This man is known as Ma'sh'allah. He can read a man's heart the way a sailor reads the sea. Give him your hand.'

The convict sailors now crowded round as Rashid held out his hand. The large eyes rolled back in the thin man's head as he gripped Rashid's palm firmly between his. He stroked his fingers back and forth across the palm. After a moment his lips began to quiver.

'What do you see?' snapped the captain.

'He was separated from his brother at birth.' Ma'sh'allah spoke in the accent of one from the marshlands of the eastern gulf. 'He is travelling north.'

The captain was growing impatient. 'What else is written?' he snapped, roughly shoving one of the other men backwards for leaning too far forwards and getting in the way.

'He is looking for the eye. He thinks this eye will enable him to fly across oceans and up mountains. He wants to move the sun and challenge the will of God.' A shudder went through the thin man as though something had startled him. He dropped Rashid's hand and straightened up, pressing himself backwards against the wall of men that crowded round.

'A curse on you, Ma'sh'allah.' The captain was clearly dissatisfied. He threw a fist at the soothsayer's head, but the thin man ducked and vanished quickly out of sight. The captain now turned back to Rashid, who fully expected to receive a sound beating. The captain, however, hesitated.

'Just tell me one thing: what did this Jew ever do to you?'

Rashid considered the question for a moment before replying. 'He called me a slave.'

'May Allah watch over us in our sleep,' one of the onlookers muttered.

'Never mind Allah,' interjected their leader crudely. He stabbed the air with the point of his dagger. 'I'm not closing my eyes while this one is among us. We take turns to stand guard.'

They moved away, leaving Rashid standing alone, saved by a crime he had not committed. From that day on he walked through the prison with his head raised high, for no man dared to even look him in the eye, lest he might be smitten by some terrible curse.

CHAPTER FOUR

This is how he came into the world.

The region of Aleppo in the season of drought, some thirty odd years earlier. The esteemed silk merchant Sayed Abdelrahman al Jabri lay sweating in the suffocating silence of the listless afternoons in that intolerably long summer, when the apricots were burned crisp and brown before they could be plucked from the branches of the trees. In the orchard behind the big house the harsh sun had shrivelled the leaves into dangling, thirsty tears of amber. He had lain, day after day, and sweated the hours sleeplessly away. Through the thin drapes that hung limply from the open windows dry puffs of cloud could be seen drifting by like smoke. As far as the eye could see there was nothing but barren land. Even the joyous glint of water, usually visible high up in the mountains, a glorious, shining affirmation of life, had vanished weeks ago. An air of pessimism had fallen over the region. No one could remember the sound of rain, except when tormented in their dreams. People no longer bothered to lay out their dwindling wares in the market place, as their customers now came knocking at their door before the sun had even shown itself in order to secure whatever was available.

The thoroughly barren and savage nature of the transformation which the land had undergone began to make itself manifest in the people. Fights broke out without warning, to be resolved as swiftly as possible in the sweltering heat which resulted in the protagonists resorting to using methods that, under normal circumstances, would be loudly condemned: knives, swords, an arrow through the neck – whatever came to hand. No one could bear the thought of expending energy on a protracted fist fight. Abdelrahman's temper was similarly affected. He stalked through the house yelling commands here and there, cursing in such vulgar language that the neighbour took to stuffing wax in her ears.

So he lay there alone, day after day, sweating. There was nowhere to channel his frustration, to vent his fury and anger. God he had already called upon, on countless occasions, but to no apparent avail – the harvest was lost. Unaccountable delays prevented the caravans from reaching them. Already his trade was beginning to suffer. No one wished to venture into a barren valley such as this.

So he just lay there unable to sleep, and with each day that passed so it seemed that his irritation grew, compiling, compounding, building itself up. Then one afternoon on his way up the stairs he almost tripped over the servant girl Butheyna. She had been with the house for over a year, pleasant, but not very talkative. He had often considered whether he had made a mistake in accepting the offer of her services from a bead trader returning from business in Cairo. He took her in mostly as a favour and because it would have been ungracious to refuse such a gesture from a good customer. Her skin was the dark brown variety known from Upper Egypt and the untamed lands of Nubia beyond. He had hardly noticed her really, but had on occasion heard her sing. She sang to herself and the other servants, her voice drifting from the shambling quarters behind the house up the high walls and circling the verandas, lending an agreeable note to the quiet evenings. She sang in a low, vibrating lull which he associated with primitivity, peasants and people with mud on their hands but it was, in its own way, engaging. In all truth he realised, as he straightened himself up on the stairs, he had never looked at her properly before. She was small, and young, not beautiful, but rather plain. Her skin was smooth and, although no more than perhaps fifteen years of age, she nevertheless had the figure of a woman about her.

'This accursed dust gets everywhere,' he observed in an irritated tone. 'When you have finished here, there is a corner in my room . . .'

As he lay there that afternoon he knew he had no intention of even trying to sleep. He watched as she bent to the task, and as she scrubbed meticulously away he felt his problems lift – literally; he had found a solution to the long dry afternoons. He called her gently to his side. He took her hand in his and gazed into the round dark eyes which shone with the strength of simplicity and wisdom. He had lived for three times as many years as she and yet, when confronted with such open confidence in the face of the world, he wondered how much of that time he had wasted. His resolve, however, did not falter for long. He chattered away in a light-hearted, amusing fashion. When he asked her what she knew of the ways of men, she replied that her grandmother had told her that, 'If the prophet had been a woman, no one would have listened.'

Such a reply intrigued Sayed Abdelrahman and he asked, 'How did you come to be a slave?'

She told him that her family had been convinced by the people of the village that she was a source of evil, that her tongue was manipulated by the devil. 'Not so long ago they used to sacrifice young girls to the river gods in those regions,' she explained matter of factly, no doubt resorting to the wisdom of her grandmother again, he decided.

'Surely,' countered the master, his curiosity warming his heart, 'that was before the word of God reached them?'

The girl snorted and shook her head like an impatient mare. God or no God, bad fortune befell the village, sickness and fever. They sold her to the first traveller who came passing.

Abdelrahman was entranced by the spirit of this womanchild. A bead of sweat ran from the ridge of her neck to vanish down the front of her cotton shift. She smelled faintly of sweat and had an honesty that engaged him. He found that the animated way in which she expressed herself only inflamed his passion further. He ordered her to stop talking and to join him, which, resignedly, she did. For the next five weeks he spent the afternoons this way, struggling and cursing, gasping and moaning, pouring out all of his built-up fury and frustration into this patient, enduring girl.

At the end of the five weeks, two things happened – first of all his wife, curious about his lack of attention, decided to take matters into her own hands and insisted that he spend the afternoons in her company. Secondly, the rains came. Day after day the deluge fell, with drops as large and heavy as fish flopping and splashing through the streets in torrents. The long drought was over.

As luck would have it, in that long barren summer, not one but two children were conceived.

Rashid was born in the month of Ragab, indeed he was born in the same month and even on the very same day that Sayed Abdelrahman's wife gave birth to the son of the house – his half-brother Ismail. One might even venture that in some sense these two boys were inextricably linked, as two parts of a whole, comparable perhaps to the stars that make up Gemini, but as is the case with that constellation, they were not really equal at all but rather two separate halves of the same thing. They were born, as it is said, in one another's embrace. Although he was his father's son, Rashid would never come to know Sayed Abdelrahman as anything but a master.

Otherwise, Rashid al-Kenzy's arrival in this world was a smooth one. Butheyna lay in the bare room where they lived and felt the night air cool the beads of perspiration rolling down her body. She would not let out a single cry, not give a sign that she was even in the house, let alone giving birth. Not that she would have had much chance of being heard above the alarming racket that was coming from the upper floor of the big house.

Later she would recount to her son how she lay with him in her arms listening to the continued screams coming from the mistress of the house, whose labour continued unabated for the next nine hours, by which time most of the guests had either fallen asleep or gone home in exasperation, unable to bear the noise any longer. When Ismail finally arrived, tearing the night in two with his cries, the whole town gave a sigh of relief and turned over on their sides to get some sleep. The midwife herself said that she had never before seen a child with such a large head and departed from the house three days later muttering over her shoulder that the master would be sure to take a new wife soon since there was little hope of any man finding satisfaction where that monster had passed.

For a time the two boys grew up together. At that young age they knew little of the differences which separated them. As soon as they were able to stand, they would run together for hours, chasing through the long dusty groves of the orchard behind the house where the apricots grew. The men who worked the land laughed with them in that innocent manner with which small boys and men play. Together they entered the Kuttab school, with Rashid walking two paces behind his half-brother. Already by the age of five, Ismail had learned something from his mother.

Rashid had learned something too. He had learned from the eyes and rough comments of the farm workers that he was no longer a child, that being sent to the school was a privilege to which he was not born. They were reminding him that he was one of them. The older boys took pleasure in chasing him through the fields, but this time it was to punish him, for he had no father and everyone knew what that meant. They beat him and held his head down until he thought he would drown in the sweet, choking earth. They said that the master of the house would not be satisfied, that in addition to black slave women he also had a passion for little boys with soft skin.

And if the master's actions caused distress outside the walls of his fine house perched on the hillside of Aleppo, then they provoked at least the same degree of concern within. Ismail's mother had descended into the gulf of misery and madness since the day she learned that she had a rival for her husband's affections in the servants' quarters. Her shame consumed her. She shut herself away on the uppermost floor of the house, refusing to show herself to family or friends. She engaged a new slave girl to attend exclusively to her needs. This girl scurried down the stairs when her mistress had fallen asleep and sat in the kitchen, entertaining the wide eyed servants with her tales: the mistress had become as thin and twisted as a vine stalk; she sat with her head over a brazier of incense until all her hair fell out; she covered herself in black and scattered ashes in her wake wherever she walked.

When the boys reached the age of thirteen the feki was sent for. He arrived looking tense and worried, hurrying up the stairs, muttering to himself in that loose-lipped fashion of his. The time had come to discuss the matter of schooling. Sayed Abdelrahman stood in a favourable light. His contributions to the Sultan's tax office and indeed locally to the Wali's own purse had added up over the years to a tidy sum, but the guardians of learning were notoriously protective about who was granted the honour of entering the prestigious madrasa.

The feki spoke rapidly. It was true that in this particular case there was a great blessing upon the house. The eye of God was firmly upon them, no doubt due to the goodness which resided in the pious heart of the master of the house. Abdelrahman smiled benevolently as he always did when compliments pleased him. 'Thank you, Haj, God will surely increase your prosperity.'

The older man nodded and bowed, but was impatient to get on with his speech. He continued his enthusiastic felicitations. A son born to the house would bring great honour upon his father's name. The smile stretched from ear to ear on Sayed Abdelrahman al-Jabri's rather broad face. He looked foolish and vain. He was of course filled with paternal pride and, getting to his feet, he made for the door of the reception room and began calling for Ismail to be brought to him. The feki spluttered and coughed and nearly swallowed his tongue. There had been a misunderstanding. He had not put his case clearly. He bowed his head deeply. Perhaps he had presumed too much.

The master of the house was mystified and growing increasingly impatient with the doddery feki and his impenetrable mumblings. 'Spit it out, man!' he snapped.

Tongues were of course known to wag, began the feki. Not that he paid any attention to such malicious tongues, but he had assumed that Sayed Abdelrahman had adopted the other boy as his own, and that sending him to the Kuttab was a means of making public this fact. Sayed Abdelrahman remained unmoving, a blank stare on his face. The old feki licked his lips. It was obvious, surely, that Ismail, despite the size of his head, had difficulty in catching hold of anything, let alone retaining it. The words seemed to wander around, being unable to settle down in all that empty space. He was restless, that was his nature. He was quick to take action, but slow to consider the consequences. He had established a reputation for himself as being sullen, impatient, unforgiving and petulant. Of course the old feki was not foolish enough to state all of these things plainly. However, what was obvious was obvious. The other boy showed more promise. His mind was swift as a hawk. He did not repeat what he did not understand and he was not afraid of asking questions. The feki summed up his conciliatory argument: 'Send the two boys, sire. Together they will bring great honour upon our fair city and indeed upon this house.'

The life seemed to go out of Sayed Abdelrahman. He slumped down on the divan, his shoulders bowed. Nothing ever seemed to be simple these days. 'My wife,' he sighed. 'I once considered the matter of releasing her and the child,' he mumbled into his chest, 'but that would be irresponsible. Where would they go and what would become of them?'

The old feki nodded in sympathy. 'They would be covered in shame for having being released from service. No slave has ever found happiness that way. Why I recall—' He stopped abruptly, noting the hand which Abdelrahman held up for silence. This was not the time for dispensing anecdotes.

'They would be destitute. No one would take them in for fear that they possessed some terrible vice or, worse, carried a sickness.'

The facts of the matter were plain: Ismail would not last a week under the rigorous demands of the madrasa, but if the other boy were sent as his personal slave then . . . together . . . The feki held up his hands in a sign of cautious optimism. Abdelrahman scratched his beard. He had aged ten years in as many minutes, it seemed. He nodded his agreement wearily. 'The Almighty sees fit to teach us at every turn of the way.'

'Each day some mighty task engages him,' supplied the teacher with a smile, and no sense of irony.

It was in this way that Rashid came to pass through the gates of the prestigious school which thus marked the start of the curious and convoluted path of his education. The madrasa was divided into four rooms with an outer circular wall linking them. The first was a mosque; the second was for the study of the Hadith, the traditions, the sayings of the Prophet Mohammed; the third was devoted to the teachings of history and law. Here one could learn of the exploits of Salah al-Din and the fall of Jerusalem, of Nebuchadnezzar and his kingdom of Babylon, of battles victorious and the heroic exploits of old. The last room was for teaching the ways of the Sufis. It was here that Rashid found himself lingering, listening to the sounds of their chants and wondering what mysteries their devotions contained.

At first the two boys attended classes side by side. They were equal, although one of them was, of course, more so than the other. In time Ismail's impatience manifested itself more openly, as did his lack of concentration and his scorn for the world at large and for his teachers in particular. He was his mother's child, sighed Sayed Abdelrahman mournfully, exempting himself from all responsibility. Butheyna did not understand a word of what was going on and insisted that when Rashid came home in the afternoons he went straight to work plucking chickens and grinding flour just as he had always done. She was afraid of that stream of gibberish which came from his tongue, placed there by those turbanned greybeards from the madrasa. She would mutter under her breath, begging the Almighty to take the devil's earth from her boy's mouth. Rashid in turn explained patiently that everything they were taught was knowledge which came with the blessing of the Prophet attached to it.

'That may be all very well in the big house, but your place is here in the kitchen, and don't you forget it.'

So Rashid grew selective about what he told his mother. He did not, for example, tell her that he went secretly every afternoon to the quarters of Sayed Abdelrahman when the household was sleeping, just as she once had. The entertainment he afforded the old man was, however, of a rather different nature, for he simply recited what he had learned that day. He did not mention to her that his real interest lay in the Revealed Sciences, that is to say, science as described in the holy texts. Nor that he dreamed of the splendour and wisdom that was Samarkand. His mind wandered up and down the pages of history until he no longer knew which age he inhabited. He forgot that the days of Harun al-Rashid were over and that the observatory at Samarkand had long since been consigned to dust and ashes. He was encouraged in his quest for knowledge by one of the masters of the Sufi order which resided at the school. His new friend was named Nuraddin – the light of faith. Nuraddin taught him many things, and some years later was to lead him over the eastern mountains to the outcast colony of scholars which was known as the Valley of Dreamers.

'In the old days there was no limit to knowledge, all knowledge was one and thus equal,' Nur would tell him. 'It was the magnificent al-Kindi who taught that we should recognize every form of knowledge, no matter where it might come from, even foreign sources.' He raised a finger as he recited, 'For him who seeks the truth there is nothing higher than truth itself.'

'When was this time?' whispered Rashid.

'Hundreds of years ago. When the learning of the Greeks first came to the language of the Prophet, may God preserve him.'

'How did the Greeks become so wise?'

'They did not know everything. They were clever and could calculate things with reason. But the Ancient Greeks did not have God like we have. There is always some aspect of knowledge which Allah alone holds the key to. That is why they eventually fell into decay.'

Rashid spent hours staring off into the empty air, trying to make sense of things. His mother was driven half crazy with exasperation at the strange ways which had taken possession of her child. In time the favouritism shown him by Sayed Abdelrahman became more noticeable. Ismail's lack of ability was made all the more obvious by the bastard sibling's aptitude. Malicious tongues wagged and before long everyone knew that the master of the house had passed his wisdom and intelligence to the servants rather than to his own wife.

And so, on the night that Ismail Abdelrahman al-Jabri passed away out of this world on a most untimely tide of fever, the tragedy was complete. A cry of anguish rose up towards the heavens in a singular expression of united grief. The line of people who came to pay their respects wound out of the city gates and circled around the ancient sloping walls. Rashid found his mother weeping alone in the servants' quarters behind the chicken fences at the back of the house. She wrenched at her hair and her eyes ran with tears. 'Weep, oh child, for the world has reached its end.'

He said nothing. He knew, of course, that she was right.

The mistress of the house appeared on the veranda overlooking the courtyard and the fountain the very day after her son had died. No one recognized her at first, having not seen her in broad daylight for fifteen years. Her skin was so pale as to be almost transparent, her eyes were swollen and her hair was as white as chalk. She stood there gripping the wooden balustrade and grinding her teeth, flecks of spittle spilling from her lips. She did not have to say a word.

They fled that night. Their belongings wrapped in sacking.

The bruised eye of the moon picked out the destitute refugees in the cradle of the dark arch of night. Nuraddin rubbed his eyes and said that the situation was grave. He looked at the mother and the child and agreed that they would find little shelter now that they were relieved from service. Nobody would take them in out of respect for the name of Abdelrahman al-Jabri and out of the fear that they carried with them some evil curse. There was no alternative but to leave the country.

'It is the boy who concerns me,' said Butheyna. 'I want my son to have a chance to live his life freely.'

Nuraddin sat for a while to think the matter over. 'You are a bright boy, Rashid,' he pronounced after some time. Butheyna had fallen asleep and the Sufi was yawning. 'What do you want to do with your life?'

'I only wish to devote myself to studying the universe in all the wonder in which God created it.'

The Sufi teacher almost laughed, before realizing that the boy was sincere. He nodded his approval. 'The only freedom in this world is learning. But you cannot remain here. There is a place you can go. A place where for decades men have sought freedom from those who would shackle their minds and bodies.'

'Where is this place?'

Nuraddin smiled. 'One week of travelling, to a place that few have heard of and even fewer have visited. It is known as Wadi al Halimeen, the Valley of Dreamers. There you will be safe.'

CHAPTER FIVE

Hassan rose early and paid a call on Mrs Ernst, who informed him that her cousin had borrowed the plug from the telephone, but that she would tell him to return it as soon as she got hold of him. Hassan got into the car and drove across the top of the long fields, dropping down the winding road that cut through a narrow gully leading past the prow of the lake. He pulled off the road, leaving the car on a grass verge beside a wooden gate. There was no one around. On the sparsely wooded sides of the valley behind him there was a dappled white horse nosing in the long grass, its long tail flicking up from the dewy ground from time to time. He climbed over the wooden gate and walked down the grassy incline towards the water. The air was cold and the surface of the water calm and motionless. On the left flank, which he worked out must have been due east, there was a plantation, a thickly wooded rectangle of straight pines that marched like a column of foot soldiers towards the lake. People look at a landscape and think it must have been like that for all eternity. The idea that the ground under one's feet is reliable. The plantation trees were no more than thirty years old. Before that this would have been open, unkempt moorland shaped by the last ice age. The ground rose above the plantation in a bare and windy sweep towards a flattened shoulder where a small collection of farm buildings could be glimpsed. The elevation of the lake made the hill seem higher and sharper than it actually was. Nevertheless, it stood out from the landscape and there was something commanding about the way it rose above the lake. Above the farm buildings he could make out the excavation site, small bright squares of white canvas flapping against the dark hill.

He drove up through the trees listening to the hum of the engine. It was going to be a warm day, dry and sunny. The sound of voices reached him as he climbed from the car beside the farmhouse. A girl wearing shorts and large wellington boots walked past. She had light blonde hair tied into two sensible pigtails which rested on her shoulders. Hassan called out a greeting and asked for directions and she pointed up the hill towards a tent just above the farmhouse. He nodded his thanks and pulled his bag out of the car.

The tent was a makeshift office. Long trestles stretched the length of it and various items had already been laid out and tagged. Kneeling on the ground was a stocky figure with long, thinning strands of white hair that hung down around his face, and a thick grey beard.

'Hans Okking?'

The man looked up, peering over the top of his glasses. He dusted off his hands as he got to his feet.

'Yes?'

'I'm from the Near Eastern Institute in Copenhagen.'

Okking stared at him for a minute before speaking. 'I was expecting Jensen.'

Hassan smiled, looked around him and finally shrugged, 'Well, you got me instead.' Okking was still staring at him. Hassan shifted his briefcase from one hand to the other and began to elaborate. 'He felt that due to the nature of the material, I would be best suited to the task. He was going to try and reach you before he left for Finland.'

'I see.' Okking peered for a moment at Hassan's briefcase. Then seemed to make up his mind. He threw a hand up in the air. 'Not to worry. If you're here, then it's your job.' He led the way out into the open air. 'Let's go up and take a look, shall we?'

There was a path that wound between the small house and a number of farm buildings. A cow peered out through an open doorway as they passed. The path was sandy and well trodden.

'We've been lucky,' said Okking.

'With the weather, you mean?'

'Driest summer since records began.'

Okking's plump outline was misleading. He was powerful and shot quickly up the hill without let-up, showing no signs of strain from the fast pace. Hassan, who was half the other man's age, struggled to keep up. He arrived sweating and out of breath at the top of the hill to discover to his surprise that a complex series of interconnecting trenches had been uncovered.

In the warm sun the volunteers were hard at work. There was a light-hearted air about the team; they were enjoying the good weather. A steady stream of light conversation flowed back and forth between them. There were perhaps fifteen of them in all, some kneeling, some resting, others poring over tiny fragments. Hassan jumped out of the way just in time to avoid being knocked down by a heavy wheelbarrow pushed by a large girl whose head was shaven down to a thin covering of bristles. Okking was talking again.

'The rock is sharp edged, chiselled, not like the boulders you sometimes find which were carried here on glaciers in the Ice Age. At first we thought it was some kind of military installation, a fortification of some kind, with the trenches and the rocks.'

'Was there anything here that needed defending?'

'That is precisely the point. It made no sense. No records show anything of that sort.' Okking was leading the way round the excavation site. He was explaining about the statue of Mercury. 'He was going to do each planet in the shape of a woman,' he grinned. 'Can you imagine?'

They came to a ladder which led down into the deepest of the eight trenches. It was easily wide enough for the two men to stand side by side. At the far end a canvas awning hung down like a curtain. Okking pulled this aside and motioned for Hassan to have a look.

Hassan leaned forwards into the gloom. A space had been cleared, a neat, square-shaped hole dug into the hillside. Inside this cavity, the sides neatly brushed aside, lay the remains of a human being. The skeleton was still remarkably intact, except for the head. The body was lying on its right side, curled up – like a child sleeping, thought Hassan.

Okking was down on his knees again. 'You see here?'

'The skull is fractured.'

'By a violent blow. The body was lying with its head sticking out. Somebody, whoever buried this fellow, had not dug far enough in. He had to break the skull to make it fit.'

'You've been doing some detective work.'

A blue eye winked. 'We borrowed an expert from the coroner's office.' Hassan was beginning to take a liking to Okking.

The whitened bones were spread out like a puzzle on the ground before them.

'A ritual killing?'

Okking beamed, pushing the long hair out of his face. 'Don't let your imagination run away with you. He was in a coffin and there are no unusual signs, artifacts, items of any significance. Considering that there must have been a lot of money around at the time – to pay for the stone for one thing – it is a very humble burial. Either there was something odd going on, or it was because he died in the construction of these strange trenches.' The broad face inflated into an even wider smile. 'A real mystery story we've got for you here, eh?'

'Do you have any idea who he might have been?' It was warm in the trench, sheltered as it was from the breeze coming off the lake. He caught the faint smell of unfamiliar perspiration coming from the archaeologist as they climbed back out. Okking's face was slightly flushed with the heat. He pointed down the hill.

'There was another building on this site where that ugly modern thing is. Quite a large house, we think; some of the sheds there still have bits of the old structure in them. It burned down perhaps in the middle of the seventeenth century, maybe earlier. We would like to have a proper look down there, but the farmer is a miserable bastard and we have to have the legal thing sorted out first.' Okking stretched a finger towards the distance. 'It would have covered about four times the area of the present building. It belonged to a man named Heinesen.'

'A wealthy estate, then?'

The corners of Okking's mouth turned downwards. 'We don't really know. Records are incomplete.' He reached into his overalls for a pocketknife and produced a large red apple which he then meticulously began to peel. 'But, based on the size of it, I would say probably that is a good guess.'

'That would coincide with this,' Hassan nodded at the skeleton. Okking licked his lips and put a slice of apple into his mouth, holding it between thumb and blade.

41

'This was an area where they raised horses. Lucrative trade in those days, you know.'

'Horses?'

Okking led the way back to the larger tent. A man with thin black hair was kneeling on the ground by the entrance. Okking introduced the visitor. 'Jens, this is the man they sent to read that gobbledygook we found.'

Jens got to his feet, pushing his spectacles back up his nose and leaving a dirty smudge on the tip in the process. 'Arabic,' he said in a quick, nervous voice. 'I think it's Arabic.' He looked at Hassan for a moment without saying anything. 'I'm not sure, of course.' He turned to Okking. 'I thought they were sending Jensen?'

'He couldn't make it,' said Okking, waving the matter aside quickly. 'Come on, where did you hide it, then?'

In a roped off corner of the tent there was a collection of odd items. Jens stepped over the rope and carefully lifted one object up. Giving it a few strokes with a soft brush he produced from his pocket, he placed it on the table at the centre of the tent. There was a strip of leather, upon the inside of which there was an elaborate inscription, like a tattoo of lines and whirling letters. When this was laid to one side it revealed a small, oblong box. It was made of brass. About the size of a shoebox, although not very deep. The upper surface was engraved with more script. On the front of the box there was an intricate latch which the one named Jens slipped open. He stepped back and held up his hand towards Hassan, beaming like a waiter uncovering a culinary masterpiece.

'There you go. Your guess is as good as anyone's.'

By the time he drove back towards the house, daylight was beginning to fade. Hassan felt suddenly tired. The elation of the day's discovery was now tempered by the fact that he had an empty house to go home to.

He stopped in at the shop on his way back. The girl he had met the first time was gone, replaced now by a tall, lanky boy of about nineteen or twenty. He had jet black hair, dyed in some way, that was too long and hung down óne side of his face, so that he had to keep flicking it out of the way.

The boy's eyes moved restlessly, avoiding any kind of contact. Hassan peered around the shelves. He was not hungry. He peered into a freezer cabinet and pulled out a chicken dinner. He hesitated for a moment in front of the shelves of beer. Then, finally, cautiously, he picked up a bottle and began reading the label.

'It's cheaper if you buy a carton of six.'

'Sorry?'

The boy pointed at a stack behind Hassan. 'There is an offer on those ones. You get six for the price of five.'

Hassan looked round at the stack of cartons, then over at the boy behind the counter.

'I don't know this brand, is it any good?'

'It's a local brewery.' The boy shrugged. 'Everyone drinks it.'

'OK, why not?' Hassan waited while the boy rang the items into the till. 'Tell me,' he asked. 'The church across there. Do you know how old it is?'

A blank look came over the boy's face. He had probably lived all his life here, but it had never occurred to him. 'The church?' He shook his head finally, relieved. 'No idea.'

'It doesn't matter. I can find out.'

'The priest lives in the small house across from the church. He would know.'

'Thanks.'

The boy gave a nervous grin.

Hassan picked up his bag of groceries and said goodbye. He wondered if the boy and girl were brother and sister, if this was a family business. As he was crossing the road a car filled with young local boys screeched to a halt outside the shop. The small vehicle reverberated with the sound of laughter and the pulsing beat of music. Who cared about how old a church was?

Later that evening he sat down at the table in the living room. He cleared away the pile of books and papers he had unceremoniously dumped there the day before and set the brass case down. It was wrapped in a scrap of cloth, the corner of a grey blanket, which he pulled aside, the smell of earth filling the room as he did so. He stared at the box for a moment, then got to his feet. He went through to the kitchen and opened the last bottle of beer. He stood there in the doorway, staring at the table where the brass gleamed dully in the small circumference of light provided by the table lamp. It was off to one side, he realized, in the region only partly illuminated by the light. This, Hassan recalled, was what was known as the penumbra, an area of partial shadow such as occurs when there is an eclipse, the moment just before, or just after complete darkness. He was peering into the past and yet, he realized, he was seeing only a portion of what had once existed.

He remained there in the doorway for the time it took him to finish his beer. A single car drove by in the distance. Then there was silence. Finally he could put his curiosity off no longer. He sat down at the table and took a deep breath. Then he stretched out a hand and slid the latch to one side and slowly, carefully, raised the lid of the brass box.

CHAPTER SIX

The narrow stone chamber lies hidden far below ground. It is not an easy place to find among the endless succession of stairwells and gloomy corridors. An insular, circular chamber. At the centre of the room stands Captain Quraishy. He is short, robust and his skin is hardened and polished by sunlight and salt water. His head is bound in a grubby piece of what might once have been quite fine silk. There is a button missing from his waistcoat. He stands uncomfortably in this unfamiliar and daunting location. He was the captain of a small vessel which, although it was rumoured to have been known to carry legitimate cargo at times, was better known for its enterprise in privateering, preying on other ships, stealing what their holds contained and scuppering them in the process. Quraishy was about as untrustworthy a man as anyone could ever hope to encounter. But he could also be persistent and stubborn and it was his refusal to speak to anyone else that had eventually drawn the qadi's curiosity.

'Speak.'

The captain cleared his throat, straightened his heavy, round shoulders and looked around the room for a moment before speaking. If he felt intimidated by his surroundings, then he did little to show it. He was smart enough to know that this was precisely what the qadi had in mind, sending for him in the middle of the night, bringing him here instead of the usual public reception chamber in the main hall of the palace. He licked his lips and gave a short bow, tilting his head slightly forward from the neck and no more, and introduced himself.

'I have seen many things in the short life which the Lord of the heavens has seen fit to permit me. This story is one of those curious matters which a man happens upon perhaps once in a lifetime. The paths of our lives cross one another constantly and yet often we are unaware of what has been passed before our very eyes. It is our duty to prepare ourselves to receive the most bountiful gems from whatever unlikely quarters they might arrive.' He paused for breath. He had prepared his speech carefully and so thought it strange that he should detect a sense of mounting impatience in his audience. He continued, 'Occasionally, one is fortunate enough to arrive at that configuration of time and place which provides the most opportune of opportunities.' He gave a wink, and another, more elaborate bow.

The qadi, despite his impatience with this performance, was nevertheless intrigued by this comical, though by all accounts treacherous, wretch, and asked him to proceed.

It was almost six months previously, when Quraishy had been travelling in the Marmara Sea, *en route* to intercept a caravan of silk merchants in the market harbour of Takriri . . . Caught in heavy storms, the captain was forced to bring his boat in to shore and take shelter for some days in a small, unremarkable fishing village on the coast. Irritated about the delay, he stamped impatiently around for two days waiting for the sky to clear. One afternoon, while staring out to sea from the shelter of the house he had requisitioned for himself, the laughter of his men drew his eye to a curious figure standing in the road surrounded by two damp horses, a mule and a servant who kept sneezing.

Aram Kevorkian was an Armenian traveller who claimed to be from Macedonia, a small, energetic figure of a man with damp eyes that bulged beneath a set of extraordinarily large and completely white eyebrows. He had lost his way, having been separated from his caravan by sheer bad luck and, it seemed obvious to Quraishy, some measure of incompetence. He was planted up to his ankles in a vale of mud while the servant shivering beside him held up a sheet of canvas as somewhat inadequate protection for his master. It was a curious sight. Kevorkian's clothes showed signs of wear. In fact, everything about him seemed to suggest a man of means who had fallen on hard times. The rain and the mud, of course, did not help matters. Intrigued, and weary of the foul weather and the dull amusement afforded him by his men, Captain Quraishy invited the fellow to shelter with him. Kevorkian, although small in build, carried himself with urgency and at the same time in the manner of a man who is naturally cautious. He mounted the portico steps slowly, trying to kick the mud from his boots, while brushing in light ineffectual strokes at the rain on his clothes.

'If God had wanted us to live in water why did he make us wear shoes?' he asked, while tipping the excess out of his boots. Captain Quraishy took a liking to the older man, whom he judged to be harmless and presenting no immediate threat. He ordered a small stove to be brought nearer so that the other man might warm himself. Kevorkian nodded and gave cautious thanks, glancing around at the numerous men who hurried back and forth at Quraishy's command.

'You are a man of means, I can see,' he observed.

Quraishy shrugged and laughed. 'We are men of the sea, our lives depend on one another. In His wisdom God has seen fit to place me in the right place at the optimal time. I rely on my instinct alone.'

Kevorkian wrung out his shirt and chuckled to himself. It struck Quraishy that the man's ability to hold a conversation seemed uncommonly restricted.

'I detect a certain inquisitiveness on your part,' said Kevorkian eventually, as he settled himself beside the stove. 'And since you have seen fit to bestow upon me the kindness of your heart, I shall try to satisfy your curiosity.' The rain clouds gave way to darkness as night fell. The two men had the stove to themselves and the Armenian was beginning to feel at ease. 'You are not quite certain what line of business I am in. Well, I will tell you. Our trades are not so far removed as you might think. I too am a trader, but unlike you I do not deal in commodities, but in information.' He looked up and recognized the faint look of confusion that had crept onto the other man's face. It appeared to amuse him, although exactly why was not clear, and he showed no interest in sharing the cause of his bemusement. 'I am not a spy,' he continued, 'if that is what you are thinking, although I could easily have become such a thing. I am not in the pay of either the masters of the Roman Church, or the Spanish king, nor even of the Sultan himself, although all of them have in their turn rewarded me. I am a free agent and am able to move without restriction. No one dares harm me, for fear that they might lose something which one day could be of worth to them, or alternatively that I might carry something of theirs to the enemy.'

'Sounds like a slippery kind of business to be in, if you ask me.'

'Knowledge is unlimited, that is my principle. So long as no one is quite certain that they are in possession of every possible detail – and no one ever is – then I am secure. I deal in stories, some true, some not so true. The important thing is that I can convince them that what I tell them is so. We live in uncertain times, my friend; no one is ever completely sure of anything.'

'I prefer to deal with things I can hold in my hands,' growled Quraishy, shaking his fists.

Aram Kevorkian's face remained in the shadows. 'I find in general that bargaining with possibilities is more powerful than any amount of gold in the world.'

Quraishy was beginning to get the idea that perhaps his initial assumption that this unassuming character was harmless had been incorrect. 'Tell me,' he asked, 'if you are so good at this, why is it that your clothes are worn and that you are so obviously ill-equipped for the journey you have undertaken?'

Kevorkian said nothing for a moment. Then he bowed his head gracefully. 'Time, my friend, catches up with all of us. The truth is that I have retired and am planning to spend my final years in the town where I was born, a week's journey from here. But you have been generous and therefore I would like to repay your kindness.'

Quraishy found himself reluctant to receive anything from this man. The man clearly knew more tricks than an old fox. He waved aside the offer. No thanks were necessary. He had done nothing more than any man would have done. Giving shelter to a stranger in a storm like that? No God-fearing soul would have turned him away, and besides, he himself specialized in the redistribution of material possessions – sharing was his trade.

'Be that as it may, I am still grateful. In return I shall tell you a story,' said Kevorkian, 'a story for which I have no further use. What you do with it is your own business. In that way you could say that you have not directly received anything in return for your kindness, no?'

Quraishy's brow furrowed, but he could not think of a way

49

around this argument quickly enough and so Kevorkian told his story.

'The town of Frankfurt on the river Main, in the Hanseatic states.'

Captain Quraishy's knowledge of inland geography was somewhat limited, to say the least. He knew and traded with any man who came his way, and he had certainly no qualms about attacking Christian ships, but any language beyond the *lingua franca* of the ports made no sense to him and was therefore of little interest. He scratched his thigh and called for something to eat.

Sensing his discomfort, Kevorkian gently offered, 'It is the seat of the Holy Roman Empire, where they perform the coronation of the Habsburgs. In any case, they hold a number of trade fairs there every year. This time it was books.'

'Books?' echoed Quraishy, spitting out fishbones at his feet. He was beginning to sense that a man could easily tire of this fellow. He talked more than an old Portuguese whore Quraishy had once encountered on the island of Sicily. The other man made no indication of having had his flow disturbed.

'It was while there that I heard a curious thing,' Kevorkian continued while blowing his nose on a silken cloth he had extracted from his coat. 'I chanced to overhear a conversation whose substance struck me immedietly as being of great interest.' He paused as if to gauge whether his audience was with him. Quraishy grunted and chewed. Kevorkian bowed his head slightly and then continued.

'A young Dutchman was talking in a very agitated and rather loud manner to an older fellow. I am intrigued by such combinations. The young man spoke intensely and yet this seemed to alarm his companion. The older man seemed to regard him as being slightly mad. I would perhaps have

dismissed their conversation as idle gossip, particularly considering the fact that the young man had obviously consumed vast
quantities of beer, which is all the rage at the moment.' A low
chuckle issued from the darkness. 'I would have dismissed the
whole matter as being the ramblings of a God-forsaken soul, had
I not caught the mention of one name – Simon Mayr.'

Night had now fallen and, having bid farewell to yet another
wasted day ashore, Captain Quraishy discovered in the clear
sprinkling of stars in the night sky a faint glimmer of hope;
perhaps tomorrow would bring the weather they needed to get
on their way. He got to his feet to get a better look at the sky.
He could only discern the shadowy bulk of the other man as he
strolled to the edge of the portico to lean upon the rail.
Kevorkian took up his story again.

'The name means little to you perhaps, but for a number of
years it has been linked to the skills of stargazers. Simon Mayr is
an astronomer, a German and one of the most highly respected
names in his field. One of the two men whom I overheard, the
inebriated one, was offering an instrument to this man for a very
high price. The other man was clearly a patron of Mayr's. The
Dutchman claimed that his discovery was unique, that no one
had successfully made such an instrument before. He had come
to the fair with the express intention of selling his device to the
highest bidder.'

Quraishy cleared his throat. In the distance an owl could be
heard. Other than that there was the gentle lull of the sea on the
stony shore below them and silence. Not a cloud could be seen
in the sky.

'Forgive me,' he said, in a voice heavy with irony, 'I am an
ignorant sea captain. I know nothing of such "book" matters.
Where is all of this leading? I cannot grasp to what device these
men were alluding.'

'A telescope, an optical device,' said Kevorkian, holding up his hands to illustrate. 'Glass lenses which are placed in such a manner of conjunction as to allow the eye to perceive things over a day's ride away.'

'Useless,' dismissed Quraishy with a snort. 'Such things have been seen before. They turn a man blind.'

'You are thinking of perspective glasses,' corrected Kevorkian. 'Not the same thing at all. This instrument can see very much further, and the image is as clear as though it were right in front of you.' Kevorkian continued, explaining that he had sent word to his agents abroad to inform him of any mention of such an instrument. Within a few weeks two confirmations arrived. The first was from a man he dealt with in Antwerp, informing him that a device such as that which they had spoken of had been mentioned in an official despatch from the Province of Zeeland to the States General in The Hague. The agent sent a copy of the despatch along with his letter. The second despatch came from a source in The Hague itself and described the nervous distress that had overcome the Spanish military delegation who were in The Hague to negotiate the details of peace between the Spaniards and the Dutch. Their commander, Ambrogio Spinola, had apparently learned that the Dutch already had such an instrument in their possession.

'Obviously such a device would change the whole business of warfare. Whichever side possessed it would win, even against great odds. Ships could be spied half a day away, and armies too.' The Armenian held out his hands. 'There, the story is yours, do with it what you will, but my debt is paid. In the right hands it could be worth a lot of money. Any man to bring such an instrument to the Sultan's diwan would spend the rest of his life in luxury. But haste and stealth are required. Such a device will not remain on the open market for long.'

Captain Quraishy fell silent and shifted his stance. The qadi remained impassive; his face betrayed no trace of the repulsion which this man's presence invoked, not even when Quraishy began to scratch his belly again.

'I cannot estimate what value you place on human life, Captain, but I suspect that you judged this knowledge which you are giving me now as more valuable than at least one single life.'

'Suffice it to say that Aram Kevorkian never reached Istanbul,' said Quraishy.

'Tell me, Captain, why do you come to me with this?'

'I am only a mariner, sire. If I was to approach the palace in Istanbul they would laugh at me. I could spend a year, maybe longer, just trying to gain an audience with the right person. This is my harbour. Here, it is a little easier for me.' Quraishy paused before adding, 'I knew that in your generous heart you would find time for me.'

The two men looked at one another and it was hard to say which of them despised the other more.

'You have spoken to no one about this matter?'

Quraishy shook his head.

'The death of this Armenian was quick and discreet?'

Again the dirty headscarf bobbed.

The qadi stepped to the door. 'You are not to leave this building until the matter is resolved. I shall consult with the Dey and inform you of his decision.' He called for the guards outside to open the door. 'See to it that this man's every wish is fulfilled while he is our guest.'

Then he was gone.

'If you believe,' said the Dey, finally, 'that this man Quraishy is too unreliable for such a mission then we must find another, a companion for our good captain to ensure that the matter is dealt with appropriately.'

The qadi strolled back across the wide room. The smell of frankincense issued from a brass brazier that swung gently on long chains from the cupola of the ceiling. The window looked inwards to the mountains. There was a sheer drop to the prison yards below where the minuscule figures huddled in the sunlight.

'What is your feeling on this matter?'

The qadi raised his hands in a gesture of uncertainty. 'I do not invest much faith in the story, nor indeed in the miracles such an instrument might be capable of delivering. However, if such a thing were to exist it would ensure that our vessels gained a superiority over this coastline which we have not had since the days of Barbarossa.'

'Then we must proceed, but please, at not too much expense.'

The qadi raised his eyebrows and then, dropping them again, he turned to address the Dey. 'Sire, any man who commanded such an instrument would be far in advance of anything which the infidels possess.'

The Dey licked his lips and nodded. 'We must proceed with discretion. We must cover our tracks carefully. It is imperative that in the event of failure there is no link to us. We cannot risk a word of this reaching the wrong ears. Do we need this clown of a mariner?'

'I believe that he can be of service, up to a point.'

The Dey nodded his agreement. 'His companion must be a man of value,' his brows furrowed in concentration, 'but also someone dispensable; we don't want to risk too much on such a venture. A man of knowledge, and yet not too many of his own ideas. A man of ideals.' He yawned and leaned back on the divan. 'Do such men of principle still exist?'

'All knowledge must be tempered with guidance,' proffered the qadi.

'We are looking for a man loyal to the idea, grateful for the opportunity, and yet compelled.' The Dey turned his stony eyes on the qadi. 'Can you find such a man?'

The qadi needed less than a moment to think. 'As surely as the sun rises,' he smiled.

CHAPTER SEVEN

The first time that Rashid al-Kenzy set eyes on Captain Quraishy and his vessel, he was struck dumb. He felt the strength run out of his legs and he sank down, perching himself on the edge of the wooden trunk which contained the sum total of his worldly possessions. He remained there for a time, unable to summon the will to move, surrounded by the carpet of fishbones and the feathers of passing gulls that was sprinkled across the uneven, stony surface of the quay. The noise of the harbour receded and two things came to mind. The first was a sense of complete and utter hopelessness. The captain was a stocky, robust figure with arms that stuck out like tree trunks from the side of his barrel-like chest and legs that resembled two small midgets perched beneath him holding his torso up. He stood there cursing and shouting, clearly either drunk or mad, or perhaps both. The very sight of him convinced Rashid that all was doomed. Even the most half-witted fool to be dragged up from the lowest sewers in the harbour would be better suited to the task at hand than this lunatic. But the qadi had assured him, had he not? He had said that all steps would be taken to ensure that the mission was a success, that special precautions would be necessary to make certain that the nature of their journey remained secret. Rashid watched as Captain Quraishy threw a luckless crew member against the railings and began kicking the man viciously. The three Yani-Ceri guards who had accompanied Rashid from the prison stood and chuckled to one another.

'You were better off with us, boy,' laughed one of them.

The vessel itself was the second thing that struck Rashid, for, contrary to what he had been led to believe, it was not a robust, oceangoing craft built of the most solid timbers from the great forests of the far north. No, it appeared to be a somewhat dilapidated galley, an ancient relic of the type that had bobbed contentedly back and forth across the sea since the dawn of time, or more appropriately, since the invention of the oar, and which had long since been superseded by craft that were sturdier, easier to handle, and faster. The hull showed glaring signs of decay, not to mention damage; it had obviously been hit in a number of places by a variety of weapons, including cannon. All along the bow the lean, bony figures of the slaves hung out over the rail to call to the passing hawkers selling sweetmeats and fruit, roasted nuts, rice and soup, begging for a portion of their wares. A small crowd had gathered around a boy selling dates. They pointed over at the ship; look, they cried, this is how God deals with the infidels. There were Greeks and Spaniards and Venetians, as well as mercenaries from the far north come to seek their fortune against the mighty Turk.

One of the guards called up to the captain and began explaining who Rashid was. Captain Quraishy nodded dismissively; yes, he knew all about him. Send the wise man aboard; he had nothing to fear. The guards fell into jovial chatter with the captain. Rashid al-Kenzy turned away. It was early morning. The sun was already high above the mountains. The harbour was wide awake and the rattle of voices and movement grated against the gentle lull of the water. Moored around the

57

stone promontory were a number of vessels, small and large, tiny fishing boats and small open galliots. There were one or two larger ships – a haughty Spanish roundship on its way west to Wahran carrying silk, salt and oil loomed over the more frail craft. Out at sea another fine vessel was approaching, with taut barrels of sailcloth against the blue.

He was a boy again, scared and alone with the same aching sense of pain in the pit of his stomach as he had had on his first day at the academy in the Valley of Dreamers. The great stone arches rose up again before his eyes. The Beit al-Hikma, named after that House of Wisdom founded by the illustrious Caliph al-Mamun in Baghdad. From the distant, cool shadows beneath the elegant script which read, *'The ink of the scholars is worth more than the blood of the martyrs'*, the echoes of chanting voices reached him. He had dreamed then of visiting the great libraries of Cairo, of travelling through the world and living in an observatory, devoting himself to the science of the celestial spheres, *ilm al falaka*. He was a boy of no more than thirteen years, wishing that he could fall on his knees behind the old scholar who proudly led the way inside. He had wished then that he could weep like a child for his mother to come and take him home. Rashid al-Kenzy could not have turned his back on Captain Quraishy and his sorry-looking ship any more than he could have turned away from his fate then, all those years before. The names and the places change, he thought to himself, but the fear is always the same. Caught in the reverie of his childhood, Rashid saw himself once more as the gawky son of a slave woman with nothing but a few pots and a bundle of clothes to her name. As in Aristotle's scheme for the movement of the celestial bodies, so it seemed that his life was a series of firm shells placed one inside the other. He was not an ugly child, but he was thin and his back was bent like a bow. He was not handsome either but, when she was not scolding him for staring at the sky like a foolish bird, she showered him with love.

A galley slave poked his nose out through a hatch in the hull just long enough to send a long jet of spittle arching down towards the water and al-Kenzy decided to himself that he was lucky to be leaving this harbour of cripples and misfits, mongrels and lame women; he was lucky to be leaving it in one piece. As if in thanks for such a noble estimate of their worth, the town seemed to have assembled itself close to the walls of the defences and were waving their hands in farewell, perhaps to him, perhaps to some other.

He stood up and turned his back to the sea to gaze at the town that had been his home for nearly three years.

The Dutch optical device is like a chimera, shimmering in the distant future ahead of him. A form of magic which is not sorcery, for what could the great mathematician Ibn al-Haytham not have achieved with a such a device? How many years would he have saved in his efforts to measure the width of the blue sky? Or in calculating the curve of the sun through the substance of the air? Such a mission was indeed like a gift from above.

Rashid al-Kenzy had no wish to serve the Sultan. He had learned much since that fateful day when he had left the house in which he was born, but most of all he had learned that the world was divided into two: those who are born to rule and those to whom it is left to serve. He was a slave, and not only that, a slave who had run away. He had no standing, not even the honour of being in service, but he now had a vision. If he could achieve this thing, if he could bring back a telescope for the Dey, then perhaps he would find that peace of mind that always persisted in eluding him. His life was a catalogue of departures, all of them leading him here, it would seem. Was this the mission which he had been waiting for all of his life? If he managed to survive, to bring back this Dutch optical device, would he find the solace and content he sought?

The journey had begun, and one might describe it thus if one was so inclined; that the sea is like an open page, a blank sheet across which the ink of knowledge and history flow, back and forth on the tide. When we lift the page of our hand from the water, the words are there, but only for the briefest of moments before running away, back into the sea.

Algiers was the first knot in a long, twisted vine that would lead him westwards, slipping like a needle through the Straits of Gibraltar and then out into the wide blue western ocean over which Columbus had travelled in search of his New World. There the trail would turn north and with a stiffening of the sails the air would grow cold and the sun's rays begin to grow faint. All of this he knew. He had studied the geography of Ibn Khaldun, and the seven zones of the world. Indeed, one might say that he had prepared all his life for just such a mission.

Rashid al-Kenzy has been granted his freedom; his life has been spared. As he sits gripping the worn railings, listening to the groan of the timbers and the cries of the slaves working their oars, he looks down at the white caps of the waves below him, swirling him onwards and upwards on a circuit of the world which he cannot predict or foresee. In the small cabin below, no more than a corner of the lower deck fenced off with hanging drapes, he kneels to pray.

Time passes, the sun spins across the sky and the moon rises. The galley moves painstakingly slowly along the course which the Almighty has laid for them. The world is a sphere, perfect and round, and the sum and the stars and the celestial orbs circle about it. God placed man at the centre of this universe for a purpose, so that he might witness the wonder of his creator. The ways of the mind are utilised in trying to understand the parameters of this world, but the sacred words and the musings of the philosophers are needed to imagine what lies ahead in the world beyond.

The coast creeps along, night and day. They stop in strange towns and harbours. The men are tense, cautious and nervous of strangers. They take on firewood and food and water. Captain Quraishy knows these latitudes well. He understands every curve, every rocky outcrop by heart. He can sense a ship more than half a day away from them, and he can smell the land. He will lead them to where they want to go. The land, it seems, also knows him, for no matter where they happen to arrive each night, they are known. Captain Quraishy chooses his berths carefully. With uncanny persistence he manages to unearth gentle harbours wherever they go, with soft waves to lull them to sleep. Even on the most difficult stretches of coast he can lead them into a calm inlet where they see only sharp rocks to greet them. At every stop there is plenty of trade to be found. Goods are loaded, unloaded and loaded again. Bewildered, Rashid can hardly keep track. They have arquebus matches from Breton and Cretan wine; they have copper wire and nails, and alum and Italian biscuits and salt. Captain Quraishy has a pair of old iron cannon and he fires a salvo over the heads of the clay-roofed villages to announce his arrival. Sometimes they fire back, but it is all rehearsed, Rashid notes. 'It is a game,' he observes in amazement, simply a game.

Their progress was further delayed by yet another lull. Rashid had marked eighteen days into his diary of the voyage when they heaved to one afternoon. Ahead of them the sky was dotted with shoals of cloud like lazy silverfish gliding beneath the glassy turqoise shell. The flags went up and the deck was suddenly alive with the scurry of bare feet. The iron wheels of the cannon rolled over the wooden planks. The matches were lit with a hiss and tiny puffs of smoke appeared over the walls of the distant harbour defences, their hard edges softened by time. Curious faces peered out through gaping cracks in the walls. The small ship was rocking back and forth at anchor with the recoil. The deck was slick and the stench of the powder bit into his eyes as Rashid crawled forwards towards the captain. Thick clouds of smoke drifted slowly across the scene. A white flag rose over the clay-coloured walls. Captain Quraishy barked out something unintelligible and slashed at the sky with his battered sabre, his normally daunting appearance now marked by what appeared to be real fury. The guns, however, fell silent, and by the time they reached the quayside, music could be heard, a tremulous and stirring mixture of tabla and strings. A man was singing in Spanish. A group of women were gathered to cheer the crew into harbour. Festivities were already under way and even the slaves were released from their shackles on this occasion. Captain Quraishy stepped ashore; casks of wine were swiftly broken open. For Rashid it was like a bizarre tale that has come to him in sleep.

They remained stranded in that port for eleven days. Eleven days when nothing happened. It was an old Spanish presidio which had long since been forgotten. The Spanish king and the Sultan played dice together now. There was no more fighting. Quraishy's dramatic arrival was a tribute to the honour of the old days. Today, with the English and the Dutch privateers steadily growing in number, there were other things to worry about.

The crew lolled about on the deck, sleeping in the sunshine. The captain was nowhere to be seen. Someone said he kept a wife nested away within the siphiculean whorls of faded chalk and mud beyond the stone fortress. One thing was certain: nobody would dare to ask the captain about the nature of his business there. They simply had to wait. And when Quraishy finally returned to the ship one afternoon, he was certainly in fine humour. He arrived laden with gifts and soon the deck was strewn with sacks of dates, nets of fruit and barrels of salted fish. There was an air of gregarious contentment about him as he drew the crew around to join in an impromptu feast. In his jovial state, the captain resembled a kindly visiting uncle and Rashid took it upon himself to engage him in conversation. He was only too willing to talk. Al-Kenzy learned that Quraishy was not his true name, that he had been born in Spain of Arab blood. A Moro, he had been forced to give up his faith but had embraced Islam as soon as he set foot in Algiers. His family had perished in the massacres of the Moriscos in Granada during the time of the Pragmatic. 'Quien tiene Moro, tiene oro,' he announced with a flourish.

'I went to sea forty years ago,' he said. He had gone to Saldas in the region of Almeria with his father in order to purchase weapons from the Corsairs. 'Un Christano por una escopeta,' was how they dealt. The sailors, lolling in the sun, barely raised their heads to listen, having no doubt heard this tale countless times before. A Christian for a musket. Captain Quraishy's maritime career had begun in the way that it was to develop. His father died at sea and the young Quraishy was adopted by a band of privateers. It was not an uncommon story. Despite the hardship of such a life, the attractions were irresistible to many. They preyed on larger, slower vessels, moving swiftly in small galleys. Armed with small arquebuses or simply knives, they set out with the bare minimum of rations: salt, a little flour, a little oil. The wealth at stake was the stuff of legend. They lived like hardened soldiers, but unlike any army conscript they each had the opportunity to become as wealthy as kings, although more often than not they never did. Often the prizes were small; gall nuts and salt would not make a man rich, but a cargo of silk or timber might. They traded their prizes too, since the vessels they captured were themselves often more valuable than the cargo they carried. The Venetians themselves could no longer do anything but provide a safe haven for their fleets. The galleys of the Serenissima circled feverishly in a hopeless attempt at defending the honour and wealth of Saint Mark. The captain threw his head back and laughed in recollection of the audacity of his youth.

But things were different nowadays. The merchant ships were faster and smaller and could outmanoeuvre any galley. The seas were thick with a cruel breed of Christian pirate who reached as far as the Aegean sea. The English and the Dutch picked off the big vessels, creeping past the Spanish at Gibraltar, during the winter when the ships were at their moorings. With their galliots and barques it was said they could cross the sea from Cartagena to Smyrna in less than forty days. They had cannon made of brass that were lighter and stronger than the old cast-iron weapons. They had plenty of powder and matches and when they fell upon a ship, any ship, they stripped it faster than a plague of locusts and set it alight. Quraishy himself had lost the taste for such a life; he no longer went out of his way looking for trouble. All that remained for him was what opportunity sent his way and of course the pastime of filling the air with these tales of old. Nowadays one could risk being taken prisoner by the knights of St Stephen, who treated their slaves worse than animals. Why, they had even been known to seize ships carrying pilgrims bound for Mecca; nothing was sacred to them. Sicilians, Maltese, even Neopolitans; all had joined in to pick at the bitter scab left by Barbarossa.

Perhaps it was because of the destination which lay ahead that these tales of the infidels' cruelty seemed to carry such weight. Rashid addressed the captain that evening. 'The route to the north, how familiar are you with it?'

Quraishy did his best to suppress a confident beam, his eyes twinkled mischievously and he stroked the edges of his droopy moustache. 'Sire, I would not presume to risk your lives on the meagre knowledge contained in my charts and this humble mind.' He tilted his head in the faintest indication of a bow. 'One must be certain up there for the seas are unforgiving and the wind is cold-hearted enough to rip a man's sails apart with a single breath.' What was needed was a good pilot. He clapped Rashid al-Kenzy on the back and sent him to bed. Don't worry, sire, leave it to Quraishy.

In Cadiz, he says, there is a man.

CHAPTER EIGHT

It was on his fifteenth birthday that Rashid reached the Valley of Dreamers and was admitted to the academy. They shaved his entire body, top and bottom, and washed him in vinegar to make sure he brought no lice with him.

Light flooded the deep room in fluid columns of eggshell alabaster, draping itself over the mineral scales of dead fish. The dark bowl of the cupola holds up the sky. The air is damp and warm. A man, stripped to the waist, his bare torso as powerful as that of a wrestler, paces unhurriedly through the gloom; beads of sweat drip from his body. The heavy wooden bucket swings in his hand as he lifts it. The wavy ribbon of water unfurls itself through the air like the gentle unwinding of long, elegant fingers of light.

The young boy stands in the doorway, his head freshly shaven and still smarting. His heart leaps to his throat as a fleeting shadow grazes the band of clay latticework embedded high in the opposite wall where the light gets in, marking the passage of birds outside in the sunlight.

The water and the gloom keep the warmth at bay. The wrestler turns slowly and walks past him, head bowed, the buckets dangling from his powerful arms, beads of perspiration rising like steam from the strands of the rope handles. His breath is like the rushing of the planetary spheres past the boy's ear.

Far away down the distant corridors of the infirmary, a voice is chanting the words of the great poet Ala' al din al Mansur, telling the story of knowledge and how it came to be known here. The legend of Taqi al Din and the Tabriz observatory, and of Ibn Hazm and how the Hamama brotherhood came into being, all of this and much more is there to remind the young apprentice of the preciousness of the gift he is about to receive.

The breeze chills the high-walled corridors as it circles through the great building. It carries the musty labyrinthine scent of damp clay and blood. The smell of the womb. It touches his head and he finds himself pressed forwards, drawn past the marble slabs where the great gaping fish lie gasping their last goodnight; some of them are still kicking, rainbow slick from the morning catch. The water keeps them cool, stops the scales from curling. Droplets tick away slowly, falling from the rounded corners onto the stone floor. He moves past the tables (where he will soon be taught to use the knife) towards the group that is gathered at the far end of the long room, whose cavernous shadows are so deep and so heavy that they give the impression that one is under water. His legs are heavy and his arms hang limply by his side in the new robes that he is wearing. The sound of voices, soft and reverent now, reaches him as though from a great distance.

The wrestler is not a wrestler at all; he is bound by service, a slave. His barefoot steps have vanished to some other corner where he crouches and waits. In his white cotton and his slippers, the boy Rashid is a novice. He is free. He is here to learn.

Gathered around the table at the far end of the roaring room are the older boys. The master is slicing with a knife and the layers of the face of the dead man lift away like paper in his hands. Examine every layer, learn what mysteries are concealed in the intricacies of God's work, he is telling them.

The birds cross the light and Rashid's mind darts away.

He turns in his sleep now, hearing the sound of the crew who are spread around the wooden floor of the lower deck. It reminds him of the long room in the academy where he spent so many nights with a simple reed mat on the clay floor. The ship creaks and the deck rocks gently beneath him. He wondered then, just as he wonders now with the sound of Captain Quraishy's snores rumbling away off in the darkness, how it was that he had come to be here.

His memories come to him while he is sleeping.

For over ten years he has not spared a moment's thought for his days at the academy. He was a child then, lucky to be alive, glad to be free, determined to devote himself to some great task. In this way learning became his life, his family, his home.

The sound of the brass orbs penduluming through the air is the sound of a giant hawk breathing in his ears. He feels the rush of wings as they swing by. He feels the pull in his stomach and wishes that he could be the motion itself rather than the bird. Deep down in the belly of the observation well, the air is warm and thick, caressed by the passing of these spheres which hum by in the gloom. They are huge; two men with arms outstretched can barely reach around the largest of them. Each globe represents one of the celestial planets. They circle through the air suspended on hollow brass rods in perfect synchronism. It took ten years to construct this model. The old observatory at Tabriz was built and torn down in that time, but in that secret place, the Valley of Dreamers, the work continued.

Standing at the centre of his memory was this model of the universe: the shiny edges gleam in the fragile pillar of light that filters through the circular hole in the roof high above, one orb is located at the centre and marks the earth, for all things turn about this world. How fast they move and how beautiful it is to behold such firm precision in motion.

The observatory and the academy, with its schools of medicine and philosophy, mathematics and geography, was really a retreat for a small group of devotees, men who feared for their lives. The Brotherhood of the Dove; the Hamama Brothers. Mystery surrounded them and they encouraged it, for it preserved them. They had made good their escape and now protected their isolation fiercely. Nestled within steep-sided, impenetrable mountains, once home to a radical sect of fanatics and outlaws, it was the valley's reputation for evil and terror which had attracted the hermits to it. They were looking for isolation in order to devote themselves to the stars without disturbance from the outside world. Here no one would dare look for them. They did not seek out students and would only accept a boy if sent by someone whom they knew and trusted. It was said that they had found favour with a certain queen whose fortune one of them had revealed many years ago, thus saving her from an unhappy marriage. A favour for which she was eternally grateful. The money was used for instruments. Other than that they produced themselves everything else which they needed.

For a year he boiled chickpeas and lentils in the kitchens for them, until the smell of garlic had permeated to his very marrow. His fingers were sore and swollen from constant immersion in water. Still they would not allow him to enter the sacred sphere of learning.

At night he wanders across the moonlit pool of the smooth yard from his cell to take his turn in the observation well. The parallactic rulers as prescribed by Ulugh Bey at Maragha; the armillary spheres; the giant quadrants; the astrolabes, all have been saved from destruction, collected, preserved and improved on. He has been promoted from the kitchens to grease and polish the instruments. His hands caress their polished smoothness with the tenderness only an orphan can know.

He is most fascinated by the medical surgeons, who consult their mysterious diagrams of currents and organs and argue incessantly amongst themselves. Ancient Chinese diagrams charting the currents of the soul versus the bloody knives.

Time brought the yearning for freedom; the tiny, invisible strands which bound him to his saviours began to part one by one. The world grew bigger, more colourful, more filled with noise and light than he had ever known in that great house where he was born to serve. He unlocked the cage of mathematics, turned the key of al-Jabr's mystical language which took his name – algebra. He climbed steadily towards the sublime array of the celestial bodies. There was no sign of randomness, this was not the reckless hand of coincidence; each and every distance between the fixed stars was measured. Measured in fingers and handspans and lances. Their brightness was arranged on a scale. They fell into houses, families, constellations of such magnificence that he was moved to tears when their delight was revealed, blinking innocently in the inky, oceanic night. Their message was written there by the Creator for man to study, to awaken his senses and make him learn. The motion of the orbs could be measured in angles and distances, while the course of his life eluded all such method and order.

Azimuths, ecliptics, precession; all of these things he passed through like layers of warmth falling away as one ascends a mountain, moving steadily as the light grows ever stronger and sharper. Each advance provided a new horizon and new problems, any one of which was enough to eat up a man's life entirely. Such was the privilege of the handed down knowledge. Each layer was therefore a life, like the snake whose age is measured by the shedding of its skin. The mysteries of the heavens could not be unravelled by one simple man. But the torch was passed on, from the Babylonians and the Pharaohs to the Greeks and Persians, then to the Indians and the Chinese. The walls of the academy rang with their names, so many that it would take a lifetime of devotion simply to learn who they were and what they had done: Imhotep; Akhenaten; Ammizaduga; Thales; Anaximander; Pythagoras; Eudoxus; Aristotle; Aristarchus who invented the scaphe to measure time; Apollonius and his epicycles; Hipparchus who gave us precession; Ptolemy's *al-Majisty* which later gave Abdelrahman al-Sufi his start in plotting the heavens; Abu Mashar and Mash'allah the Jew who illuminated the Sassanian theory that all major political events coincided with the conjunction of Saturn and Jupiter.

Al-Biruni; Abu'l Wafa; Ibn Yunus; Ibn al-Haytham; Nasr aldin al-Tusi and Ibn Shatir. Was it the length of their shadows that seemed to hang over him? Did there lurk, somewhere deep in the recesses of his mind, the idea that the name of Rashid al-Kenzy might be added to this illustrious list? The minds of men are truly of the most confounding ether. With his faith and his loyalty, would personal vanity have provoked him into believing that the ways of man are of more value than the path illuminated by God?

The process of reasoning is clearly outlined by the metaphysics of al-Farabi and others. Where does the invention of man end and the intention of the Almighty begin? The mysteries of the heavens are unfathomable to any single man. And there are those who maintain that the message of the sacred Koran will only be completely understood in the fullness of time, that it is foolish vanity which causes the learned Ulama to claim that they

71

understand everything which is written there. Is it not written that the lowliest of men is equal to the noblest, that each man's faith is between him and his Creator? But such arguments are frail protection against the swords and spears of the zealots when they come, and they do come, as they did, finally, to the Valley of Dreamers.

CHAPTER NINE

The prowling Spanish galleons waved them past Gibraltar hastily, for the Bay of Cadiz awaited. Swollen with new wealth, it was awash with vessels of every description; carracks moored bow to stern in elegant crescents. Caiques, cogs, roundships, urcas from the Netherlands and Antwerp rocked gently at anchor. The huge bulk of an ancient Venetian nave swung its nose slowly towards the east. When the English had plundered this city eight years earlier they took its wealth but did not manage to steal its honour, and still it remained proud; with its pointed steeples and its wide, palmlined boulevards it stretched its tawny fingers up towards the sky in unbowed greeting.

As Rashid al-Kenzy wandered through the crowds that thronged the squares he had the sense that he had stepped into another world. The trading houses were packed; with timber and grain, beams from the Hanseatic states, silver from America, Valencian perfumes, caps from Cordoba and cloth from Toledo. Merchants and *marineros* struggled by in the confusion of people jostling for space. It took Rashid's breath away and made his head spin. Carriages rolled past, jogged by fine horses. Officers of the King's navy strolled in groups wearing plumes and shiny buttons. The tide of wealth from the mines of New Spain across the western ocean had brought with it not just the silver-capped wheels and the shiny toe caps, but had also left a deposit of human detritus, a disparate collection of outsiders, strange types scrabbling through the plazas and the thoroughfares seeking out their fortunes. They sold cheap baubles and stitched leather goods. Young girls held garlands of withered flowers aloft while pressing their bodies forwards in offering. Mothers proffered babies for a handful of coins. There were lithe Indian boys doing tumbling tricks, long-haired men with eyes like cinders who swallowed flaming torches. Rashid al-Kenzy wandered through the spectacle in a kind of daze, his eyes unable to tear themselves away from the vivid panorama and the interminable gallery of unfamiliar faces. He heard the sound of men ranting about pestilence and death, of the wrath of God and the corruption of the soul. In the grey, overcast light he had the sense of pagan, heathen spirits unleashed, presided over by the authority of the Christians which inhabited the awesome spires and looming church walls. It was a world preoccupied with itself, with matters further afield, aware that it was the hub of some much larger wheel.

The hiss of stagnant water hit the narrow street like a whiplash, splashing over Rashid where he stood in the shadows, hesitating. The bodegone was a noisy one and the heady aroma of thick wine and laughter pulsated out through the doorway into the darkened arteries of the streets. The woman retreated back inside, the empty bucket swinging from her hand. As he walked from the harbour through the streets, Rashid had been increasingly concerned about the nature of the task which lay before him. The qadi had given him a sealed package wrapped in oiled sailcloth, upon which was an address and a name. 'When you reach Cadiz it is of the utmost importance that you proceed immediately to this place and deliver the letter. It is also vital that no one, most of all Captain Quraishy, should know of

74

your affairs. The whole weight of the venture rests in your hands.'

Stepping from the shadows, Rashid took a deep breath and pushed his way through the door. It was more chaotic than he had anticipated. He felt himself being pushed and swayed by the heady fumes and the swollen antics of the drunken patrons. On the far side of the room there was a brick arch beneath which the crowd congregated. His eye was drawn to a large man who was carrying four large jugs and calling for people to make way for him. By the familiarity with which he was treated, Rashid, easing his way forward, identified this man as the proprietor of the establishment. The man turned abruptly to find himself face to face with Rashid. He looked him up and down and then made some jocular comment which brought the attention of the other men who lolled at the counter. He was about to move past when Rashid reached out to grasp his arm. The man looked at him again, this time warily. He looked at the hand on his arm and spoke again, this time in a different tone. Rashid let go of the man's arm and held out the letter. The man took it in his large hands, turned it over a few times and then threw it high in the air. The letter disappeared within the crowd of men. From out of this mayhem one man emerged. He had a face like varnished wood and a shiny, closely shaven head. Around his neck he wore a thick leather thong upon which there was threaded a collection of items: a shark's tooth, a large silver coin, a rusty key and what looked like the bones of a man's hand. He spoke in the *lingua franca* of the sea.

'What is your business here?'

Rashid gestured at the letter. 'I am to deliver this to the woman whose name is written there.'

The man looked Rashid up and down a few times and then he nodded over his shoulder. 'Follow me. I will take you.'

They left the bodegone and began to walk. After a few minutes they turned away from the main thoroughfare and entered a quiet, deserted street of tall houses. Rashid looked back over his shoulder, partly to ensure they were not being followed, and partly to take his bearings. He slipped a hand inside the sleeve of his linen coat to feel the reassuring hardness of the dagger strapped to his arm.

The tall man spoke without looking round. 'A man once drew a knife on me, you know. The hand in which he held that blade is with me now.' He jangled the collection around his neck and laughed.

They turned again and again until they reached a narrow house. The door swung open and they climbed the stone steps which curled upwards and round. A maid peered from behind the half-opened door. They entered the room and Rashid remained there, waiting by the door. The maid sat down on a small chair beside him and, placing her hands in her lap, she stared straight ahead of her, unmoving. The tall man reappeared after some moments and, walking past Rashid without a word or even a glance in his direction, he vanished through the door and was gone. Rashid looked at the maid. She looked up and then nodded towards the open door that led to the inner chamber.

At first he could not make the woman out in the starved flicker of light that issued from the brass lamps that were set in small alcoves around the walls. The room was warm and smelled of scent and fragrant oils. Rashid remained where he was, close to the doorway. He could smell the flame and the smoke of a lamp near his face. She was standing, one foot raised upon a low stool, by the fireplace where an open stove glowed. She was bathing. With her skirts drawn up to her waist she was pouring water the colour of gleaming copper over her thigh. Rashid stood motionless.

'Come closer,' she said, showing no sign of embarrassment. She looked up. Her hair was thick black curls which were loosely tied in a bundle that fell across her bare shoulders. 'Don't stand there like an undertaker. Close the door.'

He stretched out a hand, and without turning his head he pushed the door closed behind him. She raised another bowl of water from the pot which warmed on the coals of a brazier. He watched the gleaming rivulets dance their way over her skin. Her face was rounded. In the shadow, her eyes were two small black points.

'You know what this contains?'

Rashid shook his head. The letter was now unwrapped and lay on the table beside her. The outer covering was a band of cloth into which thirteen gold coins had been sewn. She put down the bowl and, stepping away from the fire, she pulled down her skirts.

'You must bring your captain to me tomorrow night at this time. Everything will be taken care of.'

Rashid said nothing. He remained where he was. 'Go now. I am expecting a visitor,' she said with a wave of her hand. He left the room, the strange combination of scents still filling his head. When he reached the street a very smart carriage was pulling up outside the house. Two footmen dropped to the ground. Rashid caught a glimpse of an older, distinguished-looking man who descended from the carriage and, with a swirl of his long cape, vanished into the doorway.

The echo of a bell tolling over the dark sea came to Rashid as he walked. He had been making his way back to the ship, but found himself turning corners and changing course in quite a random fashion. His unease was intense. He had done what was requested of him. Why then should he feel such disquiet? He walked on. The sound of a night watchman passed him by, boots clicking across stone damp with salt water. He tried to put his mind at rest. Of course it was a strange task to be given, and carried out in secret made it no easier to comprehend, but the qadi must have had his reasons, surely?'

The night was humid and in the distance came the gentle thumping of wooden hulls nudging one another on the rising tide. The trees on the Calle de San Miguel stirred languidly to the thick scented odour of mangrove swamps and papayas rotting slowly in the humid foliage an ocean away. The silver of South America rattled in the pockets of the dark-brimmed eyes of hatted merchants who hurried down the Alameda Vieja, their hands thrust into their pockets, their wealth in the hollow tarry hulls of those ships which slipped across the moonlit sand bars and the twinkling reefs of the West Indies as they glided off, singing their way west. The city was at the centre of a complex web of handshakes and agreements by which the fate of the distant corners of the world became commodities.

Rashid al-Kenzy suddenly had no wish to see the cold northern latitudes. He had heard about the climate and the dirt and the ways of the Christians who, if word was to be believed, were even more primitive than the ones who washed up in Algiers on every ebb tide. But when he thought like this, he felt old and worthless. Wrapped in the rattle of light carriages and wagons loaded down with barrels of salt fish and oil, Rashid made his way back to the harbour.

'Urgently requires my company, you say?' Captain Quraishy fixed Rashid with a curious eye. They were making their way back to the house. There were three of them, however, the captain having insisted that the bosun accompany them. This was at the captain's request and Rashid could not think of a way to dissuade him. As they made their way across the town, Rashid tried to avoid looking in the bosun's direction, afraid that he might suspect something was amiss.

'You were told to come alone,' the maid said, looking at the bosun. The captain had already gone through to the inner room. The door closed quietly behind him. The bosun turned first to Rashid and then back to the maid.

'You wait your turn,' she said in a firm voice before sitting down to her sewing. The bosun seemed to accept this. He gave Rashid a lecherous grin and began pacing the hall with long relaxed strides, his hands pushed into his pockets. Rashid said nothing. He stood there in silence. The sound of laughter came from within, and the bosun winked at Rashid. Then, for a long time there was silence. Nothing moved. The maid remained where she was, head bowed, watching the silver needle in her fingers.

When it came to him, the realization of what was happening, it came too late. He let out an involuntary cry and in two short steps had reached the door and pushed it open. The woman was standing by the bed. Her head was down and her long hair covered her face, hanging down to her gold necklace. She was buttoning the front of her white undergarment. He glimpsed the sway of her breasts which protruded through the yawning gap. As he pushed past her she made no effort to resist. Captain Quraishy lay face up on the bed. His pantaloons were around his ankles and his eyes and mouth were wide open. Rashid swung round. The woman stepped back out of arm's reach. The dark spots of her eyes deepened, as though the lamps were being extinguished by their darkness. He edged closer and stretched out a hand to push aside the dark hair. His eyes held hers as his hand slid down over the globe of her left breast. It was cold to the touch and rose and fell lightly in his hand with her breath. His fingers traced the smooth swell of the skin. The nipple was erect and hard to the touch. He rubbed his thumb across the glistening tip and lifted his hand to his nose.

'Honey?'

Her gaze still held his eyes. 'Do not put it to your tongue or it will be the last thing you will ever taste.'

He looked back at the dead captain. The woman pulled away from his hand. She half turned and resumed buttoning her clothes.

'Go now. Your business here is done. Take him with you and leave him in the street behind the house. People die all the time in this quarter.'

Rashid looked past the woman at the bosun, who had rushed into the room behind him. 'What sorcery is this?' he cried, leaning over the dead captain.

'What has been ordered has been done,' said the woman. 'Everything will be taken care of. Go now and never whisper a word of what you have seen.' She fixed the bosun with a calm look. 'Unless you wish to go the same way.'

The bosun needed no further urging. He backed away from her, knocking over a lamp in his haste to get out of the room. The woman seized Rashid by the arm as he made to leave. 'Go to the harbour, ask for a man named Darius Reis. He will take you to Antwerp on the next stage of your journey.'

'Why?' asked Rashid.

'Who knows?' smiled the woman. 'The qadi is a very careful man. Be thankful only that you were deemed more valuable than him,' she said, nodding towards the dead captain.

Rashid fell down the stairs in his haste to get out of the house. He caught up with the bosun, who was staggering down the street cursing and shouting at the top of his voice. Rashid grasped him by the arm. The man swung on him violently, with hatred in his eyes. 'Listen to me,' said Rashid. 'I had no knowledge of this plan.'

The bosun spat in Rashid's face. 'I curse the day I set eyes on you.' He wrenched his arm free, but Rashid stopped him again.

'What is done is done with God's will. You must help me find this Darius Reis.'

'Do not fear, slave, you may carry a curse with you but I was paid to take you to your destination and bring you back alive. These things I have sworn and I remain a man of honour. He may have been a harsh man, and may God have mercy on his bones, but he was also a just man.'

'Then it is agreed? Not a word of this to anyone?'

The bosun's face was weary with fear and fatigue and his eyes were swollen. In the darkened street, the faint light of the night sky made the lines drawn by the sun appear as though they were cut into stone.

'Where are you from, bosun?'

'The island of Cyprus.'

'I know it well.'

A hollow laugh trickled from the bosun's lips. 'Know one thing, slave. I come with you for one reason only, not because I was paid, nor because of any loyalty to you, but because I want to be there when death comes for you.'

The ship was a large urca, a vessel of about 120 tons. It was constructed in the northern style with a heavy, flat stern. Built in Lubeck, it had been hired out to a merchant in Seville who had sent it to Brazil on business. Damaged on the reefs and short manned, Darius Reis had been hired to take the ship back to the Hanseatic arsenals for urgent repair. The bosun had made enquiries and learned that Darius Reis was something of a free agent. His skill as a pilot was second to none and his services were in great demand. He was rarely to be found wasting his time in port, but had on this occasion been stranded in Cadiz for almost two months, having lost his last ship to two Portuguese brothers in a wager.

All of this was explained to Rashid by the bosun as they bobbed out towards the ship at sunset in a narrow caique, the short sail flapping above their heads.

Darius Reis, they discovered, was both impatient and eager to conduct his business as swiftly as possible. He was slim, with the furtive, bright blue eyes of a bird that glinted in the afternoon light. He nodded and shrugged, barely pausing to examine his passengers. He had been expecting them, was all he said.

What little luggage they had with them was taken below deck and soon they found themselves in a narrow compartment that was to be their living quarters for the voyage. Darius Reis was both dangerous and somewhat eccentric, the bosun continued.

'There are few parts of the world he has not seen. He worked for many years fetching cotton from Cyprus and oil from Alexandria. Bringing nails and timbers from the north. Tin and beams. He has travelled the length of Africa's western coast. His only friend in the world is an ape which he found in the jungles down there.'

'An ape?'

'Big as a child and smarter than a man, they say.'

'Are we to put our faith in a man who places more value on the life of a dumb animal than that of a man?'

The bosun shrugged and grunted. 'Whatever his habits might be, they say there is no better man for the task.'

The bosun stretched himself out on his bedding and closed

his eyes to sleep. There was nothing to do no but wait for the tide. But Rashid lay there in the gloom, unable to sleep. He felt alone and uncertain. With Quraishy gone he was the only person, other than the Dey and the qadi, who knew the true purpose of his mission. He turned over on his side and closed his eyes. The image of Darius Reis loomed before him. What kind of man, he wondered, had eyes like a bird?

CHAPTER TEN

'Y ou said you knew Cyprus?'
     'Yes,' replied Rashid. 'I did.'
     They sat, Rashid and the bosun, whose boredom
with the voyage had finally overcome his reluctance to have
anything further to do with his companion. It was the third day
and they were cooped up in the gloomy compartment, listening
to the timber creaking gently far above them.

   In the years after the academy in the Valley of Dreamers had
been razed to the ground, Rashid's life took on a course which
can only be described as haphazard. And it was in this manner
that he landed on the early tide, one sunlit morning, on the
shores of Cyprus. He was to enter into the employment of a
very wealthy timber merchant, Sidi Hamed Hazin, half-blind
and somewhat wilted by age. Sidi Hazin had arrived on the
island years ago, around the time the Turks finally drove the
Venetians into the sea. He bought up everything he could lay
his hands on and later made his fortune in rebuilding the
Ottoman fleet after its catastrophic destruction at Lepanto at the
hands of the Don John, the Pope's naval commander. His
wealth assured, Hazin remained on the island, continuing to
build up a list of clients that stretched from the Bosphorus to the
Bay of Biscay. His ships returned to him bearing sacks of gold
and silver. But as time went by, money became the least

valuable thing which his ships brought to him in their holds. Far more important were the luxury goods they carried home to his young wife, who was forbidden to leave the humble palace he had built for her from the stones of a Christian fort. Incense, and perfume that came all the way from India, fine silks from Shiraz; in short, whatever he thought might please her. He sent out a special corps of trusted agents on every ship, giving them express orders to purchase anything and everything which caught their eye: novelties; trinkets; musical instruments; quivering ponies; birds that could sing sweetly. As a result, the spacious mansion was filled from top to bottom with all manner of incongruous objects. Marrying the girl was the last thing he was ever to do on a whim and he would pay for this impulsivness for the rest of his days. His time in this world was running swiftly through the hourglass. Nothing seemed to work, however. The young wife, and she was very young, remained petulant and unhappy. She was bored, despite his efforts to entertain her, and she despised him – found him physically repulsive – and his palace, built on the blood of infidels, as she put it, disgusted her. It was her cage and it was like sleeping in a butcher's shop, she declared.

Rashid arrived in somewhat the same manner as the many splendid objects that cluttered the rooms and hallways of Hazin's palace. He was found by a purchasing agent while working in the bazaar in Tyre where he hired out his skills on the pavement for the writing of letters. Sidi Hazin was looking for someone to help him administrate his library, the agent explained. It was only after he had arrived on the island that he was informed of Hazin's true purpose in engaging his services. His agents had, it transpired, in the course of their efforts to gather distractions to cheer up his dissatisfied wife, amassed an enormous collection of books, thinking that the stories written there might placate her restless soul. Sadly for Hazin she showed no interest whatsoever in the growing mound of manuscripts and scrolls: poetry that wept to be read; adventures that cried out to be taken up; erotic tales of such potency that Hazin's voice broke as he pointed them out during their tour of the palatial house. He could hardly bring himself to speak. Rashid's tour was suspended as the timber trader poured out his heart. He had hoped that his final years would be spent in the hot embrace of a fiercely passionate and amorous young woman; that she would provide him with endless and incomparable nights of pleasure, make his heart young again, and in passing would spawn a pack of male heirs to inherit his wealth. He refused to take her by force which, he confessed in tears, was an indication of the sincerity of the emotion he felt for her. He had never counted on such misery befalling him at such a late stage in an otherwise blessed life. 'There is no fate more cruel than unrequited love,' he wept, placing a hand on Rashid al-Kenzy's shoulder. Rashid promised he would do the best he could.

He set about his task most industriously. He immediately began exploring and categorising the collection of texts. He divided them into the light-hearted, the moving, the entertaining, the romantic, and the worthless, which he consigned to the fireplace. Each sentiment would be applied at the exact moment to build up to the optimum effect which he sought. He worked like an alchemist, calculating measures and weights in words and emotions. Together, each class would make up the various scales on a musical instrument. He would play her heart like a lute.

Perhaps it was fate, perhaps coincidence, but whatever it was, he found himself suddenly presented with the means to quell the longing for knowledge that had built up inside him for years. For a decade in fact, since his urgent departure from the Valley of Dreamers. Without his being aware of the yawning chasm, a hollow space had developed inside him. It had manifested itself like an ailment, like a hunger for which he had not known the antidote, a burning pain to which he could not put a name.

He now had the means and the time. He also had an unwilling pupil in the form of the pouting young wife of Sidi Hazin. Every afternoon he sat with her in the pavilion on the hillside unless the weather was bad, in which case they would ajourn to the long hall in the main house, where the light was provided by smoky oil torches. But the pavilion occupied an airy space above the big house with the gentle breeze blowing through the white cotton drapes hung to keep the sharp light reflected off the bronze sea from distracting them. He laid the book open on the small stand, and sat cross legged upon the floor to begin reading while she paced the floor. The pavilion was a place for contemplation and was therefore bare of fixtures and fittings. The marble floor was a dark-veined olive hue. There was a long divan and a tall Phoenician amphora. Apart from that, only the whitewashed wooden columns, the cotton drapes and the air and the sea. It was a pleasant place to sit, and Rashid felt at ease. The wonder was that he was being paid to do what he loved most – to read.

He had been instructed to read to her for two hours of each day and this he did. Placing the hourglass at his side, he simply read what he had chosen for the day. He paid no attention to the girl, and this was just as well, for she did everything she could to distract him from his task. She wandered around, strolling, twirling, dancing even. An incredible, fierce determination came over him, focusing his mind, keeping his eyes moving in a steady rhythm along the lines, feeling their way over sounds and thoughts, the sentiments of the soul as described in words. He refused to allow himself to glance directly at her. He would enter the room, bearing his load of books in his arms, with his eyes fixed firmly on the floor. He would bow briefly in her direction before taking his place at the centre of the room. Then, finding his page, the sand would begin to run through the hourglass and he would commence. He was not, however, completely immune to her presence. Although they rarely entered into conversation of any kind, he knew that she felt it was not only a complete waste of time but also a tedious chore (sometimes she would fall asleep while he read and he would simply continue to the accompaniment of her light snores). Being convinced that disturbing her was beyond the bounds of his duties, he did not interfere with her rest.

Nevertheless, after a time, he began to have the feeling that he could sense her moods, quite instinctively, and he began to tailor his readings to match his intuitions. He changed his approach and brought with him each time a varied selection of works, so as to be sure of being able to cater to whatever her mood might demand. If he sensed that she was troubled, as was often the case in the beginning, he would for example read qassidas by the mu'allaqat writers – al Qays, Tarafah, al Harith – for their rhythmic odes were soothing. When he felt her spirits were dulled in some way, he would turn to the Abbasid poets of the ninth century, such as Abu Nuwas, when he felt that their unorthodox style was challenging. At other times he would charge through the noble smoke and flame of the *Shahname*, the Book of Kings, telling her of the battles and victories of the bold Rustum. At other times he would amuse her with the ornate descriptions of the world in al-Jahiz's masterpiece, *The Book of Animals*.

As the months went by he found himself digging deeper and deeper into the collection of written works. He was not disturbed in any way, for Sidi Hazin, like so many of his kind, men for whom wealth is synonymous with wisdom, had less regard for such matters as reading and writing than he might have wished to imply. He was, when all was said and done, a simple merchant, no better and no worse than a man selling radishes in a market square. The enormous collection of books was piled high in an unused storeroom at the back of the house. The corridor outside the room was rife with insects and mice and it was only a matter of time before they found a way through the stone and began devouring the books and precious manuscripts.

For a year Rashid spent every available waking hour of the day and most of the nights sitting at a small table he had placed in the book store, reading his way through the stacks, mountains of written works to be found there. He himself soon abandoned poetry and made his way towards what interested him the most, the stars. He began with a general interest in the Awail sciences. His route began with a slightly soiled fragment of a manuscript of Ibn Khaldun's work – the *Muqadddima*. The remaining section dealt with the advances in mathematics and sciences. In this he found references to other areas which caught his interest. The book was caught up in a pile of works which had been purchased from a man on the island of Rhodes, a man who had inherited the collection from his grandfather, one of the last surviving knights of St John wise enough to convert to Islam all of seventy years ago when the island, the keystone to controlling the eastern Mediterranean, fell to the galleys of Süleymân the Magnificent.

The stars, astronomy. He quickly immersed himself with fascination in the wonders that they presented and the secrets of their movements. He found works on Ptolemy's *Planetary Hypotheses*, on al-Biruni, Ibn al-Haytham, as well as al Farabi's *Catalogue of the Sciences* and al-Jazari's *Book of Knowledge of*

Ingenious Mechanical Devices, which held him spellbound for weeks.

So engrossed was he in this task of continuing the education which had been terminated by his flight from the valley that one might be tempted to forgive him for not noticing the changes that were taking place in the mind, and heart, of his afternoon audience of one. By this time of course they had accumulated a good deal of time in one another's company – brief, shared moments that sparkled and glittered, startling outbursts of astonishment and laughter. Startling because they broke through that veil of animosity which had at first characterized their forced companionship. Nevertheless he did not notice that anything was amiss until it was far too late. He did note at some point that his reading rhythm underwent an inexplicable transformation. Words which had rolled off his trained tongue in careful order, and at the optimum speed for which they were intended to be read, now began to form themselves into clusters in order to trip him up. They refused to emerge the way they ought to have, holding back to then stumble over one another in a knot in their haste to get out. He began to notice her physical presence, too. He had trained himself to be immune to this, involving himself so deeply in his work that it would have taken a sizeable earthquake to have caused him to falter – previously, that is. Now he found himself distracted by everything under the sun: odd scents, the song of a bird pausing on a nearby tree, the sound of crickets sawing away in the distant fields.

Time went by and his patience began to wane. He was worried that his efforts were not having the desired effect. He continued to reassure Hazin that the old man would soon be bearing the fruits of his work. The sadness seemed to have rooted itself in Hazin's eyes and Rashid had, over the course of the year that he had known him, begun to develop quite an affection for the crotchety old fool. The more he considered the girl, her complete lack of response to his selected reading, the more he was convinced that her heart was indeed made of stone. It was on a day like any other that he realised he had no idea how to proceed. He could not decide what to read. He looked at the selection beside the reading stand and he saw the confusion he was in. There was one of the most intellectual of the great poets: al Mutanabbi – which he now realized was too complex. Abu al-Atahiyah – too morbid. Omar Khayyám – delirious. His mind was spinning and he was aware of her precocious gaze fixed upon him. Time rushed by; the large eyes like two moist olives held him captive.

'Well, scholar, are you not going to begin?'

He sighed.

'Perhaps,' she said, wistfully, 'the heart cannot be won by words after all?'

Perhaps, was all he could return. He examined the geometric patterns of the small carpet upon which he sat cross legged. Each concentric shape turned in on itself until there was no way out of the maze.

'There are no words that can make me love that old man. Why should I? He lost his heart the moment he set eyes on me. He would never hurt a hair on my head. Where is the enchantment there?'.

'I have failed in my task then.'

'He asked you to use these words to find the key to my heart. What woman could love a man who asks another to do his work for him?'

'A man who is lost.' He did not raise his eyes. Did not dare.

'You believe that I do not have a heart.'

Rashid said nothing. She reached out for his hand. 'My heart cannot be conquered by absent souls, but by a man of blood and flesh.' She held his hand to her breast and through the soft silk he felt the softness, the light, rounded flutter of her soul. His eyes came up to meet her gaze. She stretched out on the carpet before him. 'Come,' she said, drawing him to her, pulling up the hem of her gown, up over her head, until she was naked. The wind fluttered through the drapes, taking his intellect with it. 'Make his wish come true, give him the heir he has dreamed of.'

He crept up onto her, feeling the soft curves flowing between his hands like water in a warm river. He pushed his hardness between her thighs and felt her body yield with a stifled cry from her lips. They rocked back and forth as one, prayers spilling from his lips like raindrops from a drowning man. She moved as though driven by a demon, her hands were everywhere at once, upon his shoulders, running down his back, there between his legs, feeling his weight, measuring him. He began to drive harder, but each blow was absorbed by her softness. The wind ripped a long banner of cotton free. It caught for a moment on the two lovers on the floor and then it slid free and away out over the rocky green landscape. When he opened his eyes he saw the strip of cloth floating up into the sky, towards the glittering sea.

They lay in each other's arms a moment. He shut his eyes to the world.

'This is madness,' he panted.

She laughed. 'I told you. One brief moment between my legs is worth a thousand years of poetry.'

He rolled over on his back, looking up at the billowing cloth of the pavilion. For a moment they were fellow conspirators. Their time together had now grown to exclude all other distractions.

'Without poetry to keep the madness at bay we are all lost.'

'Sometimes one must embrace madness to find one's own poetry.'

For many years after he would shake his head in wonder at the comfort such frivolous talk could provide. But she had a faraway look in her eyes and he was thinking of that strip of cloth blowing across the hillside, that this liaison which he had stumbled on was somehow intricately related to what he had encountered in the words and rhythms of countless qasidas, odes to love. It was the shape of the curious striations on a pebble tossed ashore by the formless ocean. It was the weight of her breast in his hand. This love which he had not asked for was strangely complete and undemanding. He knelt there, the softness of her thighs trembling against his cheek like the feathers of a small bird, knowing there was a strong chance that could be the last good thing he might ever feel in this world.

One thing was certain, from that day on, the mood in the household changed. Hazin was delighted. His young wife's humour had been transformed overnight. He rushed to Rashid's quarters the following morning before the birds had awoken and burst into the room. Rashid let out a cry of terror and began praying very swiftly. Sidi Hazin embraced him heartily.

'You must tell me, what was it you read to her yesterday?'

'Omar Khayyám,' he lied easily.

'Ah,' sighed Hazin with a wink, 'I thought so. She could not remember, but of course that old fox cannot be outwitted.' He summoned his slave into the room to throw a chest of fine clothes down. 'Your reward. A small token of my thanks.'

'Thanks?'

The old man sat down beside Rashid and took his hand between both of his. 'I must confess, I had begun to entertain strong doubts about whether you were capable of achieving victory.' He nodded slowly. 'How foolish and weak-hearted can a man be?'

'Are you saying that . . . that?'

'That last night my wife drew me to her in one of the warmest embraces I have ever experienced. Her body was like a fever. She would not let me rest.' He shook his head in wonder. His eyes were gleaming. 'I never, in all my dreams, imagined that I would live to experience such rapture again. Beyond all my expectations.' He threw his arms out wide. 'Look at me, I am grown young again.'

Rashid got to his knees and bowed his head. 'I am glad for your sake, Sidi. Now that my task is complete I beg you to release me from your service.'

Sidi Hazin frowned. 'What a strange bird you are.' A thoughtful look overcame him. 'As I suspected, you are more wise than you would have anyone believe.'

'You pay me more credit than is due one such as I.'

'I think not. Indeed I believe that you are capable of many things, but you have a weakness.'

'Sidi?'

'You do not belong anywhere. You serve me for months, indeed, more than a year has passed. I believe that you have learned many things during your stay here. You have now given me the miracle that I asked of you.' Sidi Hazin hesitated. 'I like you, Rashid al-Kenzy, but I know nothing of your heart. You give your complete devotion to the work at hand. I feel no animosity on your part, and yet . . . I have always felt certain that at any given moment you might take flight and vanish off into the blue sky without warning.'

They both fell silent for a moment.

'Go with my blessings, Rashid al-Kenzy, and may God guide you to the reward that awaits you.'

Rashid, still not quite sure whether the words he was hearing were truly sincere, involuntarily let out a cry of alarm when the old man threw his arms around him and kissed him on both cheeks.

'You have given me back my life,' he cried.

Yes, Rashid thought to himself, he might have said the same thing himself, still half convinced that Sidi Hazin was simply waiting for a suitable moment to slit his throat. Was he blessed with some special kind of baraka? He had made an old man happy in the last years of his life in this world. He had been rewarded for his work in many ways. He sat in the harbour upon a fine wooden trunk filled with gifts and gold, and pondered over the fact that whatever mysteries the stars might contain, they were like nothing compared to those concealed in the dark, fathomless whorls of the human mind.

Rashid al-Kenzy departed on a course that took him to Alexandria, and then later to Cairo and Tripoli, and eventually to Algiers. That bright morning stayed with him still. Sailing away on a fresh breeze, upon a sea of cinnamon-coloured waves, rippled like marble, with the olive trees shrinking in the distance, the sound of the taut sails was like flimsy drapes, or the silken clothes of a certain woman, to his ears.

CHAPTER ELEVEN

The moon tumbled in its vanity about the sky as they followed in its luminous wake like scattered particles of dwindling silver dust. The Feranji pilot, Darius Reis, seemed truly to be a man of great skill and the crew praised him cautiously in their unspoken, superstitious fashion. The danger lay beyond the Iberian Peninsula, where the prevailing winds blow south and can carry a ship down along the western coast of Africa for forty leagues without let-up. The course was therefore set due west, out into the huge, untamed ocean where the waves rose like giddy, trembling mountains and the ship was a short bone in the jaws of a furious dog, fluttering this way and that. The ship was sturdily built and well she was, for a vessel like Captain Quraishy's frail galley would have been crushed like a moth out here. Lying nauseous in the damp, cold ship, fearing that his life might end at any moment, Rashid considered the foolishness of his undertaking. Surely no amount of learning could be worth enduring this?

It is said that the seventh caliph of the Abbassid dynasty, al Mamun, was visited one night in his sleep by Aristotle the Greek. It must have been an awful dream for he awoke in the morning with a haunted look upon his face and claws of sheer terror clutching at his bowels. In his anguish he let out a tremulous cry which made every door in his palace rattle.

Without delay he summoned all the crusty advisors and ancient wise men of Baghdad to him and ordered them immediately to begin translating every scrap of knowledge they could get their hands on, whatever language it was written in: Greek, Persian, Soghidian, Sanskrit, Chinese; anything and everything, but especially, he wagged a finger, that of the Greeks. And that is how learning came to the language of the Prophet. Before that, the Arabs had little but legend and religion. The revealed knowledge, the Awail sciences, were virtually unknown. 'Seek knowledge wherever it may be found, even in China!' it is written in the Book of Books. The works of Aristotle and Plato and Socrates and Ptolemy subsequently appeared and their light was passed on and enhanced by the diligence and application of dedicated men. And thus the great thinkers of the Golden Age are known to us. Rashid al-Kenzy has dreamed of scaling this pinnacle of learning. He has adopted the name of his people, the Kunouz, in the hope that they too will find a place in history, to be recorded and not to go unnoticed, unmentioned. Such vanity! he thinks as he swallows another bitter mouthful of bile. He lies, green as an unripe fig, in the bowels of the ship listening to the creak of the wood and smelling only tar and vomit.

The Greeks learned from the knowledge of the Ancient Egyptians who had bound up the earth and the stars in an intricate scheme which haunted and mesmerized them. They worshipped idols: the cat, the jackal, the fish, and Sobek, the crocodile. They sacrificed children to the river. Yes, the knowledge he had acquired would distinguish him in some of the great academies of the world. But he is alone now. Ahead of him lies the challenge of a lifetime. Was this journey truly written for him in the book of his fate? He has begun, perhaps, to doubt the course that he has chosen. Or is it God that he has begun to doubt?

97

They have left behind the streets of Cadiz, with their firm cartographic perpendiculars, their unswaying narrow rules and their flat plazas. The learning which they carry with them is of little use here for they have willingly, though unwittingly, entered their own Sea of Ignorance. The past is fading quickly. They are poised on the lip of that dark horizon which is discovery. Nothing is clearer than the obsidian gaps between the stars which circle their heads above the mariners who struggle to tame the destructive djinns that play recklessly in the canvas sheeting.

Rashid fears for his life, but this night too comes to pass and leads the living to the deliverance of morning.

The bosun fears the infidels. It is an irrational suspicion, brought about by the fever which seized a hold of him the moment they headed out into the Atlantic. He calls out deliriously, convinced that the ghosts of former shipmates, relatives, dead children and murdered captains are also aboard this vessel with him, and that their purpose is to seek out the impurity in his heart. He is a sailor of seas, he groans, and knows nothing of oceans. He abandoned all hope the moment they ventured west.

Realizing that the bosun was stricken with more than simple seasickness, Rashid felt a new fear welling up inside him. All sailors are as superstitious as old maids; they distrust all passengers for any form of live cargo carries with it the risk of sickness and madness. Rashid knew that as soon as the crew learned that one of them was sick they would not hesitate in throwing him to the fish. There was, however, little he could do, although the stench in the cramped quarters they shared was enough to drive a man to thoughts of murder. Instead, he tightened his belt and as they struggled up the cold and vicious waters of the Portuguese coast he nursed him as best he could.

The light is grey and the air strangely cold and damp. They drift silently up towards the coast of France and the English Channel. Nothing is moving, not a single sign that these regions are inhabited. Another day passes and the wind drops further. A thick fog extends its clammy reach towards them. The sailors are nervous of its embrace and they whisper to one another as though fearing that they might be overheard. They do not wish to disturb the demons of the sea if they are slumbering.

In moments of clarity, when the fever relented, the bosun continued with his apparently endless tales about their pilot, Darius Reis, who was, it seems, not known for his compassion. During his privateering days he was once honoured by the Queen of England no less. He knows no loyalty other than that of silver. When Phillip II sent his armada against the English, Darius Reis was a highly respected spy; he switched sides time and again, narrowly escaping death on numerous occasions and making himself a small fortune into the bargain. He was sired, it was said, by a Turkish mariner who survived the massacre of Lepanto in 1571, when the Venetians destroyed the Sultan's fleet. An English ship picked him up clinging to a piece of wreckage and in return the Turkish mariner seduced the captain's young wife. The sea was the only constant in a harsh and turbulent life. Once, they say, when he was crossed by a Frenchman, he skinned the unfortunate man alive and nailed his hide to the main mast as a warning. Rashid decided that he would do the best he could to avoid any unnecessary dealings with their pilot.

The fog lifted and the latitudes slipped over them like the burnished rings of Ibn Yunus' giant brass armillary, big enough, it was rumoured, for a battalion of mounted cavalry to ride through. As they passed through each sunset, it was like a shining band of metal curling over their heads. The passengers

99

sailed on blindly, not knowing what lay at the end of this particular labyrinth. Rashid scoured the horizon for the Dogstar, Sirius, without luck. Stars that once were so familiar grew now more faint and distant with each passing day, each league sailed northwards.

The bosun's health deteriorated. His chest was filled with pus and blood and in a matter of days he had grown as thin and grey as boiled fishbone gruel. He could no longer hold a cup to his lips to drink.

Like a tomb.

The cabin is cold and the walls are slick with moisture as Rashid kneels beside him cradling his head to help him to sip from the cup. The water dribbles down the sides of his mouth and onto the soiled breast of his shirt. He splutters like a man rising from the depths and the milky eyes roll alarmingly from side to side.

'We must turn back,' Rashid whispers. He does not have the heart to finish the sentence, and he is speaking of his own fear.

The bosun gained consciousness for a while. He sat up, spat across the room, the phlegm hitting the wall to drip slowly down. A thin smile appeared, splitting the strained, ashen mask which had settled there these past days. 'I shall take you with me if I go, slave.' His teeth had loosened and blood seeped from the gums; the pus inside his chest had turned to hatred.

'If God in his wisdom has decided that this is to be my time, I will go.'

The bosun laughed in a hoarse fashion. 'We left God behind us with the captain, slave. We are now in the hands of the infidels.'

'The pilot knows his work. I believe he is a good man at heart.' The bosun gave a shiver and sneezed like a cat, which left him with a perplexed look upon his face. 'He is a muthadin, is he not?'

Yes, nodded Rashid, he too had heard that Darius Reis had abandoned the ignorant ways of the Christians and embraced the True Faith. But mariners were notorious for changing sides, or faiths, according to their best interests.

'We are still moving, don't let your doubts consume your courage.' Once they reached land, he assured the bosum, he would make a swift recovery.

The bosun shakes his head. 'The sea is coming for me.'

And yes, the swell is picking up, lulling gently and deeply from far below. The matter of providence as reflected in the debate of the old astrologers came to Rashid. Ibn Sina had argued that if it was all written in the stars, then one could not possibly influence one's fate through one's actions. What, then, was the point of predicting the future? And Nasr al-din al-Tusi had replied with a story. 'If a large stone is dropped from a great height, only the man who is forewarned will not be alarmed.'

He needed a sign, any kind of hint as to the outcome of this journey, as to whether he can go on. He listened to the breathing of the sick man and the creak of the wood in the hull above his head. And supposing he had known that he would be lying in the damp, stinking hull of a ship with this icy fear eating at his liver, tending a dying man, would he have been able to avoid it? No answers. There was nothing, nothing but the rise and fall of the waves and the reek of the rotting ship. The cold in his bones was like a fever that had infested his soul.

A clear night and Rashid al-Kenzy is up on deck staring at the sky, trying to make sense of what is happening there. It gives him a warm feeling, as it always does. These faint dashes of light are the closest family he has. He spies The Archer and The Lady in the Chair. As a child he would lie awake for hours on his bed beside the kitchen trying to make sense of the confusion up there. Later he learned the patterns described in the Zij of the Persian master Abdelrahman al-Sufi. Day after day sketching the lines, learning the measurements: the Finger. The Handspan. The Lance. Between the lance, the hand and between the hand, the finger, and between the darkness ... ink covered his fingers, seeping through the skin into his blood.

The Scorpion is composed of twenty-one internal stars and three external. The eighth is the Red Star whose brilliance is of the second degree and follows the seventh; together they make up what is marked on the astrolabe as the heart of the scorpion, Galb al 'Agrab, and this is the eighteenth house of the moon. Behind this is the constellation of the arc of Sagittarius, al-kous. The heavens were written in his heart more clearly than his life itself.

The Dutch optical instrument is not real. It is not sufficient to warrant this sacrifice, this cost. He would like to believe that he is doing this in the name of learning, but he knows this cannot be true. In the spirit of adventure, then? But he has no need of such a challenge. The argument that he had no choice is a frail one. He was resourceful enough to have found a way out, if he had wanted one. He could have vanished in the streets of Cadiz, could he not? No, the arrow of destiny guides him. The words, strictures, measurements, all are embedded in his fate like the diamond capillaries of the sky. The stars illuminate but a fraction of the heavens, their brightness dazzles while the key lies buried in the dark, unlit spaces between. What might these places contain, Rashid wonders, that they seek to keep it from our eyes? What aspect of his character convinced the qadi that he would take on this task and see it through? Perhaps it is the answer to this question which he seeks.

Day and night are now indistinguishable. The sails hang

limply; the English fog chokes them in passing. The faint, eerie beacon of a passing ship patrolling the Channel floats blindly by. The horseshoe moon is tugged along behind the keel of the ship.

The bosun is dying. His life is slipping through the creaking boards of the deck where he lies while Rashid, kneeling in the corner, whispers the sacred verses. He fears being alone, and so he prays over a man who would gladly have slit his throat if he could. As he leans forward, a hand reaches up out of the darkness and fastens a fierce grip around his throat.

'I will take you with me, slave,' snarled the dying bosun.

The two men struggled in the narrow compartment. Rashid was astonished at the strength of the other man. He grasped the hand at his throat and wrestled to try to break free, feeling the panic rising as he gasped for air that would not come. He kicked and flailed wildly. With one final effort he threw himself backwards, crawling through the gloom towards the doorway. He lay there, gasping for breath.

The ship is growing green with seaweed and cankerous mould, and the crew are growing more hostile with each passing day, with each fraction of latitude that drifts by in their lopsided wake. They squat in the for'ard hold, among the sacks and the flour, listening to the sound of the rats sharpening their teeth. Rashid can smell their hostility. It hangs in their clothes, catches in the corners of their eyes and in the broken nails of their fingers, like a disease. It is a sickness that is growing as the water turns cold and the silent north glides towards them. It is as though they anticipate a parting of loyalties ahead and a choice to be made.

As the atmosphere on board deteriorated it became clear that the pilot was indeed capable of murder. His voice could be heard echoing from far above as he ranted and raved, venting his invective on the crew. They were off course, Rashid realized. The pilot had no idea where they were. It seemed that Darius Reis was just about ready to start throwing the crew over the side, one by one, to deal with their discontent when, out in the darkness, someone glimpsed a light.

CHAPTER TWELVE

The telephone had stopped ringing. Hassan lay there for a moment, slumped across the desk in the downstairs room, trying to work out what had woken him up. The lights in the house were all on, and outside the night was dark and viscous as diesel oil. Nothing was visible through the window in front of him. There were no sounds from the world outside. Even the hum of the highway, which could sometimes be discerned in the distance, was now silent. A piece of paper was stuck to the side of his face. It fell away as he sat up. He looked at the telephone for a moment, trying to work out who might have been ringing him at this hour.

The cold water made him gasp. He turned off the tap and fumbled blindly for a towel. Drops of water fell onto his shoes as he dried his head. He went back to the table and cleared some of the clutter of papers and document folders to one side. Reaching for a fresh sheet of paper and a pencil, he began to jot down what he had learned so far.

Firstly the box itself: a brass case measuring 42cm by 23cm by 11.8cm deep. It was engraved with the name of the craftsman who had made it (Fateh Abdullah Ibn al Kashi), as well as the date and place where it had been produced: the year Hegira 970 in Damascus.

The craftsman's name: al Kashi. Hassan had wondered if this

meant the craftsman was in some way related to Jamshid Ibn Mad'ud al Kashi, author of the fifteenth-century masterpiece on Arabic arithmetic, or was it a reference to the town of Kashan in Persia? The year Hegira 970 he had calculated as being 1562. A relatively new piece, then, at the time of the later engraving. On the inside cover of the brass instrument there was a dedication, somewhat later in date, around 1595. The instrument was a gift from a man, Sidi Hamed Hazin of Cyprus to 'his most loyal and humble servant Rashid al-Kenzy'.

The problem, Hassan decided, casting aside the pencil, was whether the instrument had remained in the hands of this man al-Kenzy, and whether it was he who had brought it north.

Hassan's eyelids were beginning to grow heavy with sleep again and no amount of cold water would help revive him this time. He switched off the lights and went upstairs to bed.

He woke early the following morning, showered and shaved and then set off on the short walk to the corner shop to buy something for breakfast. There was a farmer standing at the counter buying tobacco for his pipe when he walked in. The tall boy looked up and waved.

'Good morning.'

Over the two weeks that he had been staying in the village Hassan had developed a friendship of a kind with the lanky boy behind the counter. He was curious about all kinds of things, about the world beyond the confines of this village. He was on the point of departing, and this was something Hassan found easy to relate to.

The farmer had decided that he was in no hurry to go anywhere. He remained by the counter, taking his time unwrapping the packet of tobacco. The boy counted out the man's change. Hassan picked up a loaf of fresh bread, a carton of milk and a couple of apples. The farmer was stuffing tobacco with thick, muddy fingers into his pipe. He was talking, narrating some long drama involving a tractor and a stubborn dairy cow. Hassan had difficulty deciphering the man's thick accent; oddly, he had the sense that the man was waiting for him to approach the counter. It was only when he got there that Hassan noticed the headlines on the stack of tabloid newspapers lying there. 'Goodbye and Good Riddance!' Beside him the farmer was now fiddling with matches and puffing at the stem of his pipe. The boy was staring at the cash register and adding up the items. The picture on the front of the paper was of a Gambian man, arrested for drug pushing in Copenhagen and now ordered to leave the country. Hassan was familiar with the story. One would have to have been deaf, dumb and blind not to have heard about it. A ruling that would once have been greeted with dismay and opposition was now being publicly applauded; the journalists would, no doubt, say that they were only reflecting the general mood in the country, and perhaps they were right. The boy had finished entering the items and, hesitating briefly, he reached down for a carrier bag and began packing the things away. Hassan reached out and lifted up a copy of the paper.

'I'll take one of these too,' he nodded. The boy shrugged and punched it into the register as Hassan reached for his wallet. The farmer was wandering towards the door in his muddy welling-tons, chuckling to himself and exuding a thick cloud of blue smoke, ignoring the 'no smoking' signs.

When he was gone, the boy seemed to relax. His shoulders slumped and he flicked his hair aside. 'Old Viggo, he's a real character. Spends all day wandering about complaining about how he has so much to do and not enough time.'

Hassan shrugged. 'I suppose he doesn't get much conversation out of his cattle.'

The boy twitched his head, in an expression which seemed like it might have been a nod, but could equally have indicated uncertainty.

The countryside was all very well, thought Hassan, but the fact was that rural areas made him nervous. He was an urban creature. It didn't matter which city in the world it was, but he would always feel more at home in the preoccupied tangle of race, tongues and creeds, than in places like this. It was too quiet; he felt his presence magnified. He stood out like the proverbial sore thumb. The truth, he acknowledged silently, was that he was as prejudiced as the next man. To him villages signified inbreeding, mental and social isolation, backwardness.

'Did you find out about the church?'

Hassan tucked his change back into his wallet and looked up.

'Middle ages, thirteenth century, that's when they used those big square blocks of stone. Before the Reformation.'

'Is that right?' The boy stopped twitching for a moment. 'It sounds really interesting, what you're doing.'

Hassan tucked his bag under his arm. 'Most of the time I spend buried in libraries. It's not that exciting really.' He didn't think it appropriate to question the boy about where or exactly how he had learned of what he was doing here.

'You're looking at the stones up above the lake, right?'

'The museum asked me to look at some of the things they found up there, that's what I do.'

'You live in Copenhagen, eh? Must be exciting?'

'Yes,' Hassan replied, not quite sure that 'exciting' was an apt description of the place where he lived. He waited, but the boy said nothing more. They stood there silently for a moment. Suddenly Hassan had no wish to continue this conversation. He did not want to regurgitate the details of his life. He was tired of the constant need to describe and explain. He said goodbye quickly and left.

He drove into town, planning to spend another day in the public records office. It was an unremarkable town to look at, little more than a large village really, with adjoining peripheral zones – industrial and service sectors. It had once been a centre of reform, and had been quite a wealthy market town. At the start of the seventeenth century it would have had a population of between two and three thousand people. Hassan knew little about its recent history. It was like so many other places, he surmised, transformed and standardized by modernization into a collection of motorway junctions, fast food restaurants and service stations.

The person in charge of the archives was a large, energetic man who moved with surprising speed considering his bulk.

'I think I have an idea,' he announced when Hassan walked through the door. He motioned for Hassan to remain where he was as he vanished silently into a long corridor of tall shelves behind him. Hassan leaned on the wooden counter and recalled his first visit to this office. He had been met with awkward apologies, delays, what could generally be described as a lack of cooperation. Something had changed, however, and he was not sure exactly why. Perhaps it was the fact that he kept turning up, day after day, with fresh requests, which finally prompted the large man to throw his pencil down in exasperation. 'You have no idea what you are looking for, do you?'

'What?'

'Look,' said the large man, folding his arms. 'Would you mind if I gave you the benefit of my opinion?'

'By all means.'

'In my experience, secrecy is a hindrance.'

'I'm sorry, I don't follow.'

'You come in here, you request this document, or that file. I fetch it. You spend a day looking at it. No help. Then you think again. You come up with another idea. You come back with another request.'

Hassan was confused.

'All I am saying is that if you tell me the whole story, then I have a better idea of what it is you need.'

The man gestured at the shelves behind him. 'I have worked here for nearly twenty-two years,' he said. 'Whatever it is, I can find it, but I need the full picture.'

Hassan wondered if this was how work was conducted in all rural archives or whether he had just stumbled on a very unorthodox man. Either way, over the next week or so he found that whenever he turned up, a small collection of documents was waiting for him.

A door to his left now opened and the large man reappeared. He placed a box on the counter. He had a grave look on his face; he took his job very seriously. 'We're not even supposed to have this lot. The Royal Library in Copenhagen sent it over three years ago for another researcher. It was never sent back. Someone filed it away wrongly.'

Hassan could not help looking slightly amazed by this confession. The man looked at the floor and scratched his left ear. 'I was on holiday at the time. It was my replacement who did the deed.' He bit his lip. 'Now I am going to have to apologize to them and send it back.'

'Can I have a quick look, then, before you do?'

'Sure,' said the large man, cheering up a little. 'That's why I brought it up. Its just what you need. It relates to his family.'

'Whose family?'

'Heinesen's, of course.'

The man vanished into his archives and Hassan sat down at the large table in the centre of the room.

Verner Heinesen.

Hassan rubs his eyes and sits up. It is late, his neck is stiff and the room is cold. He stretched his arms and sifted idly through the pages that were scattered across the dining table. He really needed more space. There was hardly room for everything. Stacks of reference books borrowed from the public library and museum were dotted around the floor. The folder open in front of him contained all the information he had gathered about one Verner Heinesen – by all accounts a curious figure. The material faxed over from Copenhagen filled in some of the gaps. He was born in the capital in 1577, the son of a nobleman. In those days people were given titles for just about anything, but usually it was for putting money in the king's pocket. Anyhow, in 1594, at the age of seventeen, young Heinesen was sent to study on the island of Hven, home of the greatest astronomer of his day, Tycho Brahe.

Hassan pushed the Enter key on the computer and waited a few seconds as it hummed back into life.

Tycho Brahe's most significant contribution was the Stella Nova, the study of a new star in the constellation of Cassiopeia, and his planetary scheme, the Tychonic Model, in which he struck a compromise between the ancient Ptolomaic picture of the universe rotating around the earth, and Copernicus' Heliocentric theory. In Tycho Brahe's model the earth was unmoving, fixed at the centre. The planets rotated around the sun and the sun around the earth.

When Heinesen arrived as an apprentice on the island in 1594, Brahe had been busy trying to finish his eight-hundred-page treatise, the *Progymnasmata*. There were only a few gaps to fill. By 1597 he had spent six years writing an introduction and a conclusion. He still was not finished. He wanted to write a defence of the Gregorian calendar, which was only finally adopted a hundred years later. Not the most productive of times, then. Heinesen was taken in as a favour to his mother, a distant relative of Brahe's. That was all there was. Heinesen had one sister to whom he was apparently very close. She lived with him on the farm. As was the custom at the time, Heinesen had spent a number of years being educated abroad. Where exactly was difficult to say; he spent some years in Vienna, Paris and also Madrid, though it was likely that he had also travelled for some years throughout Europe and maybe even beyond.

Hassan got to his feet and paced up and down for a while. His grasp of astronomy was, he realized, not sufficient for the task. It had taken him a week to piece all of this together. He put another piece of wood into the stove. He was tired and little of it made any sense any more. Why would such a man leave the capital and move out here to the middle of nowhere? In those days, Jutland was more or less another country.

The real question, however, was the instrument in the box and how it came to be buried here. He sat down cross legged on the floor and looked at it again. It was not an astrolabe, but a geographical instrument used for orienting oneself at prayer times. It was for travellers to use in locating the direction of Mecca. He lifted up the lid. On the upper surface there was a map of the world, condensed, flattened and distorted. The Indian Ocean was an enclosed lake. Despite this it was astounding evidence of how extensive the world was for the geographers of the Islamic world. Such an instrument was testimony to centuries of ease and mobility. On the lower face there was a list of the names of all the cities of the world, engraved on a brass sheet: Paris, Vienna, Kirguz, Cairo, Istanbul, Avignon, Shiraz, Kabul.

Had it been an astrolabe, he might have suspected that Heinesen had purchased it on one of his trips to southern Europe. Such instruments, many of them relics at the time, were known to be in circulation. But this particular type was of little use in purely scientific terms to anyone who was not a practising Muslim. An item of curiosity then, of such personal significance that it was buried alongside the dead man? Or was it a gift, passed on in thanks, in gratitude, for what?

The material he had gathered at the records office that morning included a letter of complaint sent to the king. Dated April 1611, the complaint was from a certain Pastor Hans Rusk, and related to an alleged case of witchcraft and the burning down of the town cathedral the previous autumn. The Heinesen household was implicated and mention was made of the complicity of the satanic powers of a stranger to the region referred to as 'The devious Turk'. Was this a reference to the owner of the instrument, Rashid al-Kenzy? Was it proof that he was here? There was also another account in the private correspondence of a wealthy local trader named Koppel. Again this was incomplete but made some reference to the tragedy that had befallen the nephew and niece of 'our dear departed friend, Heinesen', which would have been a reference to the Verner Heinesen's uncle.

Clearly the stranger's presence in the area was not widely known about. How had he come there, and why? Rashid al-Kenzy was not a Turkish name. In the seventeenth century, however, it would have been common to refer to any Muslim as a 'Turk'. The Ottoman threat to Christian Europe was at its height, and Islam remained a real threat of varying degrees up until the culminating confrontation between East and West outside the gates of Vienna in 1683.

Hassan's investigation had, in truth, begun to depart from any kind of logical procedure. The brass case would be logged and identified in terms of place and date of origin etc. But what really intrigued him was what could not be proved in any scientific manner. The dark spaces between the evidence. Who was this man al-Kenzy, and what had brought him here? What of Verner's sister, the niece mentioned in Koppel's letter? At the back of his mind Hassan knew that he was spending too much time on this matter. It had become something akin to an obsession, he realized. There was little evidence even to confirm the presence of this man in the area at the time, and yet . . . Exhausted, he switched everything off and climbed the stairs to the bedroom and fell onto the bed in a deep, dreamless sleep. His last thought was that he had promised he would call the institute three days ago to let them know when he was coming back, but he still had not done it. He couldn't let go of the story; it wasn't finished with him yet.

CHAPTER THIRTEEN

Far down, beneath the creaking deck, alongside the dying bosun, Rashid turns his head and struggles to force open his eyes against the drug of sleep. The cloth in his hand drips steadily into the bowl by his elbow. Something is stirring above. He stares at the flickering lamp.

Up above, upon the deck the air is still, as though the world were wrapped in a sheet of damp muslin. It is as quiet as a man's dying whisper. The silence is ominous. The crew can smell the approach of bad weather from the south. They all know that it is late and that they should have sought shelter hours ago. Darkness is upon them and no one seems sure of their whereabouts.

A voice cries out and all eyes turn again towards the east where briefly, moth-flickering, like a flare, the light shows itself once more. Cyclops, one-eyed demon peering out of the tar-black night at them .... The darkness licks it in quickly, but the sight of it stirs again the corners of unease which flap in the sailcloth above their heads. The pilot is ringed by his agitated crew. The helmsman wears a rough linen scarf wrapped around his face, shielding him, he believes, not only from the elements but also from the contagion he fears the passengers have carried aboard. The others are bound up in capes and distraught bundles of blankets and coats against the weather. They carry a smell about them which Rashid notices as he approaches. The pilot straightens up and folds his arms; the council parts to let him through, out of fear or wonder, rather than respect.

'Well, sir,' the pilot sneers in Spanish, 'has your servant passed on yet?'

Rashid al-Kenzy ignores the question and looks instead around the assembly of faces. He realizes that he is almost too scared to hold his voice steady. He shakes his head briefly in reply. The helmsman curses and stamps his foot. Another of the men spits on the deck. Rashid straightens his back and addresses the pilot. 'Darius Reis, what is that light?'

'Dreamers, sir! The light of dreamers, trying to lure us onto their rocks – Wreakers, you see?' His eyes impenetrable, he grins with firm, straight teeth, his long hair blowing gently in the breeze.

The others are slumped in rapt superstition; they do not like to talk in front of this stranger. The helmsman began thumping his fist against the timbers of the helm.

'Pilot! Admit your folly! If it were not for this cargo of infected worshippers of Satan we would have shelter this night.' The others were obviously in agreement and they nodded their heads like tired pack horses and mumbled glumly among themselves. At that precise moment the rain began to pour down upon them. The helmsman, who was a large man with shoulders as broad as a bull, had to shout to make himself heard.

'Throw them overboard and be done with their curse!'

There was the harsh scent of blood in the air. Darius Reis looked at Rashid. 'What do you say, Moor?' What little harmony there was left was now about to break loose from its frail moorings.

'We had an agreement,' Rashid reminded him evenly. 'Either

way, it would be inappropriate to deal with anything at the present time other than our immediate predicament.'

The deck swayed beneath them as the sea took a deep breath and the water welled up. The pilot looked at him for a moment and then nodded. 'Get below. It is too dangerous to attempt to try and make land.' He glanced upwards. 'We have to ride out the squall.'

The storm grasped the ship by the tail and shook it for nearly a week, tossing them back and forth, out into the great Northern Sea, the Green Sea as Rashid knew it from Ibn Khaldun. The waves were harsh and sharp as crystal shards and they cut through the sails like windy lances. Through the turbulent cloud swirled the strange odour of iron and stone. The water beneath them was the world being born again, firm grey pumice and foam pushing through the bottom of the earth, snarling and wrenching itself apart as the waves rippled out in sinewy, flexible boughs of iron. Like nails their teeth cut into the pliant, rotting wood. Rashid had never imagined that such fury was known to the world, nor that it could be endured by any vessel. They were caught between the venomous sea and the fiendish determination of a pilot so stubborn as to be prepared to kill any man who doubted him. The crew withdrew to begin plotting how to slit his neck and throw him to the fishes.

The ship's crew began to turn in strange, mutinous rings. Their eyes were hooded by the thick veil of cloud and relentless rain. They turned on one another and daggers were drawn. The land which they had been courting was their worst enemy, for to be sucked in towards the shore now would undoubtedly have meant puncturing the hull and perishing.

The fifth day brought a lull and Rashid was afforded a brief glimpse of the sun through the small gun port on the main starboard aisle. But as darkness dropped over them like a stone, the wind began once again to tug impatiently at their sleeves. The sails cracked and whipped and the air was thick with the shouts of men as they struggled to pull in the main sheets, their shoulders and hearts stiff with exhaustion. How much more of this could the ship endure? The current drew them northwards into the night. Waves that could wash away an entire town sent them cascading this way and that.

Rashid went in search of the pilot and found him collapsed from exhaustion in his quarters. As al-Kenzy entered the darkened room, the pilot jumped to his feet, still dreaming. 'What?' he demanded. 'How much sail do we have? What draught? Drop the plumbline.' He sat up with such a wild look in his eye that it made Rashid pull back. There was a squeak from the bed and a hairy face appeared from beneath the blankets. With a shake of his head the pilot slumped back with a blank look upon his face. The ape crawled over to his side. It was a large creature, the size of a child of five or six with reddish brown hair and a look of such intelligence on its face as to dumbfound Rashid.

'Like the crow,' croaked the pilot, reaching for a jug of wine, 'never the bearer of joy. What news do you bring, Moor?'

'My companion will be dead before morning. Our mission is pointless. We must turn about and go back.'

The pilot laughed, long and loud, his head rolling backwards. He looked at the floor and then lifted his head as if to speak. He opened his mouth, closed it again, like a fish. He tried again and this time words came: 'A corpse? You want me to give you passage back to Cadiz with a corpse in tow? Have you lost all your faculties, man?' He reached towards a pile of crumpled clothing for a shirt and wiped his face on it.

'No, not Cadiz,' Rashid shook his head. 'His home is in Cyprus.'

Darius Reis waved a distracted hand and reached for a pipe. The sweet, leafy odour of hashish filled the small cabin. 'Cyprus, Cadiz, what difference does it make? You might as well ask me to take you to the moon.' His lean face was illuminated briefly by the flare of a match. His long hair hung over his face as he peered at Rashid. 'What kind of a man are you anyway, Moor? What reward are you seeking this far north?' He dismissed his own question with a snort. 'Never mind. You would not tell me, I know.' He lay back on the crumpled cot and kicked at the wall with his boot. Rashid decided to press on.

'Our mission is hopeless. I accepted only to gain my freedom. It is clear to me now that it is pure folly and that we all risk destruction.'

Darius Reis seemed to accept this. He nodded and set the pipe down on the table. 'You are not the first man to lose his way at sea, Moor. And I dare say you will not be the last.'

'So you will turn the vessel around?'

Darius stretched himself back on the cot and closed his eyes. 'I could not do it even if I wanted to. I have no idea where we are, Moor. All I am trying to do is keep the cursed bitch afloat.'

As he was opening the door to leave, Rashid heard the other man calling him back. 'Not a word of this outside this room,' the pilot warned. 'If the crew finds out they would string me up by the balls.' Then he turned on his side and went back to sleep.

Night. The wind more fierce. Rashid dragged himself hand over hand up the ladders to stick his head up through the narrow hatch to survey the deck. Gasping for breath, he screwed up his eyes against the blast. The planks could not be seen. In their place, a dizzy luminous mirror which seemed to breathe, its swirling surface heaved and hissed. Like the hair of a woman possessed, he thought. A barrel had come loose and was sliding back and forth. The sea was a fury, intent on spitting them out, ejecting them like the stone of some bitter fruit. Water poured in past him through the hatch, threatening to wash him down below. He hung on as the icy water washed over him. When it seemed to abate he clambered up the rungs again and out over the sill. He was scared to take a step, afraid that he would lose his bearings in the turmoil. He clung to the railing to keep from being dragged across the deck. With a thunderous crash the loose barrel splintered the wood of the housing beside him. It happened very slowly, or else very quickly, he was not sure. He saw it, but he could do nothing. A wrenching, wretched sound. If it had struck an arm's length to the left it would probably have killed him. His stomach rose and fell with the waves. He was flying, he was falling. He tasted the salt on his lips. He timed himself and waited for the right moment before launching himself out.

There was an argument in progress and Darius Reis was at the helm, surrounded by his crew. They have had enough and order him to take them to land, any land. He is shouting above the wind and water. The bottom of the the sea was a field of traps, soft round sandbanks that you could not see before you ran aground on them. 'The only course is to stick out here in deep water and let the wind run itself out.' Darius Reis stood there, swaying from side to side on the unsteady deck, the great mast towering above him, his long hair blowing like feathers around his neck. Catching sight of Rashid struggling to hold himself upright, he snapped impatiently, 'Get that fool below before he takes to the wind like a sparrow.' The weather seemed to reflect the inner state of the crew's mind, almost as though the storm itself were summoned from their uncertainty.

A strange fear this, exuding from their terrified bodies like excrement or sweat. A man was weeping like a baby. 'The sun has fallen from the ends of the earth,' whispered the Sicilians cowering in the galley brace.

Teeth chattering, and shivering so badly that he could hardly move, Rashid retreated. Halfway down the ladder his wooden fingers lost their grip and he slipped and tumbled the rest of the way to land heavily on the floor. He lay on the stinking wood of the lower deck, trembling like a leaf, gagging on the salty water he had swallowed. Another barrelful pours through the hatch above and crashes down over him. He crawls on his hands and knees down the narrow corridor, the water swilling round him. He is too cold to be scared.

The bosun was the colour of the sea, dark and unfathomable. His cracked lips moved but he could not talk. He was either reciting holy passages in preparation for his final hour, or else his lips were trembling uncontrollably with the fever. Rashid crawled to him and wrapped the dying man in his arms. There was nothing else to do, nothing anyone could do now, but wait.

Then a great hand seemed to grasp a hold of the ship and with a lazy, yawning sound it awoke from its sleep and prepared to die. The keel had locked itself tightly onto the sandy spine of a slumbering creature lying hidden beneath the icy waves, and the vessel began slowly to shake itself apart. Jammed against the sandbank, the ship now bore the full brunt of the storm. Fragments of wood splintered and flew through the air as it began to dismantle itself around them. The noise was deafening as the ship trembled like a trapped animal trying to free itself. The hull seemed to flex and bend like a goatskin waterbag. The screams of men, in pain and in prayer, rose upwards as the ship undid itself, stitch by stitch, plank by plank.

Slowly, gracefully, their heads spun around in the manner of those seekers of enlightenment – the Sufi dancers aspiring, to the divine, chanting, turning eloquent unbroken spirals in Konya, in the splendid mosques of Cairo, Kufa, Hafiz and Aleppo, stretching their tall hats towards the heights. The tails of their long gowns swirling as the sails fluttered down in torn ribbons and the crew abandoned their stations and set upon one another with the fury of wild dogs. The frail sound of pistol shots punctuated the howl of the storm.

Rashid al-Kenzy's head is filled with the sound of chanting; *La illaha il Allah*, over and over again. The salt water pours through the walls around him. He imagines he hears the bosun calling to him, although he knows that the bosun is dead. When he opens his mouth to reply, the water blows the words back down into his belly. He fumbles blindly, up to his waist, wading down the black corridor which seems to be lined with heavy wool, expanding and contracting as though he were within the breast of some strange animal. He lifts himself and, grasping hold of the first rung, begins to swing himself upwards.

The deck was alive with debris and broken sails, wooden spars churning around in the writhing confusion. The ship heaved upwards as though taking its last, beleaguered breath. A large figure slid to and fro across his path as the deck tilted. Each time the ship leaned into the wind the body crashed into the fo'c's'le and then slid away again. The bundle of clothing and bones was the remains of a man. Where the head had been there was nothing but a bloody pulp, a mess of hair and white bone, bound together in a thick tangle. The whiteness of the crushed skull like a strange tooth protruding from a leather jerkin. Rashid realized with a jolt that it was the pilot, Darius Reis. He managed to pull himself over the wooden frame. When the ship tilted he slipped and fell, back down through the hatch.

He feels himself falling, a long moment when he seems to be light as a bird.

'Pray, my child,' his mother used to say to him when he could not sleep. 'Pray for the children who have no homes, for the sheep who are lost in the hills, and for the sailors whose hearts have been lost to the waves.' And long ago, warm and safe, he would begin to recite, and before long the tide of this world would swell, carrying him away and he would float out into the sea of stars.

CHAPTER FOURTEEN

It was the commotion in the street which pulled Verner Heinesen from the jaws of the nightmare which had been about to engulf him. He awoke with a startled cry and sat upright in bed, pale as a winter field, his nightshirt damp with perspiration. He had a confused look on his face and, had she been there, his sister would have remarked that in that instant he looked the spitting image of their dear departed papa. Verner Heinesen tried to recall the cause of his distress, but the dream had evaporated like dawn fog on a summer morning. It sounded like there was a woman wailing in the street below. He called out for Klinke and his shout went echoing through the musty house needlessly. Klinke, having been alerted by his master's terrified cry, was already on his way up the stairs from the kitchen, where he had been engaging the innkeeper's widow in playful banter of a most flirtatious nature. Klinke was a womanizer who specialized in preying on young widows. He liked to think of himself as particularly adept in this field, so there were a few foul words on his lips as he stamped up the steep staircase. He threw open the door and entered without knocking to find his master pointing a finger at the small window in the corner of the small room.

'That noise, Klinke, what in God's sweet name is that terrible racket?'

Klinke bowed his head to reach the tiny alcove window. He peered out and sniffed. There was a small crowd surrounding a woman who was beside herself with fear and fury, tearing at her hair and clothes. Klinke laughed quietly and then licked the grin off his lips before turning back to the room.

'Ship went down during the night, sir. Lodged on the north beach.' Klinke stepped back to let Heinesen have a look. Over the bowed shoulders of his master he could see that the woman was almost stripped to the waist. Her clothes were in shreds and blood was running down her pale face in thin dark threads that spattered onto her naked torso. The lecherous grin remained on Klinke's face. She was on her knees now, turning her face upwards and stretching her hands up towards the sky.

'Good heavens above! Has that good woman taken leave of her senses?' Heinesen straightened up suddenly, banging his head on a low beam. He signalled to Klinke to pass him his clothes so that he might dress.

'Her husband, perhaps, was lost at sea?'

Klinke shook his head. 'Foreign ship, sir. They were all talking about it when I was seeing to the horses this morning. No survivors. No men in any case.'

Heinesen stopped buttoning his waistcoat and turned to glare at the shorter, stouter man. 'Make yourself clear, Klinke. What do you mean by that? Are you implying that there were women, or livestock aboard ship?'

Klinke pushed his tongue into a gap in the uneven row of blackened front teeth. It was a habit that annoyed Heinesen intensely. Klinke dismissed the query with a shrug of the shoulders. 'Nobody knows what it is, really. You know what people are like, sir. Some are calling it a sea-monkey, a monster from the deep; others call it the messenger of the devil himself.'

Heinesen said nothing. He started buttoning his coat again.

'It's what they believe, sir.'

'The devil?'

'Black as burned wood, they say, and eyes on him like the fires of damnation.'

'You saw him with your own eyes?'

'It's what I heard.'

Heinesen's patience expired. He pushed open the window and addressed himself to the small crowd below. 'This is a disgrace,' he shouted. 'Go on, get away from here with that terrible noise. Have you no respect for yourselves this day? Have you taken leave of your senses?'

'Have a heart Herremand Heinesen, it's not every day that the devil himself sends his emissaries to our fair port,' one earnest man remarked in a pathetic whine. The crowd seemed to be in agreement with him. They were self-righteous and scared. 'This poor woman near lost her wits when she saw the creature.' There was a murmur of assent in his wake. The woman's bare flesh was turning blue with cold. She seemed to have collapsed into a shuddering heap now and was weeping inconsolably.

Heinesen hesitated for a moment and then his curiosity got the better of him. 'How many of you have actually set eyes on this beastly apparition?'

The first speaker gestured around him. 'All of us, every last one of us.'

'Well then, you should all be ashamed for such talk of demons. Is there not a God-fearing Christian among you? And cover that woman up, for God's sake.'

With that he shut the window. Klinke said nothing. 'A flock of superstitious old women, Klinke. Seeing ghouls and sea devils.'

'Sometimes it is difficult to believe things that you have not seen with your own eyes, but that does not mean that they cannot exist.'

Something about the way he spoke. Not the accent so much, with its marshy, thick rural grumble. No, it was the formulation of Klinke's words. And something else too; the smell of the sea in the open window, the salt in the air. That combination, the salt and the words, took Heinesen back to another morning – more than ten years previously on the other side of the country, looking east instead of west, from the island of Hven across the Øresund Sound towards the firm dark outline of Skaane and Sweden.

'That is where I was born,' said the distant voice.

Heinesen could hear him speaking now as though he were standing right beside him, more real than Klinke even. The booming voice is agitated, irritated over something or other. Impatient, so that the young student Heinesen could not quite understand what he was doing wrong.

'Sir, you were saying . . . about belief.'

A blank look came over Tycho Brahe's face for a second. He scratched with a finger at the place where his foreshortened nose vanished into the silver prosthesis. 'Belief? Why yes! Of course, belief!' He turned and led the way along the shore of the island. 'But not the bovine beliefs of those money-grabbing bishops and priests, eager only to line their church pockets. God would be a sad figure if He were limited to the parameters of such fools. God is far more than that, Verner.' He smiled, the kindly uncle for once; these were early days. 'We are gullible creatures, Verner. We believe whatever the good Lord puts down in front of our noses. Anything more demands the imagination of a poet, or the insight of genius. The more we observe, the more we think we can explain.'

'Do you believe that our fates are written in the stars?'

From the tone of the old master's voice he could sense that his youthful mixture of ignorance and enthusiasm was beginning to grate.

'Everything is written in the stars, my boy. But like any language, theirs takes time to learn.' And with that he stamped away along the path. He paused though, hands behind his back, nose glinting in the light air, the high grass swaying in the wind that swept in across the grey, clipped waves around Hven. 'Perhaps,' he said, 'perhaps faith is a better word than belief, eh?' He swung on his heels and marched away without waiting for a response.

Heinesen sat down heavily on the bed to pull on his boots. So long ago. How much time and opportunity had been wasted then? What he would have given to have that chance again, now, to learn what had been offered him. Now, when he was ready for it, a full-grown man rather than an awestruck child who took time for granted.

'Superstition and ignorance. In the light of all this confusion I doubt whether we will get any of our chores done today, Klinke.' Heinesen stood up and stretched his arms. He was hungry and eager to resolve his business here and return home as soon as possible.

'The carts are ready, sir. All we are waiting for is a supply of nails and lime.'

Heinesen nodded. 'I doubt we will get any sense from these marsh dwellers today. But persevere, Klinke, do the best you can, we have already delayed our return more than sufficiently. Have the horses departed?'

'They were delayed by the storm, but the captain thinks that they will sail on the early tide tomorrow.'

'Good. Then we are relieved of that worry. Let us hope that

the good citizens of London appreciate the finer qualities of our ponies. That is what our efforts depend on.'

'Best horses in the world, sir.'

'Yes, Klinke, they are at that. The carts are secured I take it?'

'All is secure. I found a man and his son, looking for work. Shall I take them on?'

'Steady eyes, Klinke. If they have steady eyes and strong backs we can put them to work.'

'Then it is agreed.'

'Good.' Heinesen was impatient. Four days of storms and now this, strange creatures and women possessed by demons. 'I have an appointment with draughtsman Andersson which will take most of the morning and then I must have words with that half-witted provost.'

'Right you are, sir.' Klinke stamped out of the room, leaving Heinesen to consider the situation. He was curious about this 'sea devil', he had to admit. He pulled on his overcoat and picked up the rolled up plans for the construction with the latest adjustments that he wanted to show Andersson. His mind began to bury itself in technical matters. 'Sea apes indeed!' he muttered, marching swiftly from the room without checking to see if his tie was straight. The door flew closed in his wake with a thump that shook the whole house.

CHAPTER FIFTEEN

The provost stalked up the stairs to his office to face the agitated figure of his ancient notary.

'What in the name of God has descended upon us today?'

'Nothing less than the devil himself, Jakobsen, and nothing more than a man.' The provost leaned himself in over the stove and allowed its heat to warm him. For once the stupid old man had not complained about the mud on his boots. His shoulders and back ached from the ride and the exertion of walking out to the wreck. This was a good day for the town. The ship which God had deemed fit to cast at their feet was loaded with valuable goods. Not a king's ransom perhaps, but good timber that would dry out and yield a tidy sum, along with the other goods they had found; silk, some coins, not much, but it was all welcome in lean times.

'What is it?'

The provost yawned. 'I told you, a man.'

'They are saying it is a sea creature. An ape of some kind.'

'They are foolish peasants and you would do well to remember that.'

The frail old man paced about the room, pausing from time to time to peer through the distorting lattice of warped glass at the crowd which refused to disperse. He fretted and sighed. 'It is not a good thing, not good at all.' He shook his head. 'Never has such a creature been seen in these parts. Why, he is black as charred wood, they say. And his eyes, bright as a full moon. Mark my words, he will bring bad luck upon this town.'

The provost, however, was not listening. He had fallen asleep by the fire. Left to his own devices again, the notary rushed back and forth to the window to measure the agitation of the crowd outside. They showed no sign of dispersing and he continued muttering to himself as he hurried to and fro, peering out time and again in the hope that they might all just disappear.

Darkness fell and torches were lit. The faces of the people gathered outside flickered in the smoky flame. Women suckled children at their breasts. Men stood in circles and nodded their heads solemnly. Occasionally someone would decide to go up and knock upon the door and the notary, who was completely beside himself with worry, would jump up from his chair and rush over to peer cautiously out. He would stand there and try to find words of reassurance. Everything would be done in due course. Of course no one was in danger. He waved a hand at the crowd. 'Go on home,' he said meekly. 'Go about your business, now.' Of course they would not go. They remained there, eyes fixed on the building.

From time to time somebody would clamber up onto a nearby cart to try to rally the crowd. Some called for justice, others spoke of revolt. One tried to explain that they should take heart from the terrible fright which they had received today, that God in his wisdom sought only to remind them of the grace from which one can fall. They breathed in all of these words like intoxicating scents for, if the truth be told, they did not know what to do. Then their worry would overcome their patience and they would surge towards the door. Stones would be hurled and sticks hammered. When their voices rose up the grey notary crawled beneath his desk and covered his ears with his hands.

The following morning the door flew open. The man who stood there was tall and lean. He was dressed in a long black coat lined with soft fur. A closer examination of the quality of the large riding boots and the material of his clothes would have belied their somewhat stained and soiled condition. He was a youngish man who wore his hair long. He strode into the room and cast his gauntlets on the table.

'Greetings, gentlemen, from the north country.'

The provost sat up and swung his legs over the side of the cot. He grunted something under his breath and spat into the fire. 'Look, Jakobsen, see what the birds have brought to cheer us this good morning.'

The notary sat in his high chair by the window and pored over his ledgers, embarrassed by his superior. The newcomer strode to the fire and sat himself on a stool to warm himself.

'What brings you to these parts, Heinesen?'

'Two dozen ponies despatched to London on the morning tide.'

The provost got to his feet and rubbed his eyes. 'Hear that, Jakobsen? The streets of London town will soon be filled with the ripe smell of Jutland's horse shit.' He stretched his arms out wide. 'Good to hear that business is going so well for you, Heinesen.'

Verner Heinesen smiled. 'And well you might, for it keeps this harbour of yours in goose feathers and hams.'

'A man of wit is our squire eh, Jakobsen?'

The notary said nothing. He dipped his pen carefully and began slowly to scratch something across the page.

'You must excuse Herre Jakobsen today. He is a little preoccupied. You heard about the wreck on the north strand?'

'I did,' nodded Heinesen. 'And I also hear you have had some trouble.'

'Nothing that we cannot deal with, in our own time,' replied the provost.

'The sailors are saying that a creature was found in the hold of this ship. Half animal – half man, they say. They are calling it a sea-ape, which I always thought was a tale spread by the widows of fishermen.'

'If I did not know you better, Heinesen, I might imagine that you were taking our predicament rather more lightly than the matter warrants.'

Heinesen got to his feet. He was as tall as the large provost, but he appeared taller. He seemed to stoop in the low-beamed room. He shook his head and nodded towards the window. 'Those people out there are terrified out of their wits by whatever it is you have found. There are men calling for this ape-man to be hung on the gallows.'

The Provost cursed and then wiped a hand across his mouth. 'May the Lord forgive me, but I have no choice. It is my job to keep the peace. I cannot risk that the townspeople take it upon themselves to right the matter of their own accord. You understand that?'

'Of course.' Heinesen was thoughtful. He had taken the stories he had heard while making his rounds that morning as the overheated banter of townspeople, working men who had little grasp of the actual facts, unlike the provost.

'Perhaps it is not so inopportune, your arriving at this time, Heinesen.' The provost buttoned up his heavy leather jerkin and pulled on his boots. 'You are a man of learning, are you not?'

Heinesen's face stiffened, but only momentarily. He nodded. 'I trained at various academies of learning, it is true.'

'Come now, sir, your modesty is unbecoming. Herre Jakobsen, our learned friend here is shy of proclaiming his achievements.'

The notary's only gesture was to lift his eyes from the ledger, long enough, as it happened, for a large drop of ink to fall from the nib of the pen. As he began to fret and dab it away, the provost gave an exhausted sigh and turned back to Heinesen. 'You studied abroad, at the fine universities of Paris, as I recall.'

Heinesen tilted his head in a bow. 'You are, as always, most well informed.'

Having finished attending to his clothes, the provost stood for a moment. 'Perhaps Herremand Heinesen would then do us the honour of giving us his learned opinion of the creature we have here?'

There was an awkward moment. Heinesen drew himself up to his full height. 'Of course, I would be honoured to assist in any way, but my time is, I am afraid, much limited by the business which I must conduct in your fair town.'

The provost met his smile with an equally broad one of his own. 'Of course, of course. I would not for a moment entertain the idea of imposing on you, or your time. However, if you have a moment now I wonder if you would not mind casting a look at something.' He beamed. 'I am sure that we could all benefit from your vast learning.'

Without waiting for a reply, the provost spun deftly on his heel and led the way through into a small antechamber. The room was completely bare of furniture, but was otherwise filled with an odd collection of various forgotten objects acquired one way or another in the name of the state. Seized as bonds, or debts unpaid, or possessions traded for monies due to the king, or unclaimed property, from the homes of the dead for example; objects, in short, which were difficult to sell.

The provost gestured. 'What do you think of that then?'

The object to which he referred was a small wooden trunk. Heinesen stepped over to examine it more closely. It was made of some fine-quality hardwood, mahogany most likely. The ornamented brass corners and reinforcements made it a very solid and very handsome cabinet indeed. The top had been carefully inlaid with sandalwood and mother of pearl in a complex pattern of intriguing geometry. It was these shapes which drew Heinesen's curiosity. The clasp had been broken roughly with a blunt instrument. Here and there the surface had been damaged by rough handling, sand and salt.

'Recovered from the shipwreck?'

'Confiscated by my men from those peasants and simpletons out there, who no doubt would have chopped it up into firewood.'

Heinesen looked at the provost with new-found respect. 'You have truly found something here.'

'You recognize perhaps some of the inscriptions?'

Heinesen smiled and went down on one knee. 'Have you looked inside?'

The provost glanced away and shook his head briefly.

'I see.'

'I have simply not had the time to devote myself properly to the matter,' the provost replied, looking away once more.

Heinesen lifted the lid and peered inside. It was divided into compartments, shelves, boxes within boxes. There were papers, many of them badly sodden, so that the script was illegible.

'What cursed language is that?'

'The language of those who worship Mahomet, I would wager.'

The provost pulled back. 'Do not say that, Heinesen. I implore you, not even in jest.'

Heinsen looked over his shoulder at him. 'I only speak my opinion. That is what you wanted, was it not?'

'Yes, yes,' nodded the provost urgently, 'but not to anyone outside of this room. Is that agreed?'

'If you wish,' replied Heinesen getting to his feet. 'Nothing but clothes, and papers which seem to be some kind of log. And this.' He held up a flat brass case, about two handspans in length and half that in width; it was about four fingers deep. It had a sliding clasp which he unfastened. Closing the lid of the trunk he set the case down on top of it. The provost and the notary peered over his shoulder, while keeping their distance.

'This looks interesting.'

'Surely, you are not going to open it?' whined the ashen-faced notary. Heinesen lifted the lid. On the upper face there was a depiction of the world. There were points marking the location of various cities and towns. Although the script was Arabic, Heinesen's knowledge of geography was sufficient for him to identify a number of them. 'Kabool, Cairo, Vienna,' he pointed. The provost shrugged.

'What purpose could such an instrument serve?'

Heinesen was intrigued. On the lower surface there was a series of names and figures. Each point on the map could be connected to a name on these lists by means of a sliding rule. His finger traced the lines as he spoke: 'I am not sure to what end it was used, but my guess is that it was for some navigational purpose.'

'Put it away, Heinesen. God alone knows to what devious purpose it was intended.'

A smile crossed Heinesen's face as he slid the clasp back into place. 'Be that as it may. It has served your purpose.'

'My purpose?' queried the provost, wrinkling his nose.

'To whet my appetite and awaken my curiosity to meet this

captive creature thrown up from the deep.' Heinesen lowered his gaze and brushed the dust from his clothes. 'Was that not your intention?'

The provost shook his head in wonder. 'You are an intriguing fellow, Heinesen.' He gestured towards the door. 'Shall we?' They waited as the notary closed and locked the door to the annexe before the provost and Heinesen made their way out of the building and down the front steps to the street. The crowd surged towards them as soon as they appeared.

'Get out of the way. Go on, get on home, all of you!' The provost cursed and gesticulated, even going so far as to aim a kick at a gawky youth who was seated on the last step. He stopped for a moment. 'There is nothing here for you,' he announced loudly. 'I shall take care of this little matter myself.'

'What are you going to do with the devil?' someone in the crowd below him screeched. The provost placed his hand on Heinesen's shoulder. 'I have here a man with experience of just such matters. He has training at the King's academy of learning and will undoubtedly come up with a solution.'

'Be better off sending for the priest and his pyre,' called another onlooker. The thought seemed to be shared by others. 'Burn the devil now, rather than suffer the price later!'

'If anyone is to be burned,' roared the provost, 'I shall decide when and where.' Then he thrust his not inconsiderable bulk forwards and cleared a path for himself and Heinesen. They walked around to the rear of the building, where a narrow street ran. The provost marched quickly and Heinesen had difficulty keeping up with him. Behind them the crowd was trailing along. They scurried like furious mice behind the two men. Two men stood guard and the provost barked at them to keep the crowd back. He closed the door to the stable behind them with a curse and pulled a large timber across to lock it securely. He turned to face Heinesen.

'Now you see the gravity of my predicament, Herremand.'

He led the way inwards, past the looming dark shapes of cattle and horses. The room was at the very far end. The roof was low, so that both men had to bend their backs to avoid striking their heads in the gloom. The door, which was cracked and frail, was nevertheless firmly bolted. The provost gestured towards a small aperture at waist height and prodded Heinesen to take a look.

At first he noticed little but the smell. There was a narrow opening in the wall on the right, which must have faced out onto the street. Where the wall met the ceiling a band of blue light seeped through. The small room must have been big enough for perhaps ten men to stand upright in, if pressed together. The ground was covered with soiled straw. At first he thought the room empty, for he could not make out the shape of anything but the walls and the straw. Then there was a brief, almost imperceptible movement in the far corner, a flicker of something. The light had caught someone's, or something's, eye. Heinesen drew back instinctively.

'Well,' whispered the provost, 'what do you think?'

'I . . . er.' Heinesen swallowed and tried to collect his thoughts. 'It is hard to say. I can perceive very little at this distance.'

The two men looked at one another for a moment.

'You desire to enter the room, for a closer examination?'

Heinesen spoke urgently in shallow gasps. 'You asked me for my opinion. I am unable to render anything of the kind without some knowledge of what we are dealing with.'

'It is unnecessary for me to warn you of the possible dangers one might incur in such an undertaking. You have considered the matter of plagues and pestilence from wherever it comes?'

Heinesen was rapidly losing both courage and patience. 'Just open it. Let me see.'

The bolt was pulled aside and the door swung towards them. Heinesen stepped inside. The smell was much stronger. It was animals that had soiled this room, not humans. They must have settled on the first secure stall to hide their problem away from curious eyes. He looked back towards the door and saw the provost's face pressed against a crack in the door. He moved towards the centre of the room. He heard a light rattle of chains moving.

'Do not be afraid,' he said. He repeated the words, louder and in as many languages as he knew. Finally there was a long pause and Heinesen was wondering what to do next when he heard a grunt from the shadows.

Where?

The word was pronounced in the rough *lingua franca* of southern harbours, but was sufficiently close to the Spanish word for Heinesen to guess what was meant. 'Where? . . . Where you are, now?'

Where?

'The country of Dania. You are in the southern region of the peninsula of Jutland.'

How did I get here?

'Your ship ran aground. You were rescued by the villagers.' This seemed to draw some temper from the man, who began to speak rapidly in another language which Heinesen could not immediately grasp. The little he could understand was sufficient for him to hazard a guess at the portion which remained obscure.

'They are scared of you.'

Scared? Of one man?

'They believe you to be a demon of some kind, a devil.'

Again the other language, which Heinesen now guessed was either Turkish or Arabic.

The others on the ship?

'You were the only survivor.'

The provost was hissing from the door, trying to draw his attention. Heinesen ignored him and took a step closer towards the corner, treading as he did so on the pile of rinds and pulped oats which had been overturned there to feed this strange creature from the sea.

'Come forwards where I can see you.'

Silence.

Heinesen decided that it would be wise not to push for too much at once. He was also finding it hard to concentrate with the provost flapping his hand through the door and calling him back.

'I will return to see you tomorrow.'

There was no response forthcoming, so Heinesen turned and began to make his way back towards the door. The voice followed him to the door.

They will have killed me by then.

Heinesen stood for a moment and then turned to rap on the door. The provost could hardly contain himself. He wrung his large hands together in excitement.

'I knew my faith in you was not misplaced. I have to confess that we have not always seen eye to eye, but at heart I always had a suspicion that you were a man of great worth.'

'You are keeping him like a wild creature.' Heinesen paced around the gloomy stables.

The provost was at a loss. 'But of course. How are we to know whether he eats the flesh of babies for his supper? I have a responsibility to the people of this town. I cannot let him loose among them.'

Heinesen rounded on the man. 'Nor do you need to throw him in a place of such filth as to be unfit for even swine to inhabit.'

They had reached the door and Heinesen lifted off the bar and cast it to one side. The provost hurried after him, brushing aside the hands and demands of the people who had waited for them outside the stable. His patience was drawing towards its limits. He stood his ground, stamping his foot in the middle of the street.

'Herremand Heinesen, you are being unreasonable. I demand that you lessen your pace.'

Heinesen pulled up and turned back to face him. Past the provost he saw the curious, grubby faces of the onlookers. Young men, eager for blood; older men who should have known better. Sailors with harsh grins on their leathery faces. Girls clutching babies. Women who were obviously drunk.

'What would you have me do? Honestly now, if you were in my position.'

Heinesen beckoned the provost to him and patted his shoulder.

'I have lodgings nearby here and a cask of sherry from a happy customer in England. I insist that you join me.'

A short time later found them seated by the fire at the inn. The provost raised his glass of English sherry to let the flames play in the dark liquid.

'Curious, don't you think, that they are aware of our existence, they even have our towns plotted on their instruments and yet we know nothing of them?'

The provost rubbed his fleshy face and drained his glass. 'It has occurred to you that their mission might have had a military aspect to it?'

Heinesen laughed. 'Come now, do not let your imagination get the better of you, my dear man.'

'Well, admit it. It makes no sense. I believe they were lost. Whatever their mission might have been, God, in his own way, saw fit to bring it to a swift end. I must deal with the matter at hand.' The provost helped himself to the sherry before proceeding. 'You understand, Heinesen, that I am in a difficult position. I am constantly in danger of being undermined by the priest. The bishop sees fit to visit us only when absolutely necessary and this man is shamelessly ambitious. He would stoop to anything to gain more leverage in these parts. God knows, these are simple people who do not understand the ways of words, as you or I might do. They understand the bite of the whip across their shoulders. They fear God only marginally more than they fear the devil.'

Heinesen lifted his eyes from the fire. The provost nodded. 'I know. You would not expect to hear such words from a man like me. It is damned close to heresy.' He lifted his chin. 'Now, Heinesen, I am in your hands.'

'You have no reason to concern yourself on that matter,' Heinesen said, lifting the cask under his arm and filling both their glasses. 'But I know only too well the danger that you face.'

The provost leaned urgently forwards. 'Then you must sympathize.'

'There is no question that you have my sympathy.'

There was more.

'You would help me then?'

Heinesen sat back and loosened his necktie. He held up his hands. 'I have barely spoken to the miserable fellow. I do not know if I can get any more sense from him than you might.' He sighed. 'But if you so wish I can delay my return for one day and seek to communicate further with him tomorrow.'

'That is not enough.'

'That poor creature was right. It is only a matter of days before you cast him to the mob.'

The provost set down his glass. 'There is only one alternative to that. You must take him with you.'

'You are mad, sir.'

'It can all be taken care of discreetly. I will arrange to have it rumoured that we cast his body back into the waters where it came from. It is the only way. I will not give that priest the satisfaction of lighting his pyres in my town. God knows I have no great sympathy for whatever misery this creature has endured, but I will not let him be used to usurp my authority. And the only way that I can avoid that happening is to get him gone from here. Take him north with you, Heinesen. There he is not known. They will assume he is some curiosity you uncovered on your travels. With your assurances there will be no commotion. On your estate, away from townspeople, your workers will take you at your word that they are in no danger.'

'What would I do with him?'

'You are building.' Heinesen raised his eyebrows. The provost floundered in the air with his hand. 'It does not matter, I have heard as much. You are seeking men, are you not, to help with the construction of some annexe to your estate?'

Heinesen said nothing for a moment. He had not expected that his plans would remain secret for long. It appeared, however, that the nature of his work was still unknown.

'I am not a reckless man. Such an undertaking is not without risk. You are asking for an unconventional solution which in

143

itself risks bearing the wrath of the king. You are willing to give me a certificate of receipt?'

'I will give you anything you desire to satisfy your concerns.'

'You are indeed mad, or perhaps I was over-zealous in filling your glass?'

The provost shook his head. 'Neither. I am afraid I am all too sane. It is the world which is mad.' With that he got to his feet and lifting his hat he made for the door, turning once to whisper mischievously, 'Or perhaps it is God who has had too much English sherry?'

CHAPTER SIXTEEN

Not even the rain could disperse the onlookers. They sat huddled beneath a cloak of old blankets and yards of grubby sailcloth in the middle of the road. Like ducks. The ashen-faced notary watched from the small window beside his table as they indulged in sessions of cleansing flagellation. This now took place several times a day. A collection of women had taken this task upon themselves. They were of all ages, about sixteen of them. They would form a circle at the centre of the crowd, close to the foot of the steps. Then they would move in a circle, each whipping at the back of the one in front of them with a horse switch, a flail, or a handful of branches.

'When will they give this foolishness up?' the notary cried out, getting up and then sitting down again suddenly in despair. The provost grunted and struggled to his feet. He staggered across the room, rubbing the sleep from his eyes. He peered from the window and winced at the sight of the blood which mingled with the rainwater.

'The women are worse than the men.'

'Yesterday I heard that a contingent of peasants from the Lolland region is making the pilgrimage here to help with proceedings.' The notary was growing thinner and more grey by the hour. 'Think, if rumours spread we will become tainted for all eternity. People of every twisted persuasion of the body and soul will flock here, not to mention the more fervent of the religious believers. People will come here to cure us, to heal us, to bathe themselves in the evil, or simply to stand outside my window and stare.'

The provost stamped his foot on the floorboards. 'I have gathered the gist of your sermon, thank you, Herre Jakobsen.' He rubbed his face. 'You are right of course, we must get the little devil out of here as soon as possible.'

The priest arrived around mid-morning accompanied by a tall, sombre-looking man and a boy carrying a large trunk on his back. The provost gritted his teeth as they entered the room. The priest had an upturned, eager face, a receding forehead and sharp, pointed ears. He was dressed entirely in black, save for the ruffled white collar which ringed his neck. He examined the office carefully as if expecting to find evidence of spiritual depravity lurking in every cobwebbed corner.

'We are here to lend our services in the matter of this unfortunate messenger from hell.'

'And what manner of assistance did you have in mind to offer?' asked the provost, one eye on the tall man who remained straight as a tree standing beside the door. The priest smiled that ready smile of his and gave a small bow.

'It is my duty to inform you, all of you, that there is much fear among the good people of this town. There has been talk of omens and dark portents.'

'Surely, it is your duty to inform the good people that they have nothing to fear from a solitary, scared mariner who lost his way at sea?'

'If you would permit me to explain. The work of God is never finished. I am well aware of the dangers of such unbridled distress. I have, of course, as is fitting, done my best to allay such fears. However, it is also essential not to underestimate the depth of such feelings and for measures to be manifestly and openly applied in our efforts to find an effective remedy.'

'What would you suggest, priest, that we take him out and let them burn him?'

'Come now,' the priest smiled thinly. 'We must not allow ourselves to be smitten by the fever which appears to be running rife among our common brethren.'

The provost took a deep breath. The tall man, who so far had remained silent, now stepped forwards. The most striking feature about him was the shape of his head, which was like an egg pointed upwards. The staring eyes were motionless and milky coloured and protruded noticeably from the clean-shaven, angular face. The skin was grey and resembled a kind of flaky stone. His forehead rose upwards and backwards in a clean bald sweep that culminated in a thin band of brown hair. He was taller than any man in the room. Indeed, he was taller than any man the provost had ever seen in his life.

'If I might be so bold.' He spoke in a clear, composed manner. 'I might be able to supplement the knowledge we have already gathered about the creature. Might this not, in turn, help to allay the concern about its nature?'

'Who is this man?'

The priest gave another bow. 'This is our surgeon, Manson. He studied in Bologna and Basel. His knowledge of the human corpus is unrivalled.' The provost made no attempt to greet the tall man formally; hard as it was to imagine, the provost found surgeons even more despicable than priests.

'It has been suggested that Herre Manson perform his examination and return his verdict to us so that we might judge the best course of action.'

'The good bishop has made his thoughts known?'

147

The priest turned away with a cluck of impatience. 'I hardly need to remind you that you bear a good deal of responsibility for the disturbance and unrest caused by this event.'

'No, you hardly need to.'

The priest glared at the provost. 'You should have let the wretched creature drown at sea.'

'And you a man of God.' The provost raised his eyebrows in mock astonishment. He waved to the surgeon to send him on his way. Manson turned and swept from the room in three long strides, the boy behind him struggling with the large case.

The provost sighed.

The priest sniffed. 'Well, at least we shall ascertain whether or not he is carrying some evil pestilence.'

'Don't be so sure,' growled the provost. 'I never had much faith in the jibbering nonsense of surgeons. I never heard of them curing anyone of anything serious.'

The three of them stood and waited in silence. The priest turned towards the window. The notary threw a small log on the fire. The sound of the crowd gathered around the front steps was not unlike that of a stiff breeze rustling through a patch of trees.

The grey, scaly figure removed his coat and rolled up his sleeves. He tied on a shiny leather apron and ordered the boy, whose hands trembled, to strip the clothes off the creature. The tall man rolled up his shirt sleeves and took a bucket of scalding hot water handed to him by the guard who waited outside the door. He cast the contents over the huddled, naked form and then called loudly for another. He then began casting handfuls of powder around the room. Acrid smoke rose in thin wraiths from the damp stone. The boy, who had retreated into a corner, began to cough, tears filling his eyes, until finally he managed to stagger from the room. The surgeon tied a cloth around his mouth and nose and approached the dark creature across the room.

'Come here, my little beauty,' he snarled, stretching out a bony hand. For the next two hours he prodded and poked at every corner of the creature's anatomy. He rubbed its skin with alum and its fingertips in gunpowder. He stuck wooden rods up its rectum and copper pipes down its throat. He kneaded it and stretched every muscle and ligament, bent the joints this way and that, looking for gills, valves, ventricles, features that should not be there. He examined the spaces between the fingers and toes for signs of webbing. He prised long thin needles into its belly to assertain the positioning of the vital organs. From its armpits he drained a good quantity of blood into an iron pot which was then set by the boy to boil. He wrapped iron rings around its temples and poured lilac fluid through a funnel into its ears. He weighed and measured every available inch of its body, including the penis, which he held in his hand for what seemed a little longer than necessary, although by this time the subject was quite beyond caring. When the surgeon left, packing all his instruments into a large leather trunk, the devil slumped naked and retching on the cold floor. Even the guard who had witnessed the examination seemed to take pity, for he returned briefly to drop a rough linen blanket over the shivering creature.

The days went by. Rashid crouched on the floor stuffing discarded cabbage stalks into his mouth and chewing them urgently. High up on the wall was a narrow iron grill which, because of the way the stable sloped downwards, was on the level of the small street at the back of the building. People could kneel here and look in on the prisoner. They collected there like leaves. They chanted and cursed the misfortune which the sea had brought upon them. Small stones clattered between the bars from the street above. They called out taunts and threw small sticks and stones. Some of them were on their knees praying for forgiveness, while others kept up a steady litany of curses. They knew that he was a creature from a strange forest far across the sea, further south than the place where all men turned black and the devil lived in luxury in his palace of sin. They knew that one look from him could bring them out in a rash of boils and inflict such pain as they had never known upon their bowels, but they could not stay away.

The rain sputtered onto the stone cold floor, the water ran down his neck when he was huddled in the corner to sleep. He hopped from one foot to the other to prevent himself turning into a frog.

CHAPTER SEVENTEEN

Verner Heinesen squinted through the window of his room, upstairs at the inn. The glass was dark with impurities which shaded the town in a variety of browns, yellows and greens. In the distance, beyond the steeple of the church, he could see the shimmer of waves breaking on the submerged ridge of sandbanks that stretched north and south along the coastline. To the north the houses and buildings that formed the centre of the town gave way to open fields and the long wavy grass of the marshland. He had been here for over two weeks now and was becoming impatient to return home. He watched as a cart loaded high with timber lurched across the uneven stones beneath him. A woman carrying a chicken under one arm called out to the driver leading the cart.

There was still so much to do. He had laid in orders for most of the material he required with the shipping office and had already secured carts and drivers to transport the large timbers when they arrived the following spring. Everything was possible, he thought to himself. All that was required was that one planned everything out, down to the most minute detail. That morning he had concluded his business with Andersson the draughtsman. The house where he lived and worked faced onto the west side of the church. The room was large and wide with two long working benches and an impressively large fireplace kept well stoked by a young houseboy.

Andersson had a tightly chiselled face, with small eyes set close together that were like hard blue mussel shells.

'You are a man of some ambition, Heinesen.'

'You think that I am being foolish.'

Andersson thrust his chin out and looked away for a moment. 'Any man who would dare to attempt such a feat is either a fool or very brave.' He looked back at Heinesen. 'I cannot decide which one of the two you are.'

Heinesen sat down on a stool with his back to the fireplace. He liked this room. It had a cosy, comfortable feel to it and an intensity that he respected. He liked the man seated in the chair opposite him, too. The Anderssons of this world were few and far between. He would have traded a hundred noblemen for one such as this.

'The plans are sound, you say. The structure would hold?'

'In itself the structure is undoubtedly sound. The work you have done is thorough, I must say.'

'I sense, nevertheless, that you hold some reservations.'

Andersson leaned forwards in his chair. 'Heinesen, you must be clear about something. An undertaking such as this is more than a mere construction. An observatory like this will draw great attention. If you fail . . . well, I would not like to think of the consequences which your name will suffer.'

'Andersson, I came to you because I respect your judgement, and not solely in connection with your skill as a surveyor. Please, you must speak freely.'

'Very well.' Andersson clasped his hands together and sat back in his chair again. 'I shall speak my mind. Herremand Heinesen, this project of yours is a dangerous one. The financial investment itself is staggering. You are a wealthy man, from a noble family. Your income from the family properties and from the horses on your late uncle's farm is a sizeable one. Many men of your age would be content to settle down and enjoy the benefits afforded by such comforts.'

Andersson fell silent for a moment. 'What I am trying to ask you is this: why do you want to engage yourself in this undertaking?'

'The answer to that question is obvious. Were I a poet perhaps I could content myself with the life you describe. I am not heartless. I could, with some labour on my part, manage to find a suitable wife and, as you say, settle myself to the material comforts of this life. But that is not sufficient.'

'Not sufficient?' Andersson gave a gruff laugh. 'You dream of the stars, Heinesen. Be careful that their light does not blind you.'

'Not a dream.' Heinesen shook his head. 'The Spanish have made their colonies in the New World and found their silver. The Portuguese cut through the darkness which enclosed Africa and thus penetrated the eastern reaches of Persia and the ocean beyond. No, there is nothing more to be done in that field.'

'Indeed?' Andersson seemed quite bemused by Heinesen's fervour.

'Of course,' Heinesen went on feverishly, 'the work will continue. Each king sending out his fleets to place his flag on every unmarked corner they can find. But nothing new.'

'The heavens are new?'

Unable to sit still any longer, Heinesen got to his feet, unintentionally knocking over the stool as he did so. He began to pace in front of the large fireplace. 'He was so close to seeing how it must be, as described by the Pole, Copernicus. He lost his nerve, don't you see? He was afraid. That is why nothing good can come from a man of science being in the pay of a monarch. They concern themselves only with self-serving prophecies.'

'You are referring, I take it, to Tycho Brahe.'

'Old "Ironbeak".' A gleam had come into Heinesen's eye. He gave a nervous laugh and touched a hand to his nose. 'He lost the tip in a fencing duel in his young days.'

'You were an apprentice of his on Zealand.'

'On the island of Hven.'

Andersson poked at the fire. 'Fighting duels does not immediately strike one as being the mark of a man lacking in courage.'

'Perhaps in some way you are right. The fact of the matter remains that he compromised.'

'This is what you want?' asked Andersson slowly.

'I want to prove what the ancients knew, what the Hermetica texts show, that Copernicus was right, that the sun is the centre of all things.'

'Heinesen, I admire your courage, your devotion, but to take up this matter is to take up arms against the Church.'

Heinesen was dismayed. He had truly hoped that Andersson would give him at least a modicum of moral support.

'Tycho passed away, did he not?' enquired Andersson.

'In miserable exile, in Prague, seven years ago.'

'Why do I sense that there is unfinished business between you and your former master?'

'I was an assistant, nothing more. Privileged, as I was frequently informed by His Grace, for being allowed to join their company.' Heinesen's eyes grew distant as he recalled the sound of footsteps retreating down long stone corridors, of the light through the windows in the great halls of Uranienborg. 'So much could have been done. Indeed, so much was accomplished and yet he was unable to resist trying to find a compromise, a way out. He wanted everyone to be satisfied with his work.'

Andersson appeared to be growing bored with the conversation. He got to his feet and said something about getting back to work. He saw Heinesen to the door.

'You wish to build your little empire of the stars, and you are young enough to attempt it. But be sure that you are entering into this engagement for the right reasons.' He smiled. 'Who knows, you might even succeed.'

But Heinesen ignored the intended irony. 'The age we live in, Andersson, is the most exciting in history. In the next one hundred years we will learn more about ourselves and the universe in which we live than in all the centuries that have passed since the dawn of time.'

A knock at the door disturbed Heinesen's train of thought and brought him back to the present.

'Who is there?' He called out sharply. Klinke came in, pushing the door open cautiously and pulling off his hat. Heinesen looked at him blankly for a moment. Klinke had been in the service of his uncle since he was a small child. He remembered him from the few occasions when he and his sister had come to visit, when they were children. Klinke stared mournfully round the room, aware that his young master was not in the best of moods today. With his scruffy beard, his heavy boots and leather jerkin, he seemed to fill the small room. Heinesen raised a smile in greeting. 'What news from the front, Klinke?'

'The wagons are loaded and ready to leave on your command, sir.'

'Then let us depart without delay. I am eager to return to work as soon as possible.'

'Very well, sir.'

As he was climbing into the lighter, two-wheeled carriage, he surveyed the collection of heavier carts that were to follow on later carrying the goods back north. A thought struck him and he set down the reins. He called Klinke over to him.

'Go to the provost and speak to him in confidence. Tell him that I have decided to make good on the purchase we spoke of. You must be discreet, Klinke, raise no attention to your actions. The provost will understand and help to make arrangements. The man in question is to be entered into our service.'

The space between Klinke's two chestnut eyes folded itself steeply into an expression of confusion. Heinesen patted him on the shoulder. 'Not so glum, Klinke, I would not have marked you down as a superstitious old woman.' And with that he drove off, calling a postscript over his shoulder which only added to the bewilderment on Klinke's face. 'Tell him not to forget the trunk.' He rattled out of town across the cobbled stones, horses gathering speed.

The following morning, shortly before dawn, the small, cracked door in the damp stables swung open. A guard hurried in with a blanket in his hands, which he threw over the stranger's head, much as one might dress a horse. His companion helped to steer the way along the length of the cavernous cellar towards a doorway and a shallow ramp. The chipped edges of the stone arch where they emerged were picked out by the first watery rays of dawn. Upon the flat square behind the stables was a rough, short-ended wagon with heavy wheels and bars along the side. Two sturdy horses waited patiently. One guard tucked a small loaf of bread under Rashid's arm as he scuttled up the steps in his bare feet, the blanket over his head like a shroud. Standing by the wagon was the solitary figure of Klinke with a sombre look upon his face. He looked the figure over as he approached. Then he stepped back and indicated the back of the wagon. The two guards bundled the strange figure into the back of the cart, where a man and a small boy huddled together under the canvas cover. Klinke tied the sailcloth down firmly over the top of the wagon and then, climbing up into the seat, he shook the horses into life. The heavy wheels turned and the wagon pulled slowly and unobtrusively out of the town before the sun had time to open its one good eye.

CHAPTER EIGHTEEN

His name was Martin and he was named after his grandfather who was buried in the graveyard behind the village church. They were walking up the narrow path that curved across the grass towards the small grey building. Hassan had put his work aside, deciding that he needed some fresh air. Having looked across at the church through his kitchen window countless times, he felt it was about time that he paid it a visit. He had just pushed the low gate closed behind him when the boy from the shop hailed him from the road below. Hassan waited for him to catch up. It was raining lightly and the flagstones on the path were slick with water.

'They used to dance here,' Martin went on, still catching his breath, 'in the olden days.'

'Your grandparents?'

'No,' the boy laughed. 'The heathens. They used to dance here, naked. And they used to sacrifice people too.'

'Well, it's true that a lot of churches were built on sites formerly used for other forms of worship.'

Martin stuck his hands in his jacket pockets and walked backwards ahead of Hassan. 'You see? We do know a thing or two out here.'

'I never doubted it for a minute.'

They had reached the front of the church. The original

building consisted of a rectangular box shape constructed using quite large blocks of roughly hewn limestone.

'Little fish,' said Martin, poking at the shell fragments visible in the rock.

'Molluscs, not fish.'

'Molluscs?'

Hassan shrugged. 'Seashells. You know, like you find on the beach.' He carried on walking round the outside of the church. The original building had been added to, probably more than once.

'Where did you learn all of this stuff?'

'The usual places. School, college, university.' He looked over at Martin. 'How old are you? Sixteen, seventeen?'

'Eighteen.'

'Finished school? What are you planning to do?'

'No idea.' Martin gave a lopsided grin and reached out a hand to touch the wall of the church. 'So what do you think,' he asked, gesturing. 'Interesting enough for you?'

'Yeah,' nodded Hassan. 'It makes a nice break from all those books I have to read. I think I'll take a look inside.'

The sound of a car horn came from the road and Martin waved to someone. 'I have to go.'

'Listen,' Hassan turned, 'I don't know, but if you're interested I can ask if they could use an extra pair of hands on the excavation.'

'Really?'

'Sure.'

His head bobbed up and down and the greasy hair fell forwards to cover Martin's face. 'I'd like that.'

'OK. I'll talk to them.'

'OK.' He repeated the word several times as he turned to go. 'Thanks,' he shouted from the gate. Hassan waved a hand. He heard a door slam and the sound of the engine as the car drove away.

Inside, the church was dark and smelled of wood varnish. There were rows of empty, high-backed pews, each with its own little gate which opened onto the aisle. Hassan lifted the latch and stepped inside to sit down close to the back of the church. It was cool and quiet, and really quite spartan. There was a stand which displayed the numbers of the hymns that had been last sung here. He made a mental note to check on the history of the church. Perhaps Martin was right and there had once been heathen ceremonies held on this site.

He took a deep breath and turned his mind back to Verner Heinesen. What had the man been hoping to achieve, building some kind of astronomical observation tower out here in the middle of nowhere? And what was the connection to the name on the brass instrument? What had happened here nearly four hundred years ago?

What kind of a man was Heinesen? Hassan had managed to gather some information about his apprenticeship with Tycho Brahe on Hven. Letters, sent to the sister apparently, had been uncovered in a private museum close to Helsingør. Brahe, one of the most well-known astronomers of all time, did not sound like a lot of fun to work for.

Tycho Brahe was born into a family of nobles in the province of Skåne, now part of Sweden, to the east of Copenhagen, across the Øresund. The island of Hven was granted to him for life by King Frederik II in 1576. For the purposes of his research he was given an extensive estate in Norway and another at Roskilde, along with a pension of two thousand crowns from customs duties gleaned from the traffic passing through the sound into the Baltic Sea. He spent years building the audacious Uranienborg and later Stjerneborg. The community on Hven was a mixture of artisans, pupils, visiting nobles from all over Europe, including King James I of England. At the time there was no scientific centre in Europe to rival Hven. Here Brahe was the uncrowned king of all he surveyed: buildings, mills, ponds, gardens, springs, and a printing press. There were iron foundries for the construction of measuring instruments – enormous armillaries and measuring quadrants. There were chemical laboratories, livestock, and good fishing. The island was self-sufficient; they even produced their own paper for the printing press.

Fifteen ninety-six, and the nineteen-year-old Christian IV finally succeeds to the throne. Christian was the same age as Heinesen; he was born in 1577, which meant that he was eleven years old when his father Frederik II died. It was King Frederik who had supported Tycho Brahe's work. In the intervening years a council took care of matters for the young king and Brahe was not popular; there were many who openly disapproved of the late king's fondness for him. By all accounts Brahe was not an easy man, and he certainly made his share of enemies. Many of these were now gathered around the young monarch. The climate changed for the astronomer. He was accused of letting the church at Roskilde fall into ruin. Also of exploiting the small local community on Hven, who were apparently terrified of all the mischief he was creating with his meddling in alchemy and astrology. His privileges and income were gradually whittled away. He packed up all his belongings and instruments, leaving behind only those which could not be moved, and departed for Prague. Emperor Rudolph II gave him one of his own castles and there Brahe remained until his death, of a burst bladder, in 1601.

One other thing, Hassan noted, Brahe had a twin brother who died at birth.

By the time Hassan got home it was early evening. He had just sat down to work again when the telephone rang. It was his wife, Lisa.

'Where are you?'

'At my sister's place. I think I'll stay here for a while.'

'I see.'

'I need to know . . . I need to know what you want to do.'

'I don't know. I mean, I'm very busy right know.'

'How long are you staying over there?'

'I'm not sure.'

'Just tell me one thing. I think I have the right to ask. Are you in love with her?'

Hassan stared at the empty screen. The cursor flickered on and off.

'Are you still there?'

'Yes,' he said, finally, 'I'm still here.'

'Take all the time you want,' she said. 'Just don't expect me to wait for ever.'

There was a click as the line went dead. The sun had gone down. The room was silent. He remained where he was. Nothing moved.

CHAPTER NINETEEN

Late afternoon, and Klinke urged the horses on with a curse. The cart slipped past the lake to follow the curling path up the hill. Peering out from under the tarpaulin, Rashid looked down through the trees at the long ellipse of water. The tired horses plodded their way up through the stooping trees to emerge onto the prow of a sparsely wooded, windswept ridge.

Ahead of them was the large house.

'Helioborg,' grunted Klinke. Beside him on the seat were the man and the boy whom he had taken on. The father shook himself awake and the boy stretched. Rashid lay back on his lumpy bed of sacks filled with lime and boxes of nails. He rolled over and lifted his head to look up the hill.

The 'Castle of the Sun', as it was now known, was situated upon a flat stretch of ground about halfway up a broad, rolling hill overlooking the placid lake. Horses cantered through the lower fields, rushing back and forth, tossing their manes. The air was growing cold with a damp, biting edge that burred tenaciously at the bone. The carriage rattled across stones and stiffened ruts in the ground, shaking his bones loose. As they climbed the gentle slope of the prow, Rashid gazed down at the long, calm stretch of water and the horses which seemed content with these damp pastures. They were sturdy legged, robust creatures. He gave up trying to count how many there were. As the house drew near, he could see that it was not one building but a collection of several adjoining outhouses and barns arrayed around a square, cobbled yard.

Rainwater gathered in pools between which the heavy wheels jolted and swayed. The cart swung in a wide arc to draw to a halt in front of the main house. Two women set down their pails of milk to watch their arrival. The rain had stopped and the sun cut through the veil of cloud in vivid splashes of bright light. The tarpaulin was pulled aside and Rashid blinked his eyes, picking out the size and shape of this new place. The two women remained where they were in front of a long low building which he was later to discover was the workers' lodgings. There was a rather barren look about the whole place, as though it had been left too long to the wind and the rain, or perhaps lacked the one vital ingredient that would make it a home. The main house faced south and was large compared to what he had seen so far, but it had the same frailty of timber and mud wattling that made it seem almost a part of the landscape. As he climbed to the ground, his chains rattling, he was aware of their eyes upon him. The women stared in astounded silence. Their features were rough and their skin pale and watery. Rashid did not dare look directly at them; instead, he observed them out of the corner of his eye, a furtive instinct that would grow into a habit of self-preservation.

They called out to Klinke, asking him what in Satan's name he had brought along with him. Klinke snapped back with a curt comment which made them pick up their pails and move on their way. He was busy now, moving around the cart, untying ropes, calling for help with the unloading. Two men came and stood for a while, hands on hips, exchanging words with Klinke and the other drivers who had also now arrived.

The yard was filled with movement. The boy and his father who had ridden alongside Klinke were handed things to carry and they seemed glad to be given some task to complete. They staggered away towards the open door of the large stable on the east side of the compound.

Rashid felt the chains loosen. He saw the arc of the iron rings as they curved through the air, and heard the thump as they landed in the back of the cart. He heard the long breath exhaled by Klinke as the shadow of those broad rounded shoulders turned away. The house rises up in front of him. His gaze travels slowly upwards past the grey stone of the front steps, past the iron railings that curved their way to the olive-green door, up past the frame and the name carved in stone. The intersecting wooden spars were painted a thick ochre-red colour. The timbers criss-crossed one another producing triangles and squares of chalked wattling. A single drop of silver rain clung to the corner of one of the protruding beams. There were eight windows along the upper floor. He counted them.

The lodging house was a large, cavernous building. The floors were all covered in straw for warmth. The room was divided into numerous chambers by wooden partitions which made it resemble a stable. Faces peered out of the gloom at Rashid as he was led through. Some of the men had families with them and would take over a whole compartment to themselves, while many others were left unoccupied. Small children ran past, chasing one another, laughing. It took three paces to measure the width of one of these wooden construc-tions. They showed few signs of habitation, a bundle of clothes here, a sack there, but mostly they contained straw cots for sleeping on. Rashid found himself beside the opening of an empty stall at the far end, close to the wall. Klinke pointed at the ground and put his hand to his face to indicate sleep. It was damp and dark, and yet he did not mind. He was still savouring the feeling of lightness that he felt, having been relieved of the chains around his ankles. He looked up to find the other man still watching him. Klinke muttered something and turned on his heel, vanishing into the shadows. Rashid's clothes were, on the whole, in a state of considerable distress. The long woollen tunic was more holes than garment, and as he clutched the old horse blanket around his shoulders he had the impression that were he to let go, all the rags would simply fall apart – like a knot being undone.

His hands and feet were clusters of bloody sores and blisters. His front teeth felt loose and there was an awful smell issuing from his body. He had not washed for over a month. He smelt like death, he decided. He looked a good deal worse. His hair was long and knotted and his beard contained a number of small animals which he discovered had taken to living there.

He crawled into the corner allocated to him, curled into a ball and slept.

Klinke returned the following morning carrying a bundle of clothing – trousers made of thick wool and a working shirt of horsehair. Taking no chances, Rashid pulled these on over the thin rags which were left of his clothes. The trousers were big, but he pulled them up as high as he could and he tied them with a piece of rope, then he rolled up the bottoms of the legs. He curled up his toes in the stiff leather bindings of his new slippers. He noticed the boy watching him. He was smiling. Rashid smiled back.

The great building which addressed the whole yard was obviously the master's house. It faced south onto the square compound formed by the lodging house on the one side and a long stable on the other. The southern side was fielded by a walled shelter which housed a number of carriages. As he

166

followed the sturdy shape of Klinke's shoulders across the yard, Rashid turned this way and that, trying to take in everything that he saw. Ducks strolled about from one puddle to the next. The air was still and warm with the sun on his face. Summer is gone and the sunlight is sharp and clear, and the air carries a chill to it. They were passing through the gap at the right-hand side of the main house where a path curled away up the hillside. They passed a strip of birch trees and then emerged onto the open hill.

Up above, the hillside is alive with movement, tiny incessant particles of motion. The men are working, bare chested, and a light air of sweat and human voices hangs over the proceedings. Rashid is drawn in without ceremony. He is handed a shovel and told where to dig.

As the weeks go by he will learn the flavour of this earth. The sweet, vibrant ring of metal against sod and soil. The feel of blisters swelling in his palms, the raw fingers and the ache in his shoulders. As the sun begins to bow its humming arc close to the horizon, Rashid al-Kenzy becomes a part of the many-limbed creature that is swarming over the hillside. Gradually she begins to yield beneath the weight of hands laid upon her flanks. Trenches like deep weals course into her flesh as she lays herself down beneath this assault with the patience of eternity.

He grew to know the ways of his fellow workers. They paid him little attention as they worked side by side, for the only task which lay ahead of each one of them was marked on the hill. They rose before dawn, moving clumsily in sleepy movement through the cold, dark stables, past the large fireplace and the table which passed for a communal living area. He was handed a ladleful of thin soup and a piece of black bread. He sat alone, his head down, savouring each sip, each mouthful of the salty bread. He heard their comments, but he learned to ignore them.

He learned to let it pass him by like a gust of wind. They were simple people and in the manner of such people he knew that he had nothing to fear. They did not know who or what he was. What they did not know they would treat with caution, and so he learned to respect the power of silence. He watched them without looking at them, for he was curious about their manners. He was amused by the way in which they treated their women, for the men seemed to be in constant rivalry over their favours. He recalled Ibn Fadlan's description of travelling to the land of Rûm 300 years ago and he suspected that the women of these latitudes coupled with whoever they chose, although they did this furtively and gave no indication of having any contact with one another. There seemed to be no bounds of law or belief to constrain them in this matter. He could not work out who was married to whom, and the matter of the parentage of the children who spent all day running about the yard, he could not even venture to guess. It struck him that these people were different from those whom he had first seen in the harbour town where he had landed. They too were strangers here it seemed, and had the transient nature of casual workers about them, in a similar fashion to what he knew from his travels.

He had no idea what purpose their endeavours were to serve. They scraped the ground flat, cleared the bushes and shrubs, the sinewy trees, the rotten, dead wood. They were digging out rocks, making a wide flat space. He imagined it was for the construction of some form of dwelling. He wondered what it was to be used for. From the highest point of the hill the view was unhindered in any direction. It was a flat country, of no significant elevation whatsoever. One had the sense that one could look straight out to the sea, if only one's eyes could reach that far.

Gradually, through the daily shuffle of give and take, he

began to gain the respect of the men whom he worked alongside. He never complained, never shirked any task that was given him and he worked hard. He gave no thought to the future, nor to the matter of escape. He needed time to regain his strength and find his bearings.

Soon the days grew short and the nights long. They walked up and down the hill in darkness. The weather remained clear for many days at a time and when the rain came it was thin and hard as nails and it was cold enough to bring pain to your fingers, to make them sting as if they had been burned by fire. Rashid's ability to think was now severely reduced. He stuffed straw into his trousers and jacket to keep himself a little warmer. All his efforts were expended on the basic matter of finding comfort for his body, of staying alive in this inhospitable climate.

More than anything, he is grateful for this new lease of life, for having been delivered from the cruel and painful death that he had faced upon emerging from the sea.

CHAPTER TWENTY

The moon's bones are made of white silver. They gleam with audacious voracity. Their keen edges protrude sharply, cutting through the taut drum of this world. This lizard's eye finds the bars of the cage where our hero lies rotting. And if the bones of the moon are silver then the sun's heart is made of stone. Rashid al-Kenzy recalls the moment in his sleep. His body hangs limply between his last breath and death. He dreams that he has crossed the Seventh Sea and the sorcery of that green ocean is charted in his mind. He has been touched by the earth, as they say. He is delirious and his eyesight is blurred. His skin is burning. He is back in the harbour where he first landed. He is locked in a small room that smells of animals. They open the door just wide enough to throw in the bucket of cabbage stalks, potato rinds, fish skins and dry bread. They are afraid that he is the carrier of some repulsive contagion. They poke at him with a stick to force him into a corner when they venture in to see if he is still alive. They do not realize that he has already died and come back to the world as an animal.

His fingers are twisted, his curved shoulders ache with longing for the touch of the sun. The pulse in his neck ticks away the pages of his life. Slowly he recalls the clamour of urgent voices awakening him from the deepest sleep. There were people stepping over him, around him, everywhere, limbs in motion. The ship is disintegrating, but it is no longer the work of the sea and the elements: it is tiny insects, people, scurrying like rats, falling over one another in their haste to secure the best of that which is left. The timber splinters, nails yawn free, sailcloth rips apart, walls come crashing down. Their footsteps can be heard scurrying all around him, above and below. He pulls himself into a dark corner and draws his knees up to curl himself into a ball.

What barbed fate has now befallen us? he asked himself. The stiffening, swollen remains of the bosun lie beside him, stripped of their clothing. His naked body has the dark green pallor of dead oceans. A woman is exiting through the door, a cloth held up to her face against the stench. She looks back and their eyes meet momentarily. She gives a cry that is halfway between laughter and fright. He clings to the corpse, drawing it to him. The body is stiff and cold as clay, the life sucked from its marrow. A long black slug crawled across the lifeless thigh towards the belly. With a cry, Rashid knocked it away. He drew himself back into the shadow close to the wall, listening to the sounds of people moving through the ship around him. He is among the dead and drowned.

Gradually he realizes that the ship is no longer moving. There is no more water. They were aground. Feet clatter across the deck above his head, human, living feet. He kneels up to see a grey gull making a wave-like motion past the narrow window. Its very brevity seems to suggest that his freedom is now limited. A vaporous, smoky light pours in through the hatch above him as he stands in the dark corridor hesitating. He hears voices above him. Everything around him has been stripped. Lanterns, fittings, nails, wood. There are gaping holes in the hull. Anything that could be prised loose with fingers and teeth has been taken, leaving behind only the blood, hair and skin of their frantic urgency. He has been left for dead. He should stay here until dark and then make his exit. But his hand is already reaching for the ladder. The wind hums in his ears. He moves through the hull of the ship to the forward hatch. He is moving away from the noise of these creatures. His heart is beating faster than he imagined it could. He pulls himself up the wall and cautiously sticks his head out.

The light up there is blinding. The sun is shining and he shields his eyes in pain. Before him stretches a beach, long and wide and covered in white sand. The deck is swarming with them, strange creatures, dressed in heavy, dark clothing, their stench hitting him like a fist. First their smell, which is unfamiliar and vaguely repulsive. Then the sight of them. They are heavy of build. Their hair is the colour of dirty straw. Their skin is white. Their hands are big and out of proportion to the rest of their bodies. He drops back down into the safety of the hull, shaking. He sits, pressed up against the hull to listen. There is a high-pitched screeching sound which is somewhere between man and beast. Ghosts of dead mariners. It takes him some time to realize that it is the ape, Darius Reis's monkey.

The light confuses him. Perhaps it is still night and they have blinded the world with the light which comes from their hair. He crawls forwards, and climbs up again, tentatively pushing his head into the air. They seem not to see him. They have cornered the ape in the bow and are prodding at it with long sticks. They have drawn much attention and, emboldened by this, he swings a leg over the hatch and stands. People, they are just people, like the *feranj* he has seen before in the harbour towns. He sees women and children too now. He looks around him in bewilderment, trying to make sense of what he is witnessing. They brush him aside with their sacks and awkward loads, in their haste to get by. Someone carrying an armful of blankets. Two women struggling with a bulky cabinet. He now becomes spirit and passes, invisible, through the crowd. Upon reaching the railing he peers over the side. There are horses and carts on the sand, mules, old men staggering under great weights, their legs shaking like straws. The beach is littered with sacks of rice and cases of dried figs, which they are sniffing suspiciously. He has never seen the likes of this before. A thin trail of figures is making its way back and forth from the sparse tufts of grass that mark the line of distant dunes. He turns the other way and looks seaward. The water is a thin, ash-blue shell in the distance. How did the ship manage to strand itself so far from the sea? The ripple of white told them that the tide was coming in, which explained the haste he saw around him.

His eyes returned from the sea to notice a little girl standing beside him. She stood absolutely still, staring up at him. He stared back. She opened her mouth and strange sounds came from her throat. He froze. The girl pointed a finger and began to shout in a loud voice. A large-waisted woman burst into Rashid's line of sight and crushed the girl to her chest. Within moments he was surrounded by a crowd of people. This time they saw him. They stood open-mouthed, staring in silence at him. A thin woman with wide eyes and a bony face the colour of sand reached out a tentative hand towards him. He smiled and lifted his hand. She screamed and drew back. A man appeared before him. Dropping a barrel to the deck he stepped in between them. He looked at the faces gathered around and then he looked at Rashid. He peered at his face, lifted a hand up and rubbed at his chin. Someone behind him shouted a warning, but the man turned and held up his fingers to the crowd. Then, as though alerted by a signal, they all rushed in. Rashid felt himself being lifted into the air. He felt himself being pushed and shoved and then he was being carried to the side and lowered to the beach.

Handed down, arm over arm until he reached a gang of furious men whose tongues were disjointed by unfamiliar thorns. They speak the language of forest creatures. They push him and he hears their shouts. He is aware that he is shouting at the top of his voice. He has never known such fear. He is turning in dizzy circles trying to seek a way out of this maze. He lands on his face, gasping like a stranded fish on the sand.

The masts are like elegant keys suspended from the sky. Rashid al-Kenzy looked for the sun and, finding only a pale, distended aureole in its place, he rolled onto his knees and, turning roughly in the direction of the Mecca, he touched his forehead to the ground to give thanks to the Lord of the Heavens for His compassion. His final hour had come. He closed his eyes to prepare for death.

Slowly he became aware of two things: the blows had ceased and the men around him were laughing. He looked around him in disbelief. The laughter faded away as he got to his feet. They thrust the carcass of the ape into his face. It has a rope around its neck and appears to have been garotted. The expression on its face stays with him. It is that of a man suddenly grown old in the moment of death. He wonders if this is how his face will look, for in a short time they will surely have assigned him the same fate. His hands are bound roughly behind his back. They peered at him in curious amazement, poked at his arms and chest. A noose is slipped around his neck. They shook their heads in wonder. A bold hand reached out and clapped him on the back of the neck. They tug the rope and he is propelled forwards, towards the dunes. He had one last glimpse of the ship, its crushed hull sitting oddly on the flat sand. The rising tide was already swilling about the shattered bow. Rashid could see the last of the men wading back through the water. The column of people was moving, turning its back and walking towards the long grass and the marshes. They collected in a loose group upon the high ground and watched the foam flooding through the breaks in the shattered hull. Rashid saw his past crumbling in bursts of white foam as the ship subsided into the water. He felt the shove between his shoulder blades and he found himself dragged along a pathway trampled in the reeds and the long grass, surrounded by a people the like of which he had never known existed. His only thought was to stay upright, on his feet, for as long as he could.

A collection of buildings appeared out of the flat marshlands. Houses of mud wattling and timber. Larger houses of stone, a tall steepled building. The streets were crowded. Women stifled their cries with their hands and clutched children to their sides, unable to decide whether what they were looking at were man or beast. His blackness was a disease, somebody nodded knowingly, a curse. He was the child of Satan in the employ of the devil. No doubt, they agreed. Curious fingers were withdrawn. The whispers and hisses attached themselves to his back like a cloak made of fish hooks. A rift opened up in the small crowd. He looked around him in bewilderment. A woman whose eye he caught collapsed in a heap on the slick cobblestones. There were gasps of amazement and groans of disgust. He stumbled and almost fell. The only thing keeping him on his feet was the thought that these people would surely rip him to shreds if he fell. The men – there were six of them now – were big and burly and he felt, oddly enough, secure with them by his side; although he reasoned that although they may well have been leading him to his death, their strength would ensure it was a swift one.

Fascinated, unable to resist, the crowd tagged silently along, growing in size and excitement as it had since the moment the procession had emerged from the long grassy marshes and entered the town. They passed down the narrow streets of the harbour town, pulling others along with them. People stood on their doorsteps and called out, asking what was happening before they too joined the parade. They climbed on one another's shoulders. They huddled in doorways. The whole world was in a state of agitation. And by the time they had reached the stout, square shape of the church it seemed as though the whole town was following in their wake.

They drew to a halt outside a stone house on the eastern side of the church. The bloody, broken, sandy carcass of the ape was strung up over the branch of a tree. It swayed there, rocking gently back and forth. The crowd were making such a noise that it would have been impossible to imagine that the inhabitants were unaware of their arrival. The door swung open and a man appeared. He was a frail, grey-haired man, as thin and threadbare as a length of old rope. A discussion ensued between the old man, who stood at the top of the short flight of stone steps, and the leader of the men who had led the procession. No agreement could be reached, it seemed to Rashid. He was pushed and prodded back and forth. Cries of anguish still issued from the crowd of onlookers around him. The old man appeared to be asking for calm, imploring the people to allow patience to prevail. His task was not an easy one for the atmosphere among the crowd was rising to a state of hysteria, and soon he withdrew, bolting the door firmly in their faces.

A commotion ensued somewhere far behind, and a current seemed to go through the assembled villagers. A shout went up and the crowd fell away to reveal a new arrival. He was certainly a commanding presence. A large man, wearing a dark hat and a leather vest of some kind. His face was covered in thick whiskers from which a large protuberant nose emerged. Around the horse upon which he was seated there were a number of what looked like soldiers.

The bulky man leaned forwards over the large horse and swung his leg free. For a moment he hung there, lying across the horse's broad back before dropping to the ground. He carried a thin staff in his hand. Across one shoulder was a broad, shiny leather strap from which hung a short, straight sword. He walked up to Rashid. Bending forwards he peered into his eyes, a frown on his face. He straightened for a moment, turning to survey the crowd. The frown had turned to a scowl when he turned back. He pulled off a large gauntlet that smelled of horses and with his right hand he grasped hold of Rashid's jaw. There was a sharp intake of breath from the crowd. Rashid tried to pull away but, taking a firm grip, the man forced him to open his mouth. He examined Rashid's teeth. Rashid did not let his eyes meet those of the large man. Nor did he try to pull away for fear that the man would do him more harm. His hands were tied. He could smell the man, feel his breath on his face. This was a man, not a demon, not a spirit, simply a man. He grunted, let go of Rashid's jaw and then, stepping back, the large man faced the crowd. He signalled and the guards began to lead Rashid away. He found himself being dragged through a stable filled with cattle and horses. At the back of the building there was a small, dark room. A large door swung open and he found himself hurled inwards.

The moon's bones are made of white silver. They gleam with audacious voracity. Their keen edges protrude sharply, cutting through the taut drum of the world. This lizard's eye finds the bars of the cage where Rashid al-Kenzy lies rotting. He has died and come back to the world as an animal.

177

CHAPTER TWENTY-ONE

Up on that dark bruise of a hill the work continued. The men walked up each morning in a long trail of limbs, sticks, axes and levers. All clicking, ticking, snapping their way up the worn shoulder. They rose early, eager for the fray. They dug deeper into the cold, immobile fundament, digging shovel by shovel into the unwilling flesh. A shipment of large blocks of stone arrived and the men formed a long chain that snaked up through the foggy drizzle, dragging the carts up and down, their voices cutting from time to time through the opaque silence like ancient, forgotten echoes. Slowly the pile of rocks moved its way up the hillside as though time were running backwards and the crumbling mountain were rejuvenating itself.

It has grown colder with the passing weeks. The damp is beginning to bite and the wind has grown teeth. The muddy ground upon the hill has grown thick and black as tar, clutching at the boots of the bone-weary labourers as they stagger down in the darkness, coated from head to foot in the silvery mineral flakes that cling like fish scales to their hands and faces in the frail twilight; an army of Ethiopians on the retreat. The earth is against them, it chews up their trowels and spits their shovels back into their faces. Every morning they wander out in the darkness before dawn, mumbling their prayers, hoping against hope that the trench which they dug out the day before has not filled up with water while they were sleeping. This is not the season for building, they grumble. Klinke dangles the whip over their heads. Their master will double their wages for every week saved. They will never have to work again for the fortune they stand to make from this. But they know that this is not true. They walk up the hill each morning because God is in His heaven and the world was created by Him and He has deemed that this be their existence. They work because they have no choice; they have families and wives and babies with hungry mouths waiting for them somewhere who will starve if they do not bring home the money to see them through to summer. There is no other work this time of year and a curse on the man who says it is not so.

Autumn has come early this year. One week the sky is clear and blue as a lake and the next it is muddy, like the mind of an apostate.

He has begun to live among them. Their fear is breaking down with each handful of earth he claws away, each stone he lifts. This change comes grudgingly and is not complete, for he has, in their eyes, made many mistakes. There are things about them he does not understand, cannot comprehend, just as he knows there are many things about him which they will never grasp. They still know nothing of him. He is a mute, God-forsaken creature from the ends of the earth. He is the dreaded Turk who raped and pillaged his way across the Holy Land, skewering innocent Christians with burning pokers on his way. He alone is responsible for every ungodly act committed between here and the Church of the Holy Sepulchre. He is alone, however, and this makes him vulnerable. He is constantly reminded of this, of his darkness, of his alien nature. He stretches out a hand and they pull back.

At night the men sat around the smoky peat fire in the lodging house, talking in loud voices amongst themselves. They passed the clay jugs between them, which he guessed contained some kind of wine. He withdrew from their presence to the safety of his stall, listening to the mice creeping through the straw. The evening meal was the high point of the day. Afterwards the talk became gentle and contented. The voices of children in the stalls around them would be light and easy. Rashid passed the evenings quietly, alone, wrapped up in his thoughts. He seemed to spend more and more time thinking of his childhood. He found comfort there. The only one who had shown no fear of him was the boy who had travelled with him here in the cart along with his father. Sometimes he would show this boy rope tricks that he had learned on ships. The boy was keen and eager to learn, watching intently. He laughed in amazement and quickly reached out to try his hand.

One evening they are in high spirits. He does not understand why. It is something of their tradition which they are celebrating. The language which they speak remains as obscure and unfathomable as ever. The boy comes for him, drags him unwillingly from the shadows to the light around the big table. The effect is to induce instantaneous silence. There are a few grumbles and muttered curses. They have been drinking their intoxicating brew, he realizes as he stands there and surveys them. The boy is the only one who does not fear him, does not see the sign of the devil inscribed on his dark skin. The boy opens his mouth and sings. The men relax and the noise begins again as they fall into laughter and conversation. Then the boy turns to him and signals, by gesturing with a hand to his mouth, that it is his turn to sing. Rashid looks at the boy. The others are impatient, but they too have lost their tongues and seem to be willing to wait and see what might ensue.

So Rashid al-Kenzy begins to recite. He recites in a lilting lyrical fashion, the way he was taught as a child, when he was the same size as this boy who now urges him on. The words come to him from the number of times they have circled around in his head. He pours forth his comfort. And he has sung these opening lines before, to great applause, for his voice acquires a beauty of its own when it takes to song.

They sit open mouthed and listen to this strange sound. 'Guide us to the path which is straight, the path of those whom You have favoured, not that of those who have angered you nor of those who have gone astray.'

There is no response at first. They stare at their big hands, the calluses and blisters, the cuts made by the stone, the blackness engrained by the earth. Their silence is applause enough and Rashid steps back from the light. They boy smiles as the men begin to talk among themselves again, slowly, easily, in subdued stops and starts, and it is clear that, despite the fact that, although they have not understood a single word, nor do they have any inkling of where such sounds come from, he has illuminated some common strand between them.

He is among them, but he will never be one of them. He feels himself succumbing to the constant isolation of his being. The world from which he comes does not exist to these people. As far as communication was concerned, it was a matter of gestures and signs. Although he had once prided himself on his linguistic skills, he had not grasped any of the language which they used among themselves; to him it still sounded like a long, unbroken and very garbled grunting sound. They cursed him, of course, and occasionally he stood there as someone, often Klinke or the other foreman, yelled into his face for a few moments. In return he could provide nothing but a blank look. He did not despise them for their impatience, nor did he pity them for their ignorance. He accepted them, just as he felt they, for the most part, accepted him. Every morning they climbed together in silence, no matter whether it was sunshine or pouring rain, it seemed to make no difference to them. This, he observed, was truly remarkable. And every day they retraced the familiar steps of the day before, and the day before that, and yet on each new day the ground seemed unfamiliar, as though unperturbed by the light tread of man upon her surface. In this way the days and weeks proceeded. Each day they reconquered her flanks, imposing their marks upon her, and each day they retreated, stumbling down the hill, eyes propped awake by exhaustion and the faint falling rays of sunset.

When they were not working he was alone. When they broke at midday for the food brought up from the house by the women, he sat a little to one side from the others. The women usually came together. There were three of them in all and they seemed to enjoy the attention they received from the men as they walked among them distributing the food. None of them dared to come near Rashid. Instead they would hand his portion to Klinke who would come over with it. At first he had thought that this was purely due to fear. One night, however, as he lay wide awake in the lodging house, he heard a whimpering sound in the darkness. He crawled to the edge of partition and peered round.

Two figures were struggling furiously on the ground. From the sounds of their voices he knew it was a man and a woman. Such clandestine couplings had occurred before. Rashid slept in the most remote corner of the lodging house; there were no others on this row of stalls, which explained why it was favoured for such liaisons. He was about to crawl back into the corner to curl up and try to sleep when the man let out a series of urgent grunts followed by silence. A moment later a figure could be seen scurrying away down between the stalls to turn left at the end, towards the centre of the building and the others. Rashid remained motionless. The woman, he could not be sure which of them it was, remained almost out of sight. He could barely discern the outline of her within the straw. There was a long moment of silence and then he heard the straw rustling again. She got to her feet and stepped into the aisle. The moonlight squeezed itself through a cross-shaped aperture high up on the western wall. She stood there for a moment, looking up at the light. She was dressed, or partially so, her skirts up around her waist as she adjusted her under garments. Then she too turned to go back, which would bring her past his stall. Her upturned face was painted blue by the moon, but he recognized her now as the dark-haired woman, the older one. She was the mother of a number of the children, he had noticed.

She turned in his direction as though his thoughts were too loud. He closed his eyes, pretending to sleep. He remained deathly still. She too, for a moment, and then she took a step or two nearer, until she was right in front of him. The smell of her reached him now, a blend of unwashed skin, sweat and the unmistakable odour of a woman. Next, she did an odd thing. Bending down on one knee, she stretched out a hand towards him. First she stroked his leg, and then moved up towards his waist. He remained motionless, fearing what might happen should he respond. She found the hardness that told her he was awake. Getting to her feet quickly, she vanished into the darkness, the sound of her light laughter echoing behind her like a cape.

Perhaps individually they were not afraid of him at all, perhaps it was only together that they feared him?

The weather turned thick with black rain that gushed from

183

above in an unbroken torrent, night and day. The work began to slow down until it was almost at a standstill. It was as though for each step they took up the hill they slid two steps back down. The stones which they carried up refused to remain in place but instead began to tumble and slide in the slippery mud. The hill was waking from its slumber and now seemed set on repelling them.

Heinesen was up there every day, from dawn till dusk and beyond, struggling to hold his idea up towards the sky. He had constructed himself a shelter of leaves and sailcloth and sticks which the wind tore down every night. He stood there trying to keep his papers dry. He had also enlisted the help of a listless, rather pompous engineer who arrived every morning from the nearby town, coming trotting up the drive in his flimsy carriage, never showing any signs of urgency. Together they stood upon the hill and pored over their drawings, the water running from the brims of their wide hats.

It was one day, after more than two weeks of this weather, that it happened. The wind rushed across the rippled surface of the lake and slapped itself against the hillside like an open hand. The house rattled and moaned. Water kicked and spat its way down the turbid flanks. It dripped from the trees, and gushed from the eaves of the buildings in the yard, from the woodwork, from the carts. The leather of Rashid's sandals had started to rot and they began to come apart. Water oozed from every crack, every corner of the earth.

He closed his eyes, breathing softly, leaning against the wall of the trench, exhausted. He climbed out and began to move. The wind was picking up. His numb fingers felt for the stiffened cloth and he tightened the scarf across his face. The men around him stumbled and fell. He moved to join them as they leaned their weight into the levers and prised a large flat stone upright.

There were six, seven of them, all trying to manoeuvre the thing. The rain was falling in waves, blowing horizontally across the exposed hill. The light was a blue sliver against bruised grey. He slipped again as the weight shifted and went down on one knee. Behind him he heard voices rising in anxiety. The boy had apparently lost his footing and slipped down into the trench. There was a moment of laughter, of relief. A glimpsed corner of a smile and a wave to indicate that he was all right. Then the wind caught hold of the stone. Rashid reached out instinctively and touched another man's hand. The man gave a cry and pulled his hand away. It was a singular moment, an instinct, a stupid thing. It happened slowly. The stone beginning to tip, veering slowly earthwards, twisting out of his hands, his fingers, downwards, into the core of the hill.

They worked relentlessly within the deluge, which fell on them now in reproach, counting out their names in its gaze, listening to their breath in its roar. It took them an hour, perhaps longer, to dig the sides away, to clear enough space to move the square, flat stone from where it had fallen. The boy's father simply looked on. He did not cry out, did not scream, did not tear at the earth until his fingertips bled. He simply sank down on his knees on the rim of the trench and covered his ears with his hands to stop the sound of the rain. He remained like that, immobile. He did not blink, did not breathe, just looked on in silence.

It was the rain which had taken the boy's life. He drowned in its light, swallowed so much of that pure liquid that there was no room left inside for his soul. The weight of the stone held him pinned down, his face in the icy water until the life gave way and slipped loose. The men did not speak. They simply lifted the limp collection of bones and threads to them and carried the dead boy down from the hill.

The shovels and mallets, heavy iron hammers and chisels for splitting stone lay scattered around. Discarded, dismembered limbs, lifeless notes that trickled away down the tarry gash in the raven's back. The men were gone. The soft mud flooded into their footsteps behind them. A single drop fell into a boot-sized pool, and when the ripples ceased the hill was silent.

CHAPTER TWENTY-TWO

Hassan woke up in a fever, his mind racing and his breathing shallow and laboured. The bedsheets were cold and clammy, sticking to his back when he swung his feet to the floor and sat up. The room was spinning.

He made it down the narrow stairs, washed his face in the basin and noted that his urine was a dark green colour. He was shivering and crawled up the stairs and fell into a deep, swirling sleep which, to his surprise, lasted well into the afternoon.

He lay there watching a long-legged spider edge its way across the pinewood slats above his head.

'Life in the country,' he thought to himself. He crawled out of bed again and went downstairs. As he surveyed the chaos of papers and books strewn all around the living room, he was filled with an overwhelming sense of hopelessness.

He slept through until the following morning when he felt the urge to do something. Getting up, he went downstairs and stood there in the kitchen, unable to make up his mind what to do next. His legs felt so weak he could hardly stand up, and he was just about to crawl back upstairs to bed when there was a knock at the door. The boy from the shop, Martin, was standing there looking at the sky.

'Hi,' he said, thrusting his hands into his jeans. He frowned. 'You don't look too good.'

'No.' Hassan rubbed a hand across his face. He was wrapped in a blanket and shivering. 'I think I caught a chill somehow. I feel feverish.'

'You need anything? Aspirin, something like that?'

Hassan was a little taken aback by this. 'Well, actually, yes. I mean . . .'

Martin nodded. 'Just make out a list. I can run over and get it now.'

It was after he had left, and Hassan was sitting in the kitchen trying to account for the change in the boy's mood, that he recalled he had promised to take him up to the excavation that day. By the time Martin returned, carrying a bag filled with fruit juice and medicine and a jar of honey that he said his uncle had made, Hassan was washed and dressed.

'I'll just take some of this and then we can go.'

'Are you sure? I mean, you know? We can do it another day.'

Hassan gulped down a mouthful of a bitter-tasting hot lemon drink. 'No.' He shook his head. 'I'll only feel worse if I stay in all day.'

He regretted his decision almost as soon as they had set off in the car. Not that he was not glad to be out of the house; it was a glorious day, the sun shining bright and warm as they cut over the top of the valley which was thick with heather and lavender. But Martin was, for the first time since he had encountered him, in a very talkative mood.

'Someday I'd like to travel, you know? I mean I would like to go around the world. I don't have anywhere specific in mind. You know, you hear so much about all these places? I don't think there is any one place that is the answer to my dreams or anything. I want to find my own special place. It might be in India. Have you ever been to India? That is one place I am definitely going to go.'

And on it went. Perhaps he was nervous, thought Hassan. In any case, he only stopped talking as Hassan nosed the car slowly up the narrow track and pulled into the row of cars that were parked on the stretch of grass allocated by the farmer.

Okking was standing on the shoulder below the hill with a small group of people. He looked up when Hassan and Martin appeared. 'Ah, good, just in time. See what we have here.'

Between them they were holding out a large sheet of paper. Upon the topographical outline of the hill a series of lines had been carefully plotted.

'You can see how they are related.' The trenches clearly formed a triangular shape with the apex pointing north. The two main arms opened towards the south.

'It is quite an odd structure.' The man speaking was a land surveyor. He took the pipe from his mouth and pointed with the stem up towards the brow of the hill. 'There is no evidence of human settlement up there, no reason, so far as I can see, for building it.' He spoke in rather a ponderous fashion, chewing on his pipe like an elder statesman.

Okking turned towards Hassan. 'What do you think?'

'What about UFOs?'

Everyone turned to look at Martin. Hassan cleared his throat. 'This is Martin. I told you about him. He would like to help with the digging?'

'Oh yes, of course.' Okking took Martin by the arm and pointed him up the hill. 'Go straight up to the tent there and tell Jens I sent you.'

Martin wander cheerfully off up the hillside. Okking turned back to Hassan. 'Now, you were saying?'

Hassan looked down at the map again. 'Well, Martin may not be too far off, in a manner of speaking. I think it does have something to do with the stars.'

'How so?' The surveyor took the pipe out of his mouth.

'I think they were building some kind of structure for observing the stars.'

'Out here?' Okking looked sceptical. The surveyor chewed on his pipe and looked down at his map again. 'We had better call that young man back,' he said, with a chuckle, 'he may know more about this than we thought.'

CHAPTER TWENTY-THREE

The great monoliths of stone continued their journey in the absence of men, their straight sides and pointed tips projected at odd tangents at the moon, like reversed sun dials, as they sank deeper into the sodden ground. The stubborn blocks lay abandoned in disorderly heaps, suddenly useless and clumsy, their great density seeking a way back into the black shining earth. The hill was dark and brooding. The drainage work remained incomplete. The foundations lay damp, naked and exposed, as though tended by invisible souls. All the pulleys, levers, tools, everything, lay ready and waiting. The rain was relentless. It was not an observatory he was constructing, Heinesen thought to himself one evening, standing on the rim of that bleak moonscape, but a tomb. The workers had vanished, without consultation or debate. They simply packed up their belongings, bundled wives and babies onto horseless carts and, seizing the yokes, they set off down the hill without looking back. The lodging house was dark and heavy, the door rattled in the wind.

From the day the boy died a dull pallor settled over the fields and the mist clung heavily to the strange hill. To Heinesen it was almost as though the closer the project came towards actual physical completion the more elusive became the idea which it contained. He became increasingly sullen, morose, taken to snapping at the slightest provocation. It was all there, in the palm of his hand, and yet it remained frustratingly ethereal, intangible, unattainable. A fiction, created in his head, which could neither be sustained nor abandoned. It began to eat him up from within. The lamp of inspiration had begun to wane and Heinesen was being tugged along with the tide. He had lived and breathed this dream for so long that it was wrapped up inside him like a larva waiting for sunlight and warmth to release it, a light that would not come.

The feathery quill scratching its beak across the thick paper. He wandered nightly through the cavernous house sleeplessly and drank himself into the breathless roar of oblivion within the big fire in the gallery. His mind was being drawn backwards in time, to the island of Hven, Tycho Brahe's little windswept kingdom.

It is winter in that distant cold place of isolation and bitter crosswinds. The shadow of the man falls over all of them as they kick the inflated pig's bladder between them to keep warm. It rises above them in a gentle arc that reveals the architecture of the great house: quadratic with four equally sized rooms based on drawings of Renaissance buildings in Augsburg and inspired by Palladio's villas in Venice. The clear air is infused with a curious mystery of the spirit, his shadow which falls over them all.

The dwarf savant tells him that at night he dreams of fishtailed women coming to him from the sea. Young Heinesan sees evil in the hunchbacked man-child creature.

The work goes on and the great man stalks his instruments night and day. He worries about the wind, digs great troughs to sink the measuring scales out of its reach.

Young Heinesen has ink on his fingers. His ears rattle to the chained cogs of the printing rack churning out the peaks and curves of Old Ironbeak's thoughts. He writes to his sister who is lodged with a deranged aunt whose house, in a dreary quarter of Copenhagen, smells of pickled herring. Sigrid delights in the tales he sends her of that odd collection of misfits, criminals, artisans, and even a dwarf, who inhabit the island with him.

'I feel I am in the penumbra,' he scratches in the feeble candlelight. 'As though I am permanently trapped on the periphery of some illumination that will shatter the world as we know it.'

He writes of Regiomontanus and the news of Kepler and again of Brahe: 'He graced me with his company today, a few words, "no smudges on the printed page, boy." I could have killed him with my bare hands there and then. Day in and day out I run his merry printing wheel. I am his apprentice and yet he spares me less time than he does his damned dog.'

At other times his writing was opaque, his mind tightly wrapped up in the realm of learning to which he applied himself daily. 'It is true that he has made some major advances, partly through recognizing that the strategy employed by the Arabs in building larger and larger instruments was founded on a false premise. What is needed now is accuracy and more accuracy. He has set the finest craftsmen to the task and one must admire his fortitude in this matter for they are a bunch of woolly headed sheep, the lot of them, and must be watched carefully at all times. His reserve is no more than a symbol of his doubt. Look at how many years it took him to publish his findings on the Stella Nova and then anonymously!'

The audacity of youth, laughs Heinesen now, recollecting.

The dwarf clutches his crotch and thrusts his hips back and forth, a manic grin on his face.

Heinesen stepped into the long, gloomy hallway. His chest hurt and he had not slept well. All night he had been plagued by thoughts which would not let him rest. He had no wish to be a saint, or a martyr, nor indeed to be burned at the stake as a heretic. He coughed and finished buttoning the cuffs of his shirt. He paused by the window looking out onto the yard. The emptiness of it drew a curse from him. Every day that went by idle was drawing them deeper and deeper into difficulty and debt. A farm needed hands to work it, to keep it alive, or else the earth would reclaim it. He would have to ride into town today to try and find help. He was worried that rumours would already have spread throughout the surrounding area. Perhaps he should go north to the fjord. All he needed was a handful of men to run the farm and see that the horses were well kept. He rubbed a hand along the window frame. The dark wood was heavy and resinous. The floor was scarred and cracked as though someone had ridden up and down it on horseback. Straw was strewn about to keep the warmth and reduce the damp. Down the middle ran a thin trail of rusted colour where someone had strewn dried flowers all along the floor – his sister. This brought a brief smile to his face. Oddly enough, the narrow passageway and the ceiling timbers reminded him, just for an instant, of the interior of a ship. One that he had sailed in, perhaps, or one that awaited him?

One rain-swollen afternoon the silence which had fallen over Helioborg was shattered by the arrival of a delegation of black hats. Sombre men, their authority cloaked in the mud-spattered sides of an open carriage which was dragged up the hill by two disgruntled-looking horses. A glint of light caught Heinesen's eye as he lifted his head from the page. They approached from the east, thin staves of sun skimming through the bare trees.

With a hiss of water on stone the carriage drew to a halt in front of the house. Three men descended and looked around the yard for signs of life. They tightened their collars and straightened their backs as Klinke hurried over to receive them. The group stood and conversed for a short while in hushed tones before climbing the steps to the house.

Like so many crows, the three black hats settled themselves around the big fire, noses wrinkling at the chaos of books, curled-up pages and diagrams that spilled from every corner of the large room, seeping from the walls, spilling down the staircases and over the tables behind them. They hummed and hah'ed, cleared their throats and nodded to themselves.

They were all very different in appearance. There was the bishop's man, Rusk, a short fellow who tugged at the cuffs of his coat at regular intervals as if annoyed with his tailor for not having spared him a little more cloth in that department. He had clear blue eyes that never rested in one place for more than the time it took him to blink. And he blinked a lot. Beside him was Koppel, a large, dull man with the blunt features of a peasant. He was shrewd and wealthy with a humble trading empire that consisted of several herds of cattle and sheep, a couple of properties in the nearby town and a small share in the ownership of a large caravel which sailed the Baltic trading in furs, timber, tallow and, it was rumoured, children, sold as cheap and devoted labour. The third man was obviously the most senior of all of them. The King's Prefect, Holst. He was older and more plump than the others. His face was red and his eyes small. He seemed to be out of breath all the time. He wore a long moleskin coat and a brown beard that was peppered with red streaks.

They turned as one when the door flew open. There were greetings and handshakes all round. It was the little one, Rusk, pulling his cuffs straight, who declared the purpose of their visit. 'Heinesen, we have come to allow you the opportunity of explaining matters to us.'

Heinesen gave a little bow. 'That is most gracious of you gentlemen, but please tell me what it is that needs explaining.' He gestured to them, asking them to be seated. They did so, all except for Rusk, who sat down and then immediately stood up again as though the chair, like the coat he was wearing, was also too narrow-fitting.

'Come now, young Heinesen, do not play games. We would not have come all this way if it were not for the urgency demanded by this unfortunate situation.'

There was silence for a moment. Heinesen looked around the three faces. Rusk tapped his foot impatiently. Heinesen beamed broadly. 'Gentlemen, I am at your service, as surely you are aware—'

Rusk cut him off abruptly. 'The boy, Heinesen,' he growled, 'tell us how he died.'

The smile remained for a while fixed on Heinesen's face. He turned towards the fire. His voice was even and emotionless when he spoke. 'A long and continuous period of rain had loosened the soil. Although it was not apparent, it nevertheless made it very unstable. Someone lost their footing and a foundation stone fell, crushing the life from the boy who was working below.' He took a deep breath and turned back to face his audience. 'An accident. Unfortunate, but not uncommon, as you gentlemen well know. There is risk in all construction work.'

Holst broke the silence, clearing his throat. 'Are you saying,' he boomed, 'that you accept full responsibility for this incident?'

Heinesen looked the portly envoy in the eye. 'I am saying that it could have happened anywhere, to anyone . . . under similar conditions.'

'But it was you who insisted that they work that day, was it not, despite the dangers invoked by the inclement weather?'

'It is to everyone's advantage that we finish the work as soon as possible. Nobody could foresee the danger caused by the weather.' Heinesen became amicable again. He held out his arms. 'I confess that your concern is touching, but perhaps exaggerated?'

There was a silent pause.

'And tell us, Heinesen,' enquired Koppel, ignoring Heinesen's words, 'what exactly is this business you are about?'

Heinesen was aware that his affairs had been the subject of rumour and conjecture for quite some time now. Stories abounded of strange, unnatural workings on the big hill. He got to his feet and stepped to the centre of the room.

'Look around you, gentlemen.' He gestured upwards. The three men raised their eyes to the gallery that rose above them.

'What you see is the beginning of a dream. But not some whimsical fancy. No, this is a vision of the world to come, as it will develop over the next centuries.' The three men were silent, transformed in an instant from a board of inquisition into a wide-eyed audience. 'The civilized world is poised on the edge of a new age. The age of the philosophy of nature. We have barely begun to understand the world we inhabit. We have a duty to try and understand the forces which animate this world of ours.'

He moved now between the tables, pausing here and there to indicate a book or a measuring instrument. 'This knowledge has been gathered since antiquity, accumulated and transmitted over centuries by the Ancient Greeks, the Arabs, the Egyptians and now us. However, never before have we been able to assimilate all of this knowledge, to forge it together into one singular pillar of light that shall illuminate the very stars themselves. Think of it, gentlemen! To see further, wider, more clearly than ever before. We shall gather the dust of centuries into our arms and breathe life into it.'

Admittedly, the three visitors were momentarily numbed and speechless. They looked at one another, unsure as to how to proceed. It was Koppel who managed to find his tongue first. 'How, Heinesen? How will you do these things?' he demanded, almost in a whisper.

'This observatory I am constructing will become a centre of learning, renowned throughout the world. Learned men will flock here. Kings and noblemen will despatch ambassadors; they themselves will come here to witness the work being done. We shall peel away the outer surface of the world to reveal the wonderous mysteries that lie at her core.' He stepped quickly to the north window. 'Upon that hill, a series of trenches and observation garrets, with the most modern instruments for measuring the distance and increments of the heavenly constellations. Here a library, an archive to which the wisest men of Europe, of the civilized world, will travel to work, to make their contribution. There will be debates, argument, all manner of discussion and—'

'Enough!' growled Holst, slapping the arm of his chair.

The look of wonder drained from Koppel's face. Rusk jerked his head forwards like a hound on a leash. 'Do you realize the audacity of what you are proposing?' snarled Holst.

'Audacity?' Heinesen smiled easily. 'You would call it audacity to examine the world in which we live?'

'Come now, Heinesen, you cannot be blind to the implications, the repercussions of such a . . . ludicrous venture. This is a matter for universities and kings, not some second-rate horse trader in the provinces.'

Heinesen took a deep breath. Koppel tried to reconcile matters. He stepped forwards to calm Holst with a gently raised hand and delivered a long speech in measured tones. The townspeople were concerned, it seemed. People had become unduly preoccupied. Rumour had spread through the taverns and market places that something most unusual was being constructed upon the top of Heinesen's hill. What people do not know, they are naturally suspicious of. Of course it was Heinesen's hill and he could do what he liked with it, but he must remember that disturbances of this kind spread quickly through such a small community and caused unrest. The town fathers were worried about what such speculation could do to the reputation of the region and, indeed, the town itself. And then there was the matter of the kind of people who would be attracted by such ventures. People who came to gaze at the stars, even those involved in the construction of the ... thing, these were the most transient kinds of foreigners who travelled the roads in search of employment. The most notorious brand of people imaginable. Lawless types who advocated living in sin and excesses of every conceivable manner and knew nothing of the ways of God.

'None of the people I have employed have been anything but of the highest character, I can assure you of that.'

'We cannot possibly judge that as there seems to be no work going on at the present time,' observed Koppel. 'Is that a consequence of this accident?'

'An unfortunate delay. I shall be engaged in employing a new work force shortly.'

'You call the sacrifice of this boy an unfortunate delay?' Holst stamped his foot in fury. 'Have you no compassion?'

Koppel intervened, raising a hand to silence Holst. 'Hear my words well, Heinesen. We did not come here to pay a social call.' He stepped close to Verner, putting a hand on his shoulder. 'We are all God-fearing men here today, and men of some learning, but we have seen the frenzy which such talk can arouse. You are undoubtedly in great danger, Heinesen, and while that remains the case it is our duty to advise you of the matter.'

'Had he been alive,' interjected Holst, 'your uncle Gustav would not have allowed such unholy manifestations to occur on his property.'

'Unholy manifestations?' laughed Heinesen. 'Need I remind you that I myself was in the employ of the king's own astronomer.'

'No, Heinesen, you need not, for we are indeed familiar with your past. You worked for the illustrious Tycho Brahe for three years. The man was a scandal and an embarrassment to king and country alike.' Holst straightened his coat, brushing some invisible crumb from a lapel. 'True, you served as his apprentice, and I am in no doubt that it was during that time that the seeds for this escapade were planted in your imagination. But I would remind you, Heinesen, that the ideas of that man were unsound. He left this kingdom in disgrace, not before time I might add. His mind was without question disturbed. A direct consequence, in my opinion, of the unreasonable degree of patronage lent him by our noble, but misguided, monarch.'

'We could debate the degree of effectiveness of his methods, but unsound he was not.'

Holst gave a gruff bark of exasperation. 'Heinesen, I did not come here to debate the finer points of superstitious stuff and nonsense as palpitated over by these astrologers and diviners of stars. The stars are out of our reach and God intended for them to remain so. All your paraphernalia does not change that fact.' With some difficulty he rose to his feet. 'I am not an ignorant man, Heinesen. I am not a fool. I am aware of the secularism rife among certain learned circles regarding the movements of the heavenly spheres. Idle minds entertaining themselves with foolish speculation. But come down from your perch, little bird.

Your ideas mean nothing to the ordinary people of this world. They know nothing but the kingdom of God. To them your indulgent imaginings are not only incomprehensible, they are also a threat.'

Heinesen was about to reply when Rusk let out a cry. All eyes turned to him. He had been standing by the window. He turned to face them, his face as white as a sheet.

'In the name of heaven, the rumours are true.'

'What are you blubbering about, Holst?' demanded Koppel, pushing the quivering man aside.

'Out there. It walks . . . on two legs.'

'Heavenly father, preserve us!' exclaimed the merchant who had rushed to the window. He spun on his heel, his face glowing fiercely. 'Have you taken leave of your senses, Heinesen?'

Heinesen could scarcely hold himself from laughing out loud. 'Come, come, gentlemen. He is a man, nothing more and nothing less. A man such as one might encounter in the sea ports of Spain or Cathargo. He is a native of Africa, I believe. A slave, no doubt in the service of the Ottomans.'

'Who?' asked Rusk.

'The Turks,' muttered Koppel through clenched lips. His words sent a fresh bolt of fear surging through the priest's veins.

'Good God above, are they here . . . amongst us?'

'What sorcery is this that we bear witness to?' puffed Holst.

'You would speak of sorcery, sir?' Heinesen parried. 'Has not the king himself made it clear that such talk is to be condemned?'

Holst rounded on him. 'Heinesen, this is no time for levity. This is pure folly. What possessed you to bring such a God-forsaken creature into these parts?'

'Curiosity, but also necessity. I have need for all the hands I can get.' Heinesen turned to meet their gaze evenly. 'Gentlemen, I would implore you to remain calm. This man is a simple fellow. He speaks nothing but the common language of the ports of the Mediterranean Sea. He works hard, however, and as diligently as a well-trained work horse.' Heinsesen beamed, knowing that he had caught their attention. 'The wealth of the Spanish colonies comes from the work of such men. They are carrying them from the coasts of Africa in great numbers.'

'His kind does not belong here, no matter what the custom is in Spain.' Holst was adamant. Rusk was shaking his head, 'Surely it is a bad omen to bring such a creature to these parts?'

'A priest that would speak of bad omens, evil portents?' Heinesen was smiling, 'Such is the stuff of superstition and speculation, I would wager. Whatever next, the devil curdling the milk?' Rusk did not share his smile, but instead looked away, shaking his head and wiping his brow.

'I shall prove to you how harmless he is.' Heinesen stepped to the door and called for Klinke to bring Rashid in.

The three men began to hum and mutter amongst themselves. Heinesen stood by the open door and signalled for Rashid to step forward. When he entered the room the three men fell back.

'Tranquilo.' Heinesen remained where he was. He lifted a hand slowly, taking care, as one might with a nervous pony, not to make any sudden movements. 'Tranquilo,' he repeated. He nodded in the direction of the guests. 'These three men would like to make your acquaintance.'

Rashid looked around the assembly, and then, not quite sure how to proceed, he gave a short bow. No one spoke.

Heinesen looked around the faces of the men. He saw ignorance and he saw fear and this gave him a moment of satisfaction. He was more convinced than ever that his efforts to bring the light of knowledge into this region of darkness were urgently necessary.

'Come, do not be afraid,' he repeated.

Rashid stepped to the centre of the room. His eyes roamed slowly around. He had never set foot inside here before. It was as though he were inside a large wooden chamber. The floor above had been cut away so that one looked all the way up to the roof. The light streamed in through the windows. He looked to the right through the one that faced towards the hill. The glass, he noted, was different in every window. Here it was a yellowish colour and bathed the room in a warm mineral glow the colour of brass. It was indeed a large room. The shadows deepened away from the centre and bulky, odd-looking objects protruded here and there from the darkness. It was as though one were peering into the bottom of a very dark ocean where life had slowed down to an almost motionless tick.

Heinesen held out a hand to usher him into the centre of the room. 'Come,' he said, gesturing. Rashid took half a step towards the table. 'Gentlemen, do not be afraid. Note the curve of his back, obviously the result of some inherent deformity. Note the eyes which convey such simpleness of mind as one might expect in a harmless creature.'

Koppel grasped Heinesen's arm and leaned close to whisper in his ear. 'How can you be sure that he is not an emissary of the Turks?'

'A spy? Come, gentlemen, let me demonstrate the simplicity of this humble soul.' He looked around and then drew a sheet of paper towards him. The others looked on attentively. Heinesen pressed the feather quill into Rashid's hand. 'Write something,' he commanded.

Rashid looked at the three men. He looked around the room, then he looked at the quill in his hand. The men leaned forwards as he bent towards the paper. He drew a series of lines and dots, strange letters.

Heinesen held up the paper with a flourish. 'A meaningless scribble, gentlemen. My point is proven.'

The three men were not convinced. Rusk gave a sharp intake of breath. 'It is a curse, surely. In the tongue of the devil himself.'

'Silence yourself, priest. It is the simple scrawl of children,' countered Koppel.

Heinesen fell silent. The prefect was watching him closely. 'What say you, Heinesen?'

Before he had time to reply to Holst's question, however, the priest was ranting again. 'Heathens, worshippers of the Antichrist, in the devil's pay, tainted in the skin to match their souls. Have you taken leave of your senses, man?'

'He was delivered here by providence.'

The prefect could not believe his ears. He could hardly get the words out. 'Providence? Caution, young Heinesen, you will be sounding the tune of the heretics soon.'

Heinesen looked around the assembled faces.

'I think,' announced Holst quietly, 'that we have seen enough.' The fire crackled. He placed his hat firmly on his head. The other men shuffled and made themselves ready. At the door, Holst paused. 'Herremand Heinesen, know that you have brought great turmoil to this region. Your strivings here may be looked upon as an attempt to undermine the authorities of this kingdom. You will be summoned to answer these charges at the appropriate time.' With that he turned away. 'We can find our own way out, thank you,' he added, glancing once over his shoulder at Rashid one last time. Koppel hesitated at the door. 'Be careful, Heinesen, know that you are not above the law. There is no greater wrath than that of righteous men. Your good name will not protect you, nor will any man stand between you and the zealots.'

Without another word he put on his hat and strode briskly from the room. The door closed behind them and the prefect could be heard calling for his driver. Klinke led Rashid back across the yard. Heinesen sank into his chair with a sigh. He closed his eyes for a moment, listening to the shouts of the driver and the clatter of the carriage over the stones and out through the port of the gatehouse.

Silence. Heinesen lifted up the sheet of paper and stared for a moment at the markings there. Something oddly familiar about them, but it was not until he laid the paper down on the table which afforded him a view of them from another angle and tilt that it hit him: the constellation of Pleiades.

CHAPTER TWENTY-FOUR

By connecting up the seemingly unrelated fractions of light, a pattern gradually emerges from the darkness. Verner Heinesen was thinking this as he watched Klinke walking towards the house. Klinke, with his stumpy farmer's legs and his large hands. Klinke was not happy. He had always been sceptical, right from the start, when Verner and Sigrid had turned up to claim their inheritance. He had opposed the idea immediately; this was no place for a nobleman and his sister. The work was demanding and required a good knowledge of the land and the ways of livestock. Better that they took a house in town and left the matter in his capable hands. Klinke had been with Heinesen's uncle Gustav for all his working life and his loyalty to the place was his first priority. It had indeed been difficult at first, but over the years Heinesen had proved his aptitude and, he believed, won some of the irascible foreman's grudging trust.

Heinesen's recollection of rare childhood visits was vague, and dominated by images of a tight-lipped older man who had little time for children. His father had never had much time for the rest of his family, believing them to be soft in the heart as well as in the head; his brother Gustav took after their mother, he said on numerous occasions. He recalled that on the infrequent occasions when his name had come up at home it had often been in despair, irritation or that mocking tone of his father's which was as constant an element of his childhood as the sound of ships rocking in their berths in Copenhagen harbour. The impression given by his parents of his uncle was of a rather eccentric man given to reckless and impulsive actions. Perhaps it was this which had sown the seeds of curiosity which, years later, had caused him to uproot himself and his sister, sell all their remaining properties and make the journey here. Stubborn-mindedness and a desire to defy all norms as set by his father. Was it this which had caused him to seek out his uncle's brand of iconoclasm? Curiosity, too, played a part no doubt, for from his earliest memories he had been intrigued as to why a man should abandon everything and retire to this obscure corner of the country to raise horses. Gustav Heinesen might as well have sailed to New Spain as to Jutland for the distance he maintained.

And now, thought Heinesen, all of Klinke's worst fears seemed to be coming true. The foreman appeared, tugging the figure of the slave with him by the elbow.

'I've got him for you.'

'Thank you, Klinke.'

The foreman remained where he was, apparently reluctant to depart from the room. He extended one foot and then, clearing his throat, he withdrew it again. It was so much like some quaint dance step that Heinesen had to repress the smile which threatened to break across his face. 'Come now, Klinke, what is on your mind?'

'Well, if you don't object, I would like to say my piece.' Klinke spoke in that awkward, stilted tone of a man wary of too many words. He was aware that his tongue was not suited to parlour rooms and the lofty thoughts that occupy men of learning.

Heinesen leaned on the railing of the gallery and looked down at the man. 'Come along, spit it out!'

'The thing is, he's brought us a string of bad luck. This place has never looked so wretched as it does today. It lacks the sound of honest men working.' He seemed to hesitate before finding his feet again. He nodded towards the man standing next to him. 'It's just that it hardly seems wise . . . keeping him about the place. He don't belong here, ought to be sent back to whatever hole in the ground he crawled out of.' He put his hat back on and muttering, 'I've said my piece now,' he withdrew abruptly from the room.

Leather creaked on wood as Heinesen descended the staircase. He dropped an armful of papers on the large table as he approached, moving forwards until they stood face to face. Rashid met his gaze and then his eyes moved.

The air in the room seemed turbid and thick, as though infused with a resinous organic incense. It caught in Rashid's nostrils and he could not tell whether it was a kind of ink, or a lubrication on the bearings of some of the large planetary models that were spread around, or a substance leaking from the wood, or the tar that coated the roof beams, or a combination of all of these things, but as he gazed around with wide-eyed wonder, he knew that what the room smelled of was energy. A rumbling, viscous, terrifying force; the energy of a reckless mind let loose on an unchecked leash of brilliance, or madness. Rashid looked at the floor while Heinesen moved about the room with restless energy, pausing here or there to indicate a tome of particular interest or an instrument he was proud of.

'What to do with you?' Heinesen asked himself out loud. He moved his hand, reaching out behind him for something whose location he knew precisely.

'This,' he held out the sheet of paper on which Rashid had scrawled, 'is the constellation of Pleiades. You knew that.'

He began to read in musty Greek, in a fashion that Rashid had difficulty at first in following. Heinesen indicated the markings on the paper. 'You not only knew the constellation, accurately, I may say, you also knew the correct spelling in the Greek.'

Rashid said nothing.

'But more than that, you chose this constellation knowing that it was in ascent at this time. You must have seen it, observed it.'

Rashid remained silent. He did not move, did not raise his eyes. He had been foolish to reveal what he knew. A moment of vanity, or playfulness, or perhaps it was simply pride? Heinesen threw the sheet of paper back on the table and paced across the room. He had switched to his own language now. Rashid looked on, not understanding a word. 'You seem to know more than would at first meet the eye, Moor. Yet why you had to display that knowledge before the king's envoy, I do not know.' He jabbed Rashid in the chest with his finger. 'You scared the living daylights out of the bishop's henchman.' Then he began to laugh. Rashid cleared his throat.

'Quien tien Moro, tiene oro,' he delivered.

Heinesen paused and looked up. He translated the saying aloud for his own benefit: 'He who is served by the Moor will be rewarded in gold.'

Rashid smiled and nodded.

'Know, then, that I bear no interest in gold.'

Rashid remained impassive.

Heinesen gave a laugh and swung away. 'Intriguing, very intriguing,' he murmured under his breath. Rashid watched him, moving among the shelves of books and scrolls, long unwieldy reams of paper, heavy wooden covers. 'Writing, knowledge,' declared Heinesen in a voice shrill with emotion, 'that is the more noble pursuit, would you not agree? The knowledge of the Egyptians is with us. I am more convinced than ever that if I had just one of their number I could crack the secrets of the universe.'

He gestured for Rashid to follow him up the stairs.

The upper level was a kind of mezzanine floor with a gallery that circled around the entire room, reached by means of the steep, varnished staircase close to the left wall. On top of the platform, where there was barely enough room to stand, there were shelves. Aisles of shelves extended into the walls. Shelves laden with pile upon pile of rolls, scrolls, manuscripts, books, charts, maps, papers of every size, shape and description. Dangling from a hook in the ceiling was an oil lamp, a rhomboid of glowing crystal. Below them, at the centre of the room, was a huge bell-shaped fireplace that rose into a chimney. There was room in there for two or three people to be seated around the warmth of the open fire. Geometric shadows dissected and curved through the maze in a wickerwork of arcing, swollen seams of light and dark.

The aisles of the gallery extended away from the central core into the dark gloom. Here and there the glint of metal described the presence of a long rule, a measuring rod, a sphere. Rashid stopped by a large brass disc. He lifted the astrolabe and read the inscription.

'Persian,' announced Heinesen over his shoulder with glee. 'I purchased it in Venice from a foul-tempered prince with enormous debts.' His Spanish was coming more easily now.

He vanished from sight, moving along another aisle. He was looking for something, stretching and ducking as he went, leaning from side to side, muttering to himself as he went.

'Aha!' The sound of banging and thumping and then something being dragged along the floor. Heinesen reappeared, pulling Rashid's wooden trunk behind him.

'You recognize it?'

Rashid bit his lip. The trunk was bruised and battered. A large crack had appeared in the side. Heinesen threw open the lid and reached inside.

'This is yours, isn't it?' He set the brass case on the top of the box. 'What are you, Moor? A magician? A sorcerer?'

Rashid said nothing.

Heinesen laughed. He slapped a hand to his forehead. 'I am such a fool.' Rashid reached out tentatively to stroke the indentations with a finger.

'Are you a lucky talisman, or another curse fallen on my head, Moor?' Heinesen waved his own question aside. He began talking at a rapid pace. 'You seem to awaken fear and foreboding wherever you go and you must wonder why that is. I will tell you. To them you are different. It is as simple as that. When I came across you the most level headed among those simple people believed you to be a spy in the pay of the King of Spain. To the rest of them you were no less than the devil incarnate.'

Heinesen lifted up the brass case and led the way back down the stairs. He stopped halfway down and glanced over his shoulder. 'How many languages have you?'

Rashid looked out into space and took a deep breath. He raised his head. 'I can read and write, with varying degrees of proficiency, Arabic, Greek, Latin, Persian, Soghidian. I also have a little knowledge of Sanskrit. I can converse in the language of the Franks and, of course, the *lingua franca* of the sea.'

Heinesen cut him short with a whoop of laughter, long

before Rashid had finished speaking. 'Yes, yes, that is quite sufficient I'm sure,' he bustled. 'How perfect. Do not let yourself be swayed into thinking that I have taken this decision purely out of philanthropic motive,' he announced, turning to take the stairs down. 'I intend to put your abilities to good use, sir. You will assist me with your skills as a translator.'

'Translator?'

Heinesen pointed up at the shelves of documents and books on the floor above them. 'Of course. I have spent years travelling throughout the continent of Europe amassing a library of works unrivalled by any private collector. Certainly it is the envy of one or two universities, I might wager.' He was feeling pleased with himself now. He nodded and repeated, 'A translator, of course. That is what we need.' He waved a hand, calling Rashid to his side. Spread out on the large raised table were the plans for the construction. With swift gestures Heinesen sketched out what he envisioned. Turrets, towers, trenches with all manner of instruments. 'I am constructing a beast to do battle with the heavens,' he said. 'And you shall help me.'

CHAPTER TWENTY-FIVE

The moon suckles the hungry stars; she grows thin as one by one they drain her milk. The months pass and Rashid al-Kenzy is living in a place he had never imagined he would see. The days are short and dark and the stars are no longer familiar. They circle in an abrupt spiral high above the skull. The Scorpion is nowhere to be seen; the Dog Star appears only briefly and even then, faint and very close to the ground. He has reached the ends of the earth, or as near as he has ever imagined it would be possible to get. The memory of the rain which washed him up the winding roads from the shipwreck and the stable where he was once chained, has now faded in intensity, leaving only a callus-shaped scar in its passing. He has lost his way. He is convinced that this is not what was planned for him, that his course should not have led him here. How to explain such a mistake? And if he himself were responsible, then where was the hand of God in all of this? If it was written that his life should pass at all through this place, then to what purpose?

The air here is as brittle as glass and one has to breathe carefully as though high in the mountains. The cold wind slices through his bones. Rashid al-Kenzy is living in a place known as the Castle of the Sun – in a land which does not know warmth. He sits in a small room above the stairs in the gatehouse. A long room over the archway that leads into the yard, low-beamed and stained darkly with time. The walls are bare. There is a wooden cot on the floor packed with straw, where he sleeps. There is a rough, three-legged milking stool over by the window where he sits in the evenings and gazes at the sky. From the window on the eastern side his view swoops down over the swollen waist of the hillside to the flat, girded loins of the iron-clad lake and the fields of long blue-green grass; there where the horses run. During the day the sun is entangled in the stiff boughs of the birch trees which resemble sharpened staves thrust into the coppery mud beyond the fields; there, where the slim ribbon of wood marks the boundary of the estate. There is a tiny aperture in the western wall that passes for a window and through which he can look up beyond the big house and see the path which leads like a fluid, bituminous river up the dark hill. At night it glistens as hard and bright as a snake.

The damp makes his bones weep and the moonlight seems misleading, oddly inappropriate, like laughter in a graveyard.

So Rashid al-Kenzy sat and pondered his fate. The main purpose of his journey now seemed beyond the realm of possibility. Time had slowed his progress to a standstill. He had strayed from his course. Even if he were able to get away from this place, it might take him years to locate the Dutchman and make his way back with the telescope. Such a powerful instrument would surely not remain secret for long. By the time he returned home the Dutch optical device would probably be sold on every corner, by every trinket seller from Paris to Peshawar. The Wazir's children would each have a miniature model made in brass for a toy.

He turned his mind back towards his present predicament. Truly the mysteries of life cannot be revealed in a day. He would take his time, the sign would surely come and then he would go. He must make his plans carefully, for although he did not fear these people, he did not know their ways, and he was afraid of what they imagined him to be. There was another bond keeping him here, curiosity. He was fascinated by the wealth of literature that he had stumbled upon. Such a library that any king would have been proud to possess. The Dey of Algiers would have wept with envy. Rashid felt a twinge of pride in his achievement, in having reached this place, that he might add this wonder to the tale of his life's fortunes and misfortunes when the time came for the telling. The relief afforded him by this thought was brief and he soon dismissed it as idle vanity. Still, he had always believed that, just as the stars have their geometry, so does each man have his. It was his duty to discover what lay at the root of the strange sequence of events which had landed him here.

He could live here, he told himself, as well as he could live anywhere in the world. He has no home, no town or village mourning his absence, no children awaiting the return of their father. He would try to learn what he could before the time came to leave. If there was any constancy in his life then surely it was this: to learn, wherever and whenever the opportunity presented itself, and then to move when the time came.

So he struggles day after day to try to fathom the knowledge of this new world. He has been drawn into a net where all that he has learned previously serves only to tie his feet more firmly. He must fight to break free, but where will that leave him? He is afraid that he will lose everything, including his mind, to end his days shackled to a post like a dumb animal, staring vacantly at the sky, his soul eaten by the stars.

His life, it has to be said, had been made more comfortable by his new appointment. He no longer had to dig and carry, dragging himself up and down the hill each day, exhausted.

215

Indeed the work on the hill had come to a complete stop since the boy had been killed. The building where all the workers used to live, where he used to sleep, was now dark and deserted. The gatehouse was warmer, no matter how cold it felt; he could not imagine what it would have been like to still be living in that draughty barn.

The house as a whole was quieter these days. There were few people left: Klinke, who slept on the other side of the staircase from Rashid's room; the cook, a large man with a loud voice, and a housekeeper who fled whenever Rashid came into view. He was led, on the first day of his new appointment, from the gallery to the cavernous kitchen below ground where he found the smoky warmth comforting. He was given hot water with which to wash and scissors to trim his hair and beard; new clothes – thick, warm breeches of wool and a shirt of fine linen. Over this a thick jacket of woven horsehair and on his feet stockings and then shoes made of wood. They fed him warm milk, into which he broke hard stumps of dark bread. From now on, Heinesen had made it clear, he was to take all his meals there in the kitchen with the others. So Rashid ate while they looked on, fascinated. The cook was a man with a generous waist and a single curl of carrot-coloured hair sticking up from the top of his head. The woman who took care of the house was apparently his wife, although he spent more time talking to his dog, a creature which never moved from its corner by the fire unless kicked. The men watched Rashid as though they had never expected him to eat. They sat down, side by side, across the table from him, throwing extra bits in his direction, which he wolfed down as fast as they came his way. He amused them for a time, the way the dog might have done, had it been a little more lively, and then they would begin to talk amongst themselves and he was left to his thoughts.

There was nothing odd about their curiosity, their guarded reluctance to come near him. He realized that he was a strange creature to them, an outsider. To the ignorant he was an object of curiosity, without past history or name. To those who could think, he was living proof of another world, one they knew nothing of and therefore distrusted. They knew him as the Turk, son of the illustrious Süleymân, notorious impaler of God-fearing Christians. He looked at the two men, at their faces and their open eyes as they spoke to one another, glancing in his direction only from time to time. They no longer feared him; they felt nothing for him, not even pity. Rashid wondered whether he would come to know these people, whether, in time, he would betray them, or they him.

The final member of the household was Heinesen's sister. Rashid knew of her existence, although he rarely saw her. Once or twice he had caught a glimpse of a slight figure passing a doorway, a shadow at the end of the hall. Once, from the gatehouse one night, Rashid had caught a glimpse of Heinesen sitting down to eat in the big room; opposite him was a woman.

Heinesen departed once again on his travels, in an endless search for financial and moral support from the nobility and princes of Europe. Each morning Rashid rose early to kneel in prayer before descending the narrow stairs from the gatehouse. He crossed between the carts and carriages and walked quickly across the yard towards the main house, his head down against the biting wind, his mind already entering the shelves of dusty parchment and paper ahead of him.

He let himself quietly into the study. He always stood there for a moment, looking around him to assertain that he was alone, before proceeding. Then he would cross the room to the table by the window. The table itself was as large as Rashid's room in the gatehouse. He had paced around it to make certain of this estimation. He climbed into the high chair and lifted his feet onto the round straw footrest. The housekeeper had been instructed to make sure the fire was lit.

So Rashid would settle down in the big chair to the sound of wood crackling in the broad fireplace behind him. Then he would bend his head and begin to read. In the beginning he could not sit still for more than a few intakes of breath before he was off again, charging up and down the stairs, in and out of the galleries, sifting frantically through what was there. He began with material in Arabic, of which there was little, mostly in poor condition and generally very aged, and progressed quickly to the Spanish and then Greek texts. He found that the words and signs came back to him quickly. Often he would be so immersed in his reading that he would forget to eat until his stomach began to pain him severely. He would then drop from the chair and stumble down the gloomy corridor to the stone steps and the kitchens. His odd hours seemed to suit the others for they still appeared to have no wish to share their meals with him. He was fed the remains of whatever was left, scraped together in a wooden bowl. The dog opened one eye and gave him a mournful look, as though he were taking food from the mouth of a dumb beast.

But he was not expected to spend his time just satisfying his own curiosity. Heinesen had set him a task to complete in his absence. He was to translate the rather bulky Toledan charts. These charts were a collection of tables for the sun, moon and other heavenly bodies, describing their movements and relative positions. This particular version was by a native of Seville, Ibn al-Ha'im, who claimed from the outset to be correcting an earlier collection. In presenting his evidence, Ibn al-Ha'im included long passages, both in Arabic and in a language which Rashid guessed was that of Castile. Heinesen, he suspected,

218

probably had no need of these measurements; solar and lunar inequalities based on al-Battani's detailed accounts of planetary stations; rates of visibility. Rashid was convinced that if he began rooting through the galleries he would uncover a more accurate version of the same tables; al Khwarizmi, or possibly the tables of King Alfonso X of Spain – Alfonso the Wise, the Christians called him, no doubt because it was he who managed to throw the Moors out of Leon and Castile. He who had remarked, 'If I had been the creator of the universe, I should have done a more thorough job of it!' An anecdote to which Rashid's mind frequently returned these days, a reminder of the shameless arrogance of the Christian mind.

The Toledan charts were, in any case, of little use. They would have to be adjusted for use in these latitudes. In the three hundred odd years since they were printed someone must have adapted them already. Heinesen was obviously setting him a test to gauge the extent of his skills.

He settles back into the creaking chair, leaning over the desk. The air has a mysterious density, laden with frail arteries of redolent ink and the moribund disintegration of brittle parchment. His eyes ache from the poor light and the effort of trying to make out the printed characters. It is written in a tongue which is familiar to him, but still the words do not come easily. His lips move as his finger traces the lines of script. The mountain of books rises up before him. The lamp burns low. He stretches his neck, rubs his hands together and blows on his fingers to warm them. How he longs for the warmth of latitudes which he recalls, the brightness of the light there which made the letters simply jump from the page. How can anyone learn anything in these latitudes where the words crawl inside the paper to keep warm?

Altitudes and azimuths, the tables, the charts of stars, all familiar to him despite the awkwardness of the language and the method used. He recognized the patterns of his ancestors, the great men whom he had grown to admire and love as though they were his family – his true family, as he thought of them. For a long time, a lifetime, he had lived with these men in his head, until they had become a part of him and he of them. How he had dreamed of joining their ranks; mathematician, astronomer, geographer. Such aspirations now seemed far away and all the more ridiculous for that. The books which filled the shelves of that great library had once suffocated and stimulated his imagination. He wanted to swallow them all whole. He wanted to dig his way through page by page, line by line until all the knowledge hidden there in signs and ciphers was his. He would drink the ink, eat the paper. These books contained the arcs of the heavens, the holy, unfathomable mystery which enclosed him, like a cocoon.

CHAPTER TWENTY-SIX

'You can't stay here for ever, you know.'

'I know. I just can't really face going back.'

'That bad, huh?'

They were sitting in the car at the junction by the shop. Martin was examining the dirt under his fingernails.

'Well, I don't know anything about it, but I always thought that having a family . . . I mean a child and a wife. I mean, there's something special about that, isn't there? I mean, something worth protecting.'

Hassan shook his head.

'It's not always as easy as that.'

Ahead of them a small blue car came racing round the corner. It screeched to a halt outside the shop. A boy got out and went inside.

'Your friends.'

'They're not really my friends,' muttered Martin. His head jerked back as he brushed his hair aside. 'They're just the only people around here my age.' He gave a dismissive laugh. 'I can't really get rid of them, I suppose.'

The sound of music came from the interior of the other car. The boy who had gone into the shop now emerged and glanced up and down the road. He caught sight of Martin and waved. Martin waved back. The boy leaned into the other car again and the sound of laughter could be heard echoing away down the otherwise deserted road. Then he jumped in and the car reversed quickly until it was alongside Hassan's car. Three or four boys could be seen inside waving and gesturing. The driver revved up the engine a few times and then let the car go, wheels spinning as it raced away with a high squeal of rubber on asphalt.

'Well, you can't say that I haven't livened things up around here.'

The note of irritation that had crept into Hassan's voice did not go unnoticed. Martin lifted his head. 'They are only fooling about, you know. They don't mean anything by it.'

'If they didn't mean anything by it, there would be no need to do it.'

'There's not a lot for them to do around here. There's not that much choice.'

'Everyone has a choice, don't they? You have a choice.'

Martin was fidgeting about now, tapping on the dashboard. 'You don't know what it's like. I mean nothing happens here. You have a life, a job, a family. I mean, maybe they wonder why you have those things and they don't.'

Hassan tried to make the boy's face out in the darkness.

'Is that what you wonder?'

Martin lifted up his hands and then dropped them again, as though the words wouldn't come. He tried another smile, but it stiffened and congealed. 'You talk as though they wanted to harm you or something. Like they want you to stop doing your work here. They know nothing about who you are or what you are doing here.'

'That's just the point, isn't it?'

Martin swung his head and looked away for a moment. 'I don't understand.'

'They don't care what I am doing here. Why should they? They don't want to know. They just want to hang on to their ignorance and fear. It grows in them, getting tighter and stronger with each passing year. Until one day its all they have and they know nothing else.'

'They're just bored, bored, stupid farmer kids . . . like me.' He wrenched at the door and climbed out. 'This is too much.'

Hassan wished he had not taken out his frustration on the boy. He tried to make amends. 'All I am saying is that you could do a lot with your life, Martin. It doesn't have to end here.'

'Sure.'

There was a moment's pause.

'What about your friends?'

Martin was looking down the road. 'They'll come back,' he said. 'They have to. There's nowhere else for them to go.'

As he drove the short distance home Hassan could see Martin in the mirror. The awkward lanky figure crossing the dark road towards the bright lights of the shop.

He was still trying to piece together the world as it was then. What was happening in astronomy at the start of the seventeenth century? What did it encompass? Tycho Brahe was employed by the king as an astrologer. In a series of lectures delivered by Brahe in 1574 he indicated that he believed that man's fate was not ruled entirely by the aspect of the heavens, but that God had given man the ability to overcome the influence of the stars. Astrology was therefore of use in helping to predict an imminent danger or threat, thus allowing man to take action to avoid it. It was the failure of astrology to predict events accurately that spurred Brahe to begin to examine his instruments. He attributed the problem with astrological predictions to a lack of precision, which was why he concentrated so much of his efforts on constructing his own instruments.

What about this man Rashid al-Kenzy? Scientific knowledge in the Arab world was on the decline throughout the sixteenth century. The Golden Age of learning peaked in the Arab world three centuries earlier. There was a huge gap. There was no mention, for example, of Copernicus' theory of heliocentricity until the end of the seventeenth century, and then only in passing. The reaction in the Islamic world would have been similar to that of the Christians; to defer the centre of the universe to the sun, away from the world and away from man would have been considered a dangerous idea. Allah created the earth and the seven heavens, did he not?

Hassan sat back and put his feet on the table. So, assuming that Rashid al-Kenzy had not attended a university in Europe he would have known nothing of the science of the day. Copernicus' ideas on astronomy were still only known to a small circle of scholars, and they were certainly not broadly accepted.

What would a man like that have made of such ideas?

Why had he travelled so far north, alone?

Why was Heinesen buried on the hillside, and who buried him? Why was the brass instrument buried with him? A gift?

He went back to his notes, the burning down of the cathedral was in 1610, which was the most accurate way of fixing the time when the mysterious 'Turk' was present in the area. What was happening in astronomy in 1610? Hassan opened up his encyclopaedia and tapped in the date. The screen flickered and the machine whirred. He clicked his way through the index. Galileo was busy building his telescope, observing the mountains of the moon. Sixteen-ten was a strange time; ideas about the way the universe worked were going through radical reform. In 1633 Galileo was condemned to life imprisonment for appearing to advocate Copernicus' theories. The sentence was not enforced, but he did spend the rest of his life under house arrest.

Hardly likely that Rashid al-Kenzy would have come looking for scientific evidence or knowledge; he would have gone to a university town. Then his arrival here would have been an accident, a coincidence. Hassan turned back to his map of Europe. He traced a finger down the coast. A ship travelling north, or south? North. His finger found Holland and he remembered something. He went back to the encyclopaedia. Galileo had been involved in controversy with a German astronomer named Simon Mayr in 1609 over the design of his telescope. The instrument in question had first been mentioned in Holland the year before. But by the time al Kenzy arrived in Europe the telescope was becoming widespread. It would make little sense to come all this way for something like that, surely? Hassan dismissed the idea, switched everything off and climbed up the stairs to fall into bed and deep, deep sleep.

CHAPTER TWENTY-SEVEN

Rashid abandoned the task set for him by Heinesen. Or rather, it abandoned him of its own accord, for he was swept off on other tides, other schemes. He had begun to turn his attention fully to the contents of the library. He was not certain what he was looking for, perhaps a clue, a way of understanding what was going on in Heinesen's mind.

From time to time he would recall his life in more familiar latitudes. He no longer recognized the person that he had once been. He slept badly. He lost his appetite. He had, in time, overcome his revulsion for the food here, and would have eaten if he could have forced anything down, but every mouthful lodged in his throat and almost choked him.

He felt as though he were being eroded, gently, like sand in the wind, like a field of maize he had once seen upon which a cloud of locusts descended. You could see the colour of the field changing before your very eyes, the green stems curling away from the ground to leave the earth naked, barren and brown. Looking back on the course of his progress it now appeared to him that his entire life encompassed a process of dislocation, from the very moment of his birth or even earlier. Even before his entry into this world he had lost the place of his birth when his mother was abducted into slavery. He had thus far lost his home, his father, his people and his beloved mother. Now he floated in a sea of voices, none of which was his. His sense of the stars was now betrayed by magic. His geography had crumbled away into confusion. In the latitudes he now traversed God no longer placed man at the centre of all creation, but off to one side, just one of many brightly spinning orbs, signifying little more than a handful of fireflies. He was among people who spoke the name of God but did not believe what their own lips told them.

He continued to plot his escape. Within the vast library there were, of course, maps, charts of the land and sea alongside those of the stars. He would make his way east to the coast and the shipping lanes that led into the Baltic Sea and the ports of the Hanseatic League and Pomerania. He was strong and was convinced that he could endure whatever hardship was necessary to secure himself a passage south, back to the world. He had made careful copies of maps of the region upon which he plotted his route. He knew where to find enough food in the kitchen stores to sustain him on his journey. He had even picked out which horses he would take with him. All was ready, and the time to move was soon, before the winter set in, before his sanity gave way. The time to move was now.

But the constellation of the heavens that circled Rashid al-Kenzy's head was unfamiliar and he was in danger of losing his way completely. Another planet was bearing down on him, unforeseen and unexpected.

It was a day like any other, until the door creaked open and Rashid lifted his eyes idly from the pages before him. The person who entered crossed the room, humming to herself as she went. Motionless, he watched her scattering dried flowers over the straw-covered wooden floorboards as she walked. She did not glance in his direction and, indeed, appeared not to have noticed his presence. It was as though he were invisible. He returned his eyes to the pages in front of him and resumed his calculations. He knew who she was. This was Heinesen's sister. Rashid was fairly certain that she either suffered from some terrible physical affliction or that otherwise her mind was in some way disturbed. Seeing her now, it struck Rashid that she probably would scarely have noticed if the house through which she walked were in flames. He turned his nose back down to the pages in front of him. She lived an isolated existence, residing in the upper north wing of the house and rarely emerging, and when she did it was as if the rest of the world did not exist, as though she were simply carried through life upon a wave of thought.

Over the next few days she appeared again, a number of times, and Rashid began to feel uneasy about her presence. He no longer felt comfortable. He harboured deep suspicions about her nature and intentions. If Heinesen was light and high in spirit, then she, Sigrid was her name, was surely the opposite. She rarely seemed to speak at all, to anyone. Rashid longed for Heinesen's return.

She was not large in stature. She carried herself with the quietude of firm conviction. Her hair was cut short and and tied out of sight beneath a plain black scarf, which ought to have lent her a somewhat dowdy appearance, but only succeeded in making her appear all the more confounding. She still appeared only occasionally and this was a small mercy for which he was truly grateful. The very sound of her footsteps filled him with fear and trepidation, although he could not describe in words what kind of threat she posed.

His eyes down, he could hear that she had stopped moving. He did not dare even peek in her direction, for fear of meeting her gaze. He did not dare, but he could not help it. The room was silent for so long, so . . . at an appropriate moment, turning the page of the big book, he let his eyes drift off the arc of paper and rise. She was nowhere in sight! His heart began to beat. Two things to be afraid of, he recalled from his old feki's teachings: the sea, and women who possess the 'eye'. The sea he had survived, but perhaps only to succumb to this more potent threat. He climbed gingerly to the floor from his chair. She had indeed vanished without trace, straight into thin air. He gave a silent curse and began reciting religious verses under his breath. His efforts to locate her became more urgent, less cautious. He stepped forwards, and then again, looking frantically about him, turned from left to right. His sleeve brushed the tip of a measuring quadrant taller than a man which rested on the floor. It began to swing. Rashid jumped to catch it and managed to save it before it hit the ground. Carefully he raised the heavy brass instrument into balance again. Then, suddenly she was there emerging from the depths, like the thin black smoke of an oil lamp rising through the glass.

Neither of them say a word. He lowers his head and returns to his seat to begin working again. After a moment or two he stops, realizing that she has not moved. He lifted his eyes again.

The light from the window, behind and to her left, fell across her face. She stood in a commanding position, her hands clasped together in front of her. She had a strong face, Rashid noted, firm jaw and a high forehead which vanished into the black scarf which she wore tightly wound around her head. From this solemn binding a tiny strand of fine hair had released itself and now danced like spun silver on the sun's beams.

Rashid wondered whether he had done something wrong. Perhaps she was aware that he was no longer carrying out the task given him by her brother.

Heinesen, he recalled, had informed him, in passing, that she composed poetry, which she recited to him in the evenings when they sat inside the big fireplace. Rashid listened to all of these praises with half an ear. He had never heard of a woman writing poetry and he doubted whether in that language of theirs, which sounded like ducks squabbling, any sentiment as sublime as poetry could be expressed.

'Whereas, I must confess, my talents lie in the computations, the precisions of quantification, measurements, her strengths lie more in the intuitive scale of the intellect. She reads the soul with great clarity and is in my humble opinion one of the foremost authorities on the mesh between the stars and the soul. She can speak for hours on the relevance of Giordano Bruno and the Hermetics; the *Prisca Theologica*; the *anima mundi*. A sphere of thought of the utmost value in interpreting the nature of man's fate as described by the stars, would you not agree?'

Of course Rashid could neither agree nor disagree, since such matters were new to him. Yes, astrology he knew and matters of magic and dream interpretation he had some knowledge of, but these names were new to him. He had no idea what significance they played. Now it served only to confirm his initial suspicions about the woman.

It had occurred to Rashid that they might not be siblings at all. Such matters had been spoken of before in Allah's presence and would no doubt continue to be so until the fires of hell consumed all involved. Odd that the two of them, both well past what was a suitable age, should not have married. A woman's fertile years are limited and while she was obviously a stern character of doubtlessly unforgiving nature, she was nevertheless a woman capable of producing children.

Whatever the case may have been, there was no doubt in Rashid's mind that with the emergence of this creature from seclusion, an air of disturbance seemed to have invaded the house. She sat scribbling furiously page upon page, day in and day out, working long into the night, until the nib broke under her hand, or the ink ran out, or some other thought came into her head to push whatever she was doing aside.

Thus it was that one day he looked up to find her asleep, her head down on the table, her hands stretched out across the solid oak. Silent and unmoving, he looked at her. For the first time being unafraid to allow his eyes to examine her. He could see little: the dark hair that emerged from beneath the border of the black scarf. As he watched, she stirred and the scarf slipped off her head. Her hair was straight and fine, like dark silk, he thought. In the middle of her forehead there was a strip of light where the hair had turned prematurely white. He examined the soft lines of her face and could not understand why he had feared her. She must have been the same age as he, perhaps a year or two younger. Surely, such a face was incapable of doing anyone harm?

Some sheets from a manuscript had slipped to the floor. He thought for a moment, leaned down and looked again. They were still there. He took a deep breath and put down the page he was holding. Still she had not moved. The fire crackled contentedly behind him. He hesitated no longer. Dropping lightly from the chair he knelt on the floor to pick up the leaves of paper that had drifted down. He turned them over and over in his hands trying to make sense of them.

It was in this way that she guided him towards the works of the heathens.

'Hebdomades,' he read slowly.

It was at precisely that moment that she stirred. He became like a stone – not even breathing. Awakening suddenly, she lifted her head. Her eyes turned towards him and then, seeing him there, she hurled herself backwards, letting out a startled scream and tumbling to the floor. They were both frozen in that position, like two frightened animals, he on his knees and she on her side, with one foot caught on the chair beside them. She was breathing heavily and began hurriedly to gather up the papers and straighten her clothes. He reached to lift the chair back up into an upright position. Her hand grazed his in her haste to complete the action herself. He retreated to his chair and then turned and buried his nose back in his work.

Silence returned to still the room. Not a word between them was yet spoken.

CHAPTER TWENTY-EIGHT

'*Hebdomades*,' Rashid heard himself say, at last. She placed her hands on the book in front of her, closed it firmly and looked up.

'*Hebdomades*,' he repeated. 'What does it mean?' She spoke without hesitation, her gaze steady and unwavering, her hands clasped lightly together on top of her notebook. 'Published 1589 in Venice by Fabio Paolini. It contains Ficino's theory of magic. It outlines the cosmology and astrology upon which magic is founded.' Her Spanish was better than her brother's.

Rashid frowned. 'What is the argument of its existence?'

'The argument of its existence is our existence.' He recalled that Heinesen had on some occasion informed him that she had taught herself to speak and read it while he himself was travelling in that country. They communicated in that language during his absence, such was her bond to her brother, and such was her determination. Her accent was, however, strange. For she had never used the language in speaking, but only for purposes of reading and writing. She spoke confidently, but with an awkwardness that irritated her, as though the words were about to slip away from the tongue as soon as they were unleashed. Her grammar was more correct than his and reminded him of the conversation of the old Jewish scholars in the Mudajarre quarter of Algiers.

She was talking now at great speed; having taken up the lead of Paolini's *Hebdomades* she rushed on, so fast that it made his head spin. Her study of the work in question was not complete, having reached its source only in passing, in the works of an Englishman named John Dee. Did he know the work of Dee? Rashid shook his head blankly. She cantered onwards.

John Dee wrote the mathematical preface to Billingsley's English translation of Euclid. He subscribed to the thoughts of Agrippa in *De Occulta Philosophia* in which the universe is divided into three worlds.

'In the first, the Natural world, the Magus operates using natural magic. In the Middle or Celestial world, he uses mathematical magic. And in the Supercelestial world the Magus operates by means of numerological configurations.' She was truly magnificent when in full flight and barely paused for breath, it seemed. He had never witnessed such enthusiasm before. 'Dee believes that one can conjure up angels by the use of numbers.'

She came to a halt as abruptly as she had begun. He was at a loss. Angels by means of magic? He was aware that the witless expression on his face must have made him resemble some bovine creature, but he was nevertheless unable to move a finger. His head nodded up and down in time with the cadence of her speech. He wanted to go on.

'I must confess that I find it difficult to see the immediate bearing of such fanciful theories.' He finally managed to find his tongue again. What he meant to say was that such matters struck him as being devoted to a kind of magic which was trivial and false and had little to do with the noble spheres. She returned lightly, coaxing him on, 'Does it not surprise you that the first Greek work which Cosimo de Medici ordered translated into Latin was not Plato, but the *Corpus Hermeticum*?' Yes, it surprised him. How could he have known such a thing? Her voice trickled through the musty room like powerful ink seeping into his head. 'Does that not tell you of the significance of this work?'

'I do not know this Hermes Trismegistus,' he murmered. Every waking hour he had spent poring over words and paper seemed to be called into question, grew faint and grey, like sunlight fading into darkness.

With an impatient ruffle of her skirts she stood, resting her hands for a moment upon the wide, ornate table at which he worked. The dress she wore was an indigo blue, heavy with starch. The buttons on her tunic were made of smooth, carved bone. The rustle of the countless layers of her skirts was like the languorous sway of undersea trees. He was learning to look at her, to face her, steadily, without trepidation or concealment, but face on, as one human being to another. His eyes betrayed him, flickering this way and that, catching only fragments, corners, loose threads hanging from her sleeves, a strand of hair floating in light.

Hermes Trismegistus was an Egyptian priest, she tells him, a contemporary of Moses, no less. He is also known as Idris. He told of the creation of man like this. First there was the creation of light and the elements of nature. Then came the creation of the heavens with the seven planets which he called The Governors. The creation of man followed this. When Adam sought the secrets of divine power he was expelled from the garden of Eden for his disobedience, but according to Hermes he regained his dominion over nature through communion with the cosmos. The seven governors loved him and each gave him a part of their rule.

Rashid's first impression was that he had stumbled upon a world of amateur speculation. Something new to him. The ideas this woman was proposing were nothing less than wild guesswork at best, and at worst they were direct advocations of pagan idolatry, the worship of nature and the planets. Silently he made a prayer to the Almighty creator that he might forgive him for entertaining such vagaries. But he has been drawn in. His ears hunger for more of these tales, for they are as seductive and filled with wonder as any story he has ever heard or read, and they are the key. He is mesmerized, spellbound. She has begun to tell him the tale of the world she inhabits, of the air she breathes. In a short time she conveys a great deal, about statues and clocks; mechanical animation. The clock was the key to unlocking the *anima mundi*, the spirit of the universe.

Time, then, is the key, he offers, grasping at straws in the wind. She shakes her head, not time alone. Time and space. Perspective.

It is all a matter of perspective, she says. Infinite space is endowed with infinite quality and this infinite quality is endowed with the infinite act of existence. She has started to talk of Giordano Bruno, the heretic. Rashid sits with his mouth hanging open, waiting for flies. For the thoughts which Bruno dared to speak aloud they bound him to the stake in Rome and burned him alive. Ten short years ago. He had claimed that the sun was the source of all life and energy. 'The earth moves because it is alive, it lives!' said Bruno. They scattered his ashes to the clouds for suggesting that the universe was limitless.

'Is that not the very expression of the wonder of life?' she asked him. He had no idea what expression it was, but it scared him, this poetic sense she made of the world. 'The earth we walk on is alive. Think of the trees and the wind, think of the sunlight—' She stopped abruptly, for she is running ahead of herself and has forgotten.

What was the difference between the ways of the infidels and the ways of the believers? He, too, would doubtless be burned alive if he returned home spouting such ideas, and yet . . .

She was guiding him along a path, feeding him fragments crumbs to keep him on the right track. The irregular motions of the planets were difficult to explain. If one followed the Ptolemaic model of concentric circles describing the paths of the orbs, how does one then explain the varying distances of the planets?

A circle, then, is no longer a circle.

Had he heard such ideas spoken of in Aleppo or Damascus, Rashid would no doubt have laughed along with the others. Is the earth now to become an idol, a god? But he is not in Damascus, he is in the belt of the Seventh Zone, unfit, according to the great scholar Ibn Khaldun, for man to inhabit. More than this, he is in the Castle of the Sun and he is alone; he must make up his own mind as to what is right and wrong.

And he has already been shown the evidence: the *Stella Nova* observed burning brightly by Tycho Brahe, Old Ironbeak, as Heinesen refers to his former master, the astronomer to the king's court in this land of ice and water. He observed a new star burning in the constellation of Cassiopeia. The angle of the star changed as the constellation climbed, proving that this new star was far beyond the planets. So there was movement and change; the stars were not fixed in a crystal latticework as Aristotle had claimed. If this were true, then what had previously been believed to be fixed and unchanging was not actually so. What had been supposed to be silent and still was no longer so. Of course, he could have been wrong, but the calculations were there, the measurements made sense mathematically. A new star.

Rashid felt his progress was slow. The speed at which he could read was improving, but the amount of information which he then had to digest also subsequently increased. His mind moved in jerks, like the limbs of a dying gazelle.

They continue onwards towards Copernicus.

Inspired no doubt by the writings of Bruno, Copernicus spoke of nature, of the motion of the earth being a natural and non-violent motion. 'Whatever happens in the course of nature remains in good condition and in its best arrangement.' Rashid's brow furrows in confusion. Was the man advocating a return to the ways of beasts? Nature superior to the ways of man? Before the one true God was known, the world was filled with the darkness of the Jahilliya. A time of ignorance inhabited by idols and pagan gods who demanded human sacrifice. Could it be that the stars themselves had become such objects of worship? Copernicus, the son of a Polish merchant, spoke of the appearance of a daily rotation belonging to the heavens while its actuality belongs to the earth. On a ship sailing on quiet waters everything beyond appears to be in motion, while in fact it is the ship itself which is moving. Such arguments sink their talons into his skull with a tenacious grip.

She goes on to speak of architecture, of the buildings of Brunelleschi and Alberti in Florence. Perspectivism conceives of the world seen through the eye. The eye of man replacing that of God. A simple shift, a small step, no more. What we see is truth.

'Your perspective is changing,' she says. 'It is nothing to be afraid of.'

It is true, the world is tilting and Rashid is terrified that at any moment he may go flying off into the blackness of the void beyond.

She beckons, and he goes. She has begun to teach him things which he has never dreamed of.

For days Rashid could do nothing. He felt helpless and numb, as though everything he had learned up until now added up to less than a handful of dust. But even this, he realized with a start, was not true.

Looking at the diagrams she had shown him, it occurred to him that this man Copernicus must surely have known of the ideas of Nasr al din al-Tusi.

'Who?' she asked.

Nasr al din al-Tusi was the founding father of the Maragha School. Rashid took a deep breath. It began with Hulagu, the grandson of Ghengis Khan, who decided to improve his certainty of victory in battle by giving his astrologers and star diviners a place in which to work in peace. He assembled the wisest heads in the land and built them an observatory at Maragha in Azerbaijan. It was headed by al-Tusi, a man of such wide-ranging ability that it was whispered that even the founder of the Mongol dynasty himself took care not to offend his sensibilities. They constructed models in which only circular motions of a constant speed were allowed. Ptolemy thought up the equant. The Maragha philosophers retained it. Thereby, for every planet there was a point, a place in the universe from which the angular velocity was viewed as constant.

Astronomers arrived from east and west, Szechuan Chinese, Goans, Castilians. All assembled in admiration of the great man of knowledge. There were no astounding revelations, however. The work was carried out cautiously and systematically. No one questioned the theory of the spheres which had come down from Ptolemy. In all the splendour of the Zij of Muhi al Din al-Maghrabi, and later Mu'ayyad al-Urdi of Damascus whose treatise on the form of the universe was referred to indirectly by Ibn Shatir, in none of these was the basic assumption that the world occupied the centre of the universe challenged.

Why should it be?

239

He had the sense some days that he was running in circles, faster and faster, a dog chasing its own tail. A part of him longed to be back in the ports of debauchery, an ignorant fugitive again.

He lay on his back, staring into the darkness. He took to going for long walks, wandering up and down through the fields, his feet frozen like lumps of wood. The chestnut brown horses stood nuzzling the ground. He admired their small, compact shape. They were no bigger than mules, some of them, but they could carry a man for days without let-up. The lines and words began to blur before his eyes. They shifted place and congealed as though melting on the page. He could not read another line. He has always relied on the evidence of mathematics. He believes in this as much as he believes in anything. If the conclusion to which these equations led him was a refutation of the word of God, then he was truly lost. Does truth change according to geography? Could it be that what held true here in these climes would not hold elsewhere? His mind was beginning to play tricks.

CHAPTER TWENTY-NINE

Invisible, the Scorpion glides along the blue angled satin of the night sky. He sees it in his mind's eye, recalling it with wonder and affection from the sky above the Academy where he spent so many nights falling asleep with the canopy of stars for his blanket. Nowadays he slept where he worked. The flame burned the candle low and the heat from the small iron stove in the wall faded. He woke up shivering with cold and stiff from his awkward position. Still feeling exhausted from a night plagued by dreams and demons, he crawled to the floor and wrapped himself in the blankets that he had and, closing his eyes again, he fell into exhausted sleep.

Even while he slept, his mind turned in restless orbits, circling through waves of warm air, looking for a landmark that would tell him which direction was the right one.

The books cluttered up his head as he eagerly absorbed their knowledge. All of this was so familiar and yet why was it so disturbing? The languages which he had not used for so long fluttered in his wrist like a nervous pulse. He could not rest. When he slept, his lips still moved as he followed the lines of the pages that had impressed themselves upon his memory.

He tells himself that the growing unease which he feels welling up inside him is due to a kind of nostalgia, is due to the change in climate, the cold damp that has set into his bones like rot. But he knows that this is not true, knows that it is not the biting cold, the ache in his back, or the way the trees seem to wither around him, or even the absence of the sun which lends to this place an air of desolation and misery hardly describable. Nor is it the absence of the familiar in the constellations that rise above his head, peering only cautiously through the mists and the cloudy miasma. What disturbs him most profoundly is the endless channels through which words are now once again leading him, blindly.

And he is filled with terror, daily.

Terror at the thought of the chaos which lies beyond the mystery inscribed in the Seven Heavens by the Creator of all things. Terror at the kind of evil that is held at bay by that simple trellis of light, a terror yet to be unleashed by man in his foolish vanity and desire for omnipotence. Terror at the fear of losing the one thing which has sustained him through all the years of his life – his religious faith. He no longer prays. It is a fear that is directly linked to the awe he feels when contemplating the sheer mathematical beauty of that intricate scheme which can describe so many motions at once. As his appetite grows, so does his belief wane. He is afraid that his course has brought him to a harbour ruled by confounding forces, too strong for him to slip free, and he despairs at the thought of whether or not his skills are capable of matching such complexity. He is afraid that all his hard-earned knowledge is about to abandon him at the first sign of the tide turning. He has begun to crawl into the dark labyrinth of doubt.

The rain is gone for ever, replaced by tiny granules of snow, sprinkled over everything as though shaken like a handful of salt. The roofs of the buildings that line the rectangular yard are now silent and still. The stables, the big house, all are decorated with this new season of strange light. Rashid sits motionless for hours.

He has seen snow before, on the tops of the sunlit mountains above the academy. He recalls now the wonder of the world, as though his senses had been numbed from so many hours spent wrapped in the inky armillary of books. He saw now how the world could transform itself so easily and so completely. Caught one afternoon on his way from the main building to the gatehouse in a flurry of light, fluffy flakes, he stood there in wonder, unaware of the amusement he afforded Klinke who stood chuckling to himself watching from the stables. The flakes landed on his nose and melted into water. He stood there like a child as the cloud, like a swarm of milky winged butterflies, swirled around him.

The course of his mind has been disturbed, perhaps permanently. Of course, he should have known this. He should have known that there is always a price, that to venture out along the unknown road has its risks. That the dangers for which one has prepared are not always those which present the greatest threat. Many things only become clear with time, and thereafter to return then requires something more than simple longing. He gave himself to learning, adopting an innocence of intention which he had encountered before and which he should have known was false. To depart demands its sacrifices. Even one such as he, whose entire life had been a succession of arrivals and departures, knew that it takes a little more courage every time. Perhaps this is, after all, his fate.

It was becoming clear to him that he had inadvertently stumbled upon something unique. An idea that was as dangerous as it was revolutionary. The divorce of faith from reason was unknown in the east. The ideas of this Copernicus would have been laughed away by his peers, by his teachers. To break the firm hold of the Almighty's seven heavens? What was left was a void. But he was becoming convinced now that this was the mission of his lifetime: to reveal. To return home bearing this knowledge was surely a greater feat than any mechanical instrument, no matter how strategically useful. In this way the course of his life signified not gradual progression but a tool of change. If he could carry this knowledge, and set the evidence clearly before the wisest minds in the Sultan's court, then he would be rewarded beyond any man's dreams, but more than that, his name would be inscribed in the books of history as the man who had shed another fragment of light into the darkened cave of man's ignorance. Surely this would be an achievement greater than any reward? On the other hand, they might just call him an apostate and slice off his head.

He returned to his plans of escape, began to assemble the necessary documents and charts. He would have to carry everything with him. He began to go back, to revise his notes, to ensure that he had not in his haste excluded something. He was now charged with a new sense of purpose and his departure from these parts was now imminent. The moment he had his evidence gathered, he would be gone. Soon.

But the stars have changed their constellation and, waking or dreaming, she comes to him. He cannot understand this strange bond which grows inside him. This desire to be near her. She was driven by something he could not fathom, whether it was truth or madness he could not tell. Either way, he was now mesmerized by her trance, and by her green eyes. He will remember this feeling, for it will return, seizing him, gripping his belly, making him writhe in his sleep. He has been touched by the earth, as they say. His mind is no longer his own.

They have begun to circle one another in the big hollow house – everything else has retreated into the background. They appear to be orbiting around the same confined space, unmarked, but sensed. The awkwardness of this space of which they are both aware, is that they are neither able to claim nor ignore its existence.

In the warm glow from the fire and the weary weight of late afternoon, he drops his head down to the table in front of him and falls asleep. The quill drops from his fingers and falls lightly to the floor. He does not hear the door open. He does not hear her move through the gently swaying boughs of his sleeping thoughts, nor her footsteps as she approaches. She leans over the table to glance at the work which is spread out before him. She hesitates as she turns to go and then, quickly bending down, she retrieves the feather from the floor and places it behind his motionless hand. Then she is gone.

He watches her for a sign. Anything to indicate that she, too, has been seized by this fever. He is curious about her age – she must be three, four years younger than he, no more, and yet he is struck by the sharp intensity of her mind. She knew so much! She has devoted her life entirely, selfishly, to learning; nothing else has ever taken her attention. In this they are bound.

His mind has become distracted and seems to wander idly over the pages the way he himself once wandered in his childhood through the orchards. The sounds of his life, the memories, the scents, all of these were buried inside his body, beneath his skin. The scent of tamarind and jasmin, of apricots. All of these things have already grown faint. He fears that in time he will have lost them, that he will no longer know who or what he is. The colours of his memory have been reduced by this frail light to varying shades of grey. He no longer inhabits the sharp linear sunlight, but fears that he is now to be found in the partial shadows such as those cast by the moon in eclipse – the penumbra. The unspoken is that which separates them and draws them together – that and the mutual unspoken conspiracy against the impossibility of their meeting.

He attempts to speak some of their language. He moves his tongue, rolling the sounds around in his mouth like stones. His efforts are awkward and clumsy and to his delight she responds with light ripples of laughter that struggle to break free of her intense frown of concentration – she is amused by his interest and not dismayed by his efforts. This humility towards herself is what compels him, the breadth of her magnanimity.

Where in this confusing crosswork of tongues could they possibly meet?

On the day that the remarkable thing happened he was sitting alone in the gallery. He was deeply buried in the study of the influence of al-Tusi's coupled mechanism upon the thinking of Copernicus. If a link could be forged between the mind of a revered scholar such as al-Tusi and the radical theories of an accursed unbeliever like Copernicus, then it would not seem so very far removed as might at first be perceived. If he could establish the line of thought connecting the two apparently separate spheres of East and West. If he could find out whether or not the man Copernicus had been aware of al-Tusi's work, then . . . then what? He is only a simple man, he tells himself. He can only understand these new ideas if he can connect them to his own knowledge. Copernicus must have been familiar with the Hermetical scripts. He would have known them as the writings of an Egyptian sage of great antiquity. There is an unclear line between what we know – what we can prove for certain – and what we believe, a line that only becomes clear after it has been extracted from the ether of intuition. Ideas of universal life, of a force of animation, these are beliefs, intuitions. Copernicus trusted his intuition and then went ahead to create an argument to sustain it.

Despite its frailty, the sun seemed about to free itself from the southern trees which had bound it to the damp earth for so many months. Rashid sat in silence wondering at how the earth could be so different. It seemed to age and die in these climes. Klinke arrived bearing an armful of dry wood and began to stoke up the fireplace with rough, clumsy thrusts. Smoke seeped into his veins and he closed his eyes to the light for a moment and, exhausted, he must have passed into a deep comfortable sleep. He was floating down a warm stream. He is standing on the quayside in Algiers. He is a teller of tales addressing himself to the ocean. His story is a demon, a fever that will not let him go. He must continue to speak; one story leads into another. He cannot stop, for if he does, what will the ocean do then?

She was there before him as though she had slipped like a minute detail from the corners of his dream. She was seated opposite him across the wide table. He coughed and cleared his throat, feeling somewhat foolish at having been caught napping. She gave no indication that she had noticed him, but he found himself wondering and imagined for a second that he could see a smile barely concealed on her face. She did not look up and the light from the low sun coming through the window filled her hair with gleaming strands of woven silver and gold. She had her head down and was scribbling away furiously. He noticed with a start the way the shadow of the window frame touched her neck. She was bent slightly away from the light. The eloquent arch of the fingers of her left hand stretched across the paper.

Then she looked up.

At that precise moment a ray of sunlight passed through her eyes, flooding the room with startled beams of livid warmth. He was adrift, floating in a sea of liquid, molten life. What had changed? These were the same eyes that he had seen and avoided for weeks and months and this was the very same sun towards which he had turned his face like a lizard whenever it presented itself; upon which he had gazed for all the useless years of his life, all the worthless years that he had lived up until this particular precise moment. But this time the light from her was focused on him. She was looking at him, and it was as though in that instant in which she looked up, that he came into being. A part of him that had been dead to the world was suddenly located; accurately, precisely charted.

She was talking, but he did not hear her words. He saw the movement of her lips and yet he could not make out a single syllable.

It was a simple, singular, solitary moment.

From that moment onwards he began to notice things, odd things: faint scents which seemed to fill the room. Scents which he had never paid attention to before. His ears became so sensitive that the very slightest creak of a footstep on the stairs sounded like a mountain falling into the sea. The skin of his fingertips became soft and sensitive as a baby's. He could barely stand the rough touch of the paper that he wrote upon. His palms were constantly damp and he felt dizzy as though he had consumed a barrel of Cretan wine. He could not sleep, nor could he summon the strength to rise from his bed in the morning. He could not understand a word that he read. No matter how hard he tried, it was as though his eyes could only graze the surface of the page without lifting a single word.

Other things, too, began to come to his attention, such as the curve of her mouth, the even rows of her teeth, the soft arc of her lips, the way the light draped itself across her cheek.

He has begun to experience pain, a real physical ailment that grips his inner organs. It is the pain of separation, and of uncertainty, and he has never known such feelings before. He lies in bed racked with fever for three days. The pain does not subside, but on the contrary increases for every moment that he is alone. He listens for the sound of her footsteps in the hall. He hears the light sound of her laughter in the creak of the night.

To her sun, he was the hidden face of the moon. He felt the shadows which fanned out from his arms and back like rigid, tarry wings, weighing him down, until he felt unbearably heavy and barely able to move. She was a gleaming mercurial pool of light and calm into whose warm embrace he longed to glide. She represented a geometry so complex and sublime as to make the latticework of stars that illuminated the heavens pale into worthless distant ornament. She was vibrant and they were tarnished baubles.

He is looking for a translation, a transformation, a change of form. A metamorphosis that would enable him to reach her. She was distant, airy and floated ethereally above the ground, while he was immobile and clumsy as a felled tree. His feet swelled and his shoulders stiffened. He bumped into walls and stubbed his toes. He spilt ink across the table. His fingers grew long and wooden, his nails became claws.

The silvery lock of hair that spilled down from her forehead was a mystical sign, making him think of astrological mystery and spells that tie up the fingers of the soul in knots. She marked the way towards a knowledge for which he felt unprepared but, more than that, unworthy.

The way her fingers curled and uncurled, their tips grazing the surface of the paper, made him almost scream out in pain, for he had become so attuned to her every gesture, every movement, that it was as though the rough paper was his skin.

As the light surrounding her swells and radiates, so does he feel himself repelled, pushed backwards into the corners of gloom, blinking like an owl in the daytime. He is the poor relative at the ceremony bringing only old bones and a much flea-bitten and scruffy hide. She is beyond his reach and yet, like an idiot or a child, he insists on stretching his hand out towards the flame.

He is suspended in mid-air, unable to fall or fly. He wishes he could offend her and have it over and done with. He cannot tread this line eternally.

Narcissus knows that the beauty which gazes back at him from the brook is not his own. His folly is that he wishes to make it so. And yet he knows that in the moment in which he reaches out to touch the shimmering chimera, it will fall apart in his hands. In the instant in which he traverses the boundary between the hand and the eye, he will destroy the very object of his desire.

And yet the fever persists. He discovers that he can detect her scent in the air; long before he even sees or hears her approaching, he is aware that she is nearby. He walks through the stables and stops still realizing that she passed this way hours ago, perhaps days. He blinks and looks around. Suddenly the very ground upon which he places his feet fills him with trepidation. His days are now numbered.

He looked from the window towards the east. A curious orange glow had appeared on the horizon. It seemed to swell and pulsate like a huge firefly. A pillar of black smoke rose into the sky. Somewhere something was burning fiercely and Rashid wondered to himself if his eyes were beginning to deceive him, or whether this, too, was perhaps a sign.

CHAPTER THIRTY

His last day at the excavation site and Okking, in a rash moment of impulsiveness, had invited Hassan to come to his house that evening for dinner. It was out of courtesy, Hassan realized, the intention being to formally mark the end of their period of working together. He also knew that it was not an easy gesture for Okking to make. People in these parts did not, as a rule, invite strangers into their house to eat. Although they had been colleagues of a kind for nearly three weeks, they still knew next to nothing about one another. Perhaps it was a hint, that he had reached the end of his time here and should begin to think about going back home. Oddly enough he now felt reluctant to leave. Nor did he feel much like indulging in the polite conversation required to get through such an evening. He stared at the blinking cursor on the screen in front of him. It was all slipping out of his fingers. He was beginning to wonder to himself what he would do with all this material when he had finished. It could not be described as an academic dissertation, for he had long since stepped over the line between the available facts and his imagination. A work of fiction then, describing the apparent arrival of a visitor from the Middle East at the beginning of the seventeenth century? An unlikely story in its own right. The facts, those that he had accumulated, were few and far between. He was certain that the man had existed, that his reasons for travelling here were probably not those for which he had been credited.

He had begun to think of Rashid al-Kenzy as a kind of catalyst. His Rashid, that is. An outside element that, once introduced, tended to accentuate the light in some way.

The Okkings lived in a large modern villa, modestly lodged down an unassuming side road on the outskirts of the town. It took him more than an hour to find it. He lost his way and had to stop to ask directions twice. It was not the kind of house Hassan would have associated Okking with. It was neat and orderly and seemed almost like a doll's house the way everything appeared to fit into place. The hallway had nice, lightly varnished wood on the floors and a large mirror at the end of it. Okking's wife was a slim, tidy woman in her mid-fifties, her dark hair peppered with grey and clipped into a tidy, business-like bob that fell almost to her shoulders. She had a thin string of pearls around her neck and wore a dark cardigan and slacks. Okking wore slippers, his glasses perched on the end of his nose and a bottle opener in his hand. Hassan thought about taking off his shoes, but the weather was dry so he settled for wiping them thoroughly on the doormat instead.

He made a few complimentary remarks about the house, determined not to overdo it. Mrs Okking, Ellen, took it in her stride, guiding him swiftly round in a casual, detached kind of way, as though she has been through this routine many times before. Okking himself made no comment. He remained civil, even a little awkward, as though the house were his wife's domain. The two of them sat in the living room while she busied herself in the kitchen. It was a long room, with one wall devoted to neatly ordered bookshelves and on the far side a wide window looked out over the pool of darkness that was the lake. A string of sodium streetlights picked out the town beyond.

'I hope that your stay here has been fruitful.'

Hassan smiled and sipped his wine. 'I am not certain how much my assistance has been of help to you.'

The large, red-faced man tipped his head to one side, in what was intended to be a noncommittal gesture of magnanimity, Hassan decided. 'Oh, all the museum people are very happy with your help. The items found could not have been identified and categorized without your assistance. Of course,' he scratched his brow, 'I hope it has not been too much of a bore for you. You have been away from home for longer than you could have expected.'

Hassan set his glass down on the table. 'Well, I have to admit that I am partly to blame for that myself. I found myself very intrigued by this whole case.'

'Of course. It is highly unusual.'

'Yes,' nodded Hassan.

'I don't think we will ever have all the facts. The gaps in the records make our understanding of the period incomplete.' Okking cocked his head to one side. 'Yes?'

Hassan shook his head. He had been about to say something. He stopped and then started again. 'I was just thinking what a shame it is that the records do not contain anything more substantial about the Arab who was involved in Heinesen's work.'

Okking shrugged his round shoulders. 'Such finds are extremely rare. Sometimes I think that the fabric of history is actually made up of holes, all the unwritten accounts, and voices which remain silent.' He was in a jovial mood, and took on the appearance of a kindly uncle entertaining a child. 'Of course, you are right. It would have been quite something.'

253

'I keep thinking of why the brass case was left behind. I mean, apart from its value, an instrument that he used in his travels to enable him to find Mecca, to say his prayers.' Hassan broke off, realizing that he had lost Okking's attention.

'More wine?'

'It just seems as though it must mean something, leaving it behind like that.'

Okking filled their glasses. 'I'm sure you are right, but it is impossible to say.'

The subject was quietly dropped. Hassan sipped his wine as Okking went out to the kitchen and his wife. He could hear the two of them talking in low voices.

The two of them emerged together. Mrs Okking sat down. Okking poured her a glass, which she sipped once and then never touched again

'Are you married?' she smiled.

He did not allow himself to be thrown by the directness of the question. 'Yes,' he said briefly. 'I have a little boy.'

The silence which followed began to close in on him. The woman sat forward with her knees close together and to one side, so that she was perched, like an elf on the branch of a tree. He knew what the silence was. He had been expecting it.

'You speak Danish very well.'

'I've lived here long time.' He spoke too quickly, too close to the surface.

She blushed. 'I didn't mean to pry, but you know how it is. We are all curious to know where people come from.'

He would have forgiven her, except for the 'but'.

'It's all right,' he smiled. 'I am quite used to it.'

Okking was making himself busy. The breezy wail of Count Basie rose from the stereo cabinet. He brought over more wine to fill their glasses.

'I have been thinking,' said Hassan, 'that I will perhaps do some more research on this case. I have contacts at the university in Cairo. Perhaps something can be unearthed from that side.'

'Well, I am no expert in that field, but I would not raise my hopes too high.' Okking sat back in the big armchair and scrutinized Hassan carefully, as though seeing him for the first time.

'Maybe I have been carried away a little with this whole experience. After all,' Hassan remarked, straining for a light-hearted note, 'I have never been to Jutland before.'

'Really?' intoned Ellen.

Okking grunted. 'A real city boy.'

They fell quiet again.

'There have been reports of visits to this country by Arab merchants, most notably Ibn Fadlan's famous account of his journey to the land of the Rûm. But there is something quite unique about this case.'

'It has caught your imagination, I can see that.'

Hassan leaned forwards, gazing at the flame of the candle between them. 'There is nothing to suggest that this man was a merchant, that his mission here had anything to do with trade of any kind. I believe that he was looking for something.'

Okking was clearly not in the mood for more talk about work. It was Friday and tonight he wanted to relax. Nostalgia was as close as he wanted to get to his profession. He laughed lightly now. 'I will tell you,' he said, 'when I first began to study archaeology I was completely obsessed. I burned with the desire to unearth the hidden stories of our ancestors.'

'He was so hard working, he hardly had time for any of us in those days,' she nodded.

'You get older, these things matter less.'

Hassan smiled along with them. He did not feel like going any further, did not wish to inform them of the hours he had spent letting his imagination guide his path, trying to get into the mind of an elusive figure, a four-hundred-year-old shadow.

The rest of the evening was, thankfully, taken up with the gentle ritual of dinner. The food was excellently prepared and quite conventional. The men made awestruck comments about the food that was served them: fluffy pastry shells with a mushroom filling followed by roast beef, very rare, with potatoes and sautéd carrots and then a small gâteau smothered in whipped, low-calorie cream. By the time they reached the cheese and biscuits Okking was beginning to show signs of wear from the amount of wine he had consumed. His eyes grew dull and he began yawning. The conversation had drifted towards their children, who were now grown up and moving away. The son was travelling around the world and the daughter was living in the capital.

'It is such a busy place. So many people, and so much happening.' The mother clasped her hands together on the table.

Hassan was wondering if this was leading towards an oblique comment about immigrants. Of course the capital was more 'cosmopolitan' than the province, she was saying, but young people today are so much better at taking care of themselves than we imagine.

They were worried. The city was hours away by train – another world, and one inhabited by people like him.

Hassan said his thank-yous and drove carefully through the sleeping town. There was hardly anyone to be seen, and very little traffic. Before long he was out on the other side, alone on the long road with the starlight and the trees.

Nothing moved in the village but his headlights. It was as he was getting out of the car that he noticed something was wrong. He locked the car and walked around to the front. The windows of the small house had been smeared in something that turned out to be a mixture of shaving foam and spray paint. Every window at the front of the house had been covered over. When he reached the kitchen door at the back he was relieved to find it still locked. There was no sign that anyone had forced their way in. A children's stuffed toy had been hammered to the door with a large nail. He pulled it off and held it in his hand for a moment, turning it over: a small, furry monkey.

He had been away too long, he decided. It was time to leave the past alone and come back to the real world. It was time to go home. Placing the monkey on the table in front of him he sat down. After a time he reached for the telephone and called his wife.

CHAPTER THIRTY-ONE

The shiny horses are coming – in a clutter of hooves, hard ground and iron on wood. The echo reverberates up the hillside, penetrating the porous silence of the big house and rattling off a chain of events. There is a stunned moment of quiet, burst by yet another round of hammering at the front door. Rashid is motionless. He hears the sound of people, many of them, hears their urgency. He steps cautiously forwards. Through the window he sees eight men standing around. They look strangely clumsy in their heavy clothes and big boots, their hands clutching long staffs, rifles, swords. The man at the centre of the group seems familiar and Rashid recalls that he was one of the three men who came when the boy died.

He does not hesitate for a moment. He moves quickly down the hallway, stepping lightly as he goes. The voices draw nearer. Heinesen, who had returned that night, has intercepted them and is loudly protesting while the other man is explaining.

Rashid descends the stone steps to the kitchen. The smell of wood burning and the trace of smoke from the fireplace. The door is ajar. He steps out into the cold air and sees the cook, who is bent with his back to the house gathering up logs from the woodpile. Rashid starts to move, slowly, carefully. Keeping his eye on the cook, he begins to climb the hill. The ground beneath his feet is frozen, and as hard as stone. It cuts through his boots, sending sharp jabs of pain through his feet. He is stumbling and his breath comes in short gasps. He is walking; he is running. If he can reach the top of the hill he will be able to vanish down the other side into the trees, and beyond that the moorland. He is nearly a third of the way up when he hears a shout from behind him. He turns to see the cook pointing up towards him. Two of the soldiers are standing there with him.

Rashid is running uphill again. For a moment it is as though nothing has happened in his life since that morning, which seems a lifetime ago, when the Yani-Ceri guards were on his heels. He still has not learned that escaping uphill is not the best of ideas. He curses his stupidity, he curses his vanity, and most of all he curses his feet for not finding a firm grip on the back of this stony carapace of a hill.

He runs with a thousand afreet after him and God in his wisdom knows that he ought to have made it, but the soldiers had horses and they were soon upon him. A blow struck him in the centre of his back, sending him sprawling. The air left his body as he crashed face down into the powdery dry snow.

They bound him up in knots and slung him like a sack of corn across the back of a horse. The others were waiting in the yard below. Heinesen shook his head in dismay as he climbed onto his horse. Sigrid said nothing, did not look in his direction. She climbed silently up onto the carriage to sit, face lowered, beside a tight-lipped Klinke. The soldiers sat astride their mounts, waiting for the order to ride off. From his position on the horse's rump Rashid watched the house receding slowly into the distance behind them – he thought it unlikely that he would ever set eyes on the place again.

The journey took most of the morning. It was a clear day. The sunlight was warm on his back. He watched the slow passing of the road beneath the horse. The town was larger than he expected. Woodsmoke rose from the chimneys of the cottages. They passed through a gap in the defences, a ridge of steep mud and straw that extended away on both sides from the western gate, disappearing down towards the glint of light on water. Muddy children stood atop this mound and jeered. One of them threw a clod of earth, and the others followed suit. A stone struck Heinesen on the forehead, making his body jerk rigidly in the saddle. The laughing soldiers abandoned their charges and bent down to begin returning fire. Overwhelmed, the children scampered away down the other side, out of sight.

Blood trickled down Heinesen's face. He shook his head to clear it. By craning his neck, Rashid could see Sigrid, her back upright, her head held high. He could not help but gaze in wonder at her poise.

They passed through streets thick with horse manure and sheep, twisted straw and broken twigs. The ruts of heavy carts like scars left by a dull blade. Men folded their arms and watched the procession pass by. Women covered their mouths in horror, some reached out to turn their children away. One man slapped his daughter in the face for staring too hard at Rashid. His eyes moved distractedly among them, their faces were grimy with sweat and dirt, their hands were hardened and bruised from work. Their clothes were simple, rough garments. He felt nothing for them, not pity, not wonder. He did not fear them; he feared their ignorance. They knew nothing but the soil in their hands, the smell of grass growing in the summertime, and the warmth of smoky fires in the winter.

The cathedral was still smouldering when they arrived. They drew to a halt at the centre of the town. Before them was a scene that filled Rashid with real fear. This was the fire he had seen glowing on the horizon the previous night; a sign, but not the one he had hoped for. The blackened stone, the wisps of smoke still issuing from among the collapsed ruins. The faces of exhausted men covered in soot and grime. People were kneeling on the ground, weeping. Heinesen descended from his horse and helped his sister down from the carriage. Hands grasped hold of Rashid and pulled him to the ground, where he remained, crouched with his hands still bound behind his back.

He watched as Sigrid began to move. She walked in light steps, absently it seemed, the way he had seen her move through the house so many times, picking her way through the debris of charred wood and burned clay and brick. The men who had fought the fire in vain slumped down to watch. She moved as though caught in a dream, stepping through the crowd as if it did not exist. Heinesen was confronted by Rusk, the priest.

'Your foul work has borne more evil fruit, Heinesen.'

'You speak in riddles, priest. The smoke has confounded your reason.'

The priest sneered, 'You would speak of reason?' He flung an arm out to point a finger at the ruins of the cathedral. 'First the death of the boy, and now this. You would claim that this was the result of reason?' He stepped past and raised his hands dramatically towards the sky. 'Good people, the house of God has burned to the ground this very night, and this man,' he stabbed a finger at Heinesen, 'this man talks of reason.'

'Get thyself in order, priest,' hissed Heinesen, but the priest brushed him aside. Rusk was beside himself. He rushed towards the crowd of onlookers. 'If ever there was a sign from above, then this is it. And what does that sign tell us? I ask you, good people, what does it tell us?' He was nodding his head, smiling in a strange kind of way. 'That there is evil among us, being perpetrated by members of our very own community. Take heed, I say, for this is a warning of the sternest kind. Our God-fearing community is being warned of the evil in our very midst.'

Heinesen turned, frantically looking for someone to appeal to. His eye caught on a figure standing on the periphery of the crowd, a man in a wide hat, carrying a fine walking stick in one hand. 'Koppel,' he cried, 'do something, for heaven's sake, man!' But the merchant simply shook his head once from side to side and looked away.

At that moment a cry went up from the crowd. Hands were pointing back towards the cathedral. Sigrid had emerged from the doorway, her clothes dotted with flames. She still walked with the same calm composure that one might expect on a sunny walk in the meadows.

'She walks through fire!'

Heinesen rushed forwards to reach his sister, but a group of men seized him first, holding him steady. He struggled furiously, but could not break free.

'What more proof of sorcery do you need?' yelled a triumphant Rusk. Three men rushed forwards to seize Sigrid. They tried to hold her without being burned and, with curses and howls of pain, they managed to beat out the flames that were eating their way up from the hem of her long dress. Klinke dropped down from the wagon and began to pull away the men from around Heinesen. A hand reached out and closed around a large chunk of brick which flew threw the air. Klinke fell to the ground with a cry as it hit him on the back of the head.

'They bring the devil himself among us, in the form of this wretched, tarry beast.' Rusk pulled Rashid roughly to his feet and thrust him out at arm's length towards the crowd. 'What purpose does he serve? I shall tell you. They have tampered with the firmament of the heavens, with their instruments and their spells. With their foul tongues and their curses.' The crowd was uncertain what course of action to take. Rashid could see the terror in their faces. A woman fainted, her eyes rolling up until the whites showed. He could smell their fear, which was like the fear of horses penned into a corner. They surged back and forth in their confusion. Rashid's legs began to give way. He struggled to stay upright, for any sign of weakness at this point and they would rip him limb from limb.

'First the death of a Christian child, and now this.' Rusk shook Rashid by the scruff of his neck. 'What evil sorcery could they not conjure up with the help of this apprentice of Satan's, whose body is the colour of darkness, a sure sign of his tarnished spirit? He carries the blackness of Lucifer into the world. What unnatural fornications has he not indulged in? Can we be sure that she is not the devil's whore, that she does not carry the fruit of his evil seed in her womb?'

The crowd began to grasp the magnitude of the danger which now stood before them. Nervously, the men were beginning to look to one another for a sign. Rashid seized his chance and, wrenching himself free, he flung himself onto the back of the carriage. He clambered to his feet, hands still bound behind his back and faced the crowd. He saw the terror in their eyes. Even they did not know what to do with this horror; they were immobilized by their own revulsion. It would take but a moment for them to gather themselves, to transform this confusion into hard-tempered hatred and then they would rip his arms and legs from his body and feed him to the birds.

Indeed, a low whisper had already begun to surface within the crowd; burn them! The darkness was closing in and Rashid al-Kenzy closed his eyes, drew a deep breath and howled like a dog, long and high and wild.

The crowd instantly fell motionless. They stopped breathing. There was a deathly silence. He surveyed them from on high.

He gasped or laughed, in exhaustion, in relief. He struggled to control his breathing.

'Good day, dear people,' he said loudly, addressing them in their own language. 'Is there food on the table? Is there fire in the hearth?'

There was utter silence for a moment. Whatever else Rashid might have been about to say, and his knowledge of their tongue was so severely limited that he would have had difficulty uttering another word, was left unsaid, for the silence was broken by the sound of laughter. It broke out in fits and starts, rolled itself into a ball and rattled around the town square in front of the charred ruins of the cathedral. They laughed and laughed and Rashid, not knowing what to do, not knowing whether this was a good or a bad thing, simply stared back at them.

'See what trickery he plays upon you,' raged the priest, frantically moving among them, trying to rouse them again, to literally shake them out of the spell. They brushed his hands aside. Rusk was left alone, raving at the sky, while their laughter echoed long and loud in his ears. The trial was forgotten, the work of the devil dismissed in paroxysms of laughter. Rashid could not believe his eyes. They had never witnessed a creature such as he speaking their tongue. He sat down in a heap, unable to take his eyes off these strange people.

Klinke was getting to his feet again. The blood had matted itself to his clothes and neck and he looked a horrific sight. He helped Sigrid and Heinesen into the carriage and then climbed up to take the reins. They pulled slowly out of town. No one tried to stop them.

CHAPTER THIRTY-TWO

Heinesen was never to recover from the trials of their ordeal that day. It was as though his very faith in man, and in himself, had been irrevocably shaken. He confined himself to his rooms, rarely emerging. He lost all interest in anything and refused to address any matter whatsoever. There was no mention of his ambitious plans. People came knocking at the door for work and left disappointed. Others arrived, bearing enquires from distant acquaintances, colleagues, friends, people wanting to know of his progress, but all of these matters went unanswered.

One day a fast carriage pulled up outside the door. Two men descended and lifted a long wooden box down to the ground. Leaving it there on the steps, they climbed back up and whipped the horses into a frenzy to beat a hasty retreat down the hillside. Rashid lifted the box and carried it into the gallery. He was alone. He undid the box and lifted out a smaller package wrapped in oilcloth. Inside this was a long varnished case. His hand rested on the smooth surface for a moment.

He pushes aside the gleaming catch and lifts the lid.

He knows what it is, knew long before he saw the long oblong box lying in the darkened hallway. His hands brushed the soft velvet and his fingers slid underneath to the smooth, gleaming, round softness of brass. He held it up towards the light and squinted at the brass plate screwed into the top: *Hans Leppershey, Mifddelburg, Zeeland*. He weighed the telescope up in his hands and shook his head at the wonder of the world.

Heinesen's condition deteriorated. His sister never left his side, night or day. Her face grew drawn and grey. Her eyes, once so filled with light, now began to flood with shadows. Rashid sat in the gallery and waited. He could no longer work. It was as though he were waiting, although he did not know exactly what for. He needed things to make their intention apparent. And so he waited.

A surgeon was summoned, a young man who seemed nervous and flustered, and ill at ease to be in the house at all. He immediately ordered that the house be boarded up and that no light should enter or leave for fear of contamination. All those in the house must remain there and all those outside should not dare to enter. Whether this was truly a measure necessitated by the sickness which ailed Heinesen, or was, as Rashid suspected, a measure imposed for the surgeon's own peace of mind, remained an unanswered question. He then insisted that all were made to gargle with salt water and told to wash their hands and feet with their own urine. An odd prescription, Rashid decided, refusing to comply with such filthy instructions. His distrust of such men was not surprising. He kept his distance and when asked he dutifully informed the doctor with a wary nod of his head that he had carried out the necessary task.

Sigrid remained by her brother's side. Rashid crouched by the small aperture in his room in the gatehouse, watching the movement of light through the upstairs rooms, knowing that it was she who carried the oil lamp. Once in a while he saw her there, standing at the window of Heinesen's room, looking out at the world. He felt the gulf between them widen with each passing moment. Closing his eyes, he imagined himself beside her; when he opened them again, the window was empty.

A week went by; the surgeon came and went each day, clattering by under the gatehouse as though demons were chasing him away from the place. The few remaining staff, the cook and his wife, lasted little more than the first week. Klinke was losing the sight in his eyes as a result of the blow he had received, and he departed one blue morning without warning. Rashid watched him stumbling clumsily down the hill, never once turning his head back towards the house.

The farm was now deserted and the stables went untended. The livestock, chickens, horses and cattle wandered freely round the yard with no one to care for them. From time to time some of them even got into the main house itself and could be found wandering about the hallway, chewing the straw on the floor and scratching at the wood with their hoofs. Hens nested under the stairs and eggs began to appear in the most unlikely of places.

CHAPTER THIRTY-THREE

He swings out through dark, starry space. The Scorpion is in the southern sky, low and elusive. Hands outstretched before him, he plummets.

A few drops of rain begin to spit on Rashid's neck as he puts his hand down into the murky black water. He was knee deep in it, but he could feel the bottom where the workers had laid the first flat stones. He lifted up his fist and clenched it, squeezing the mud from his palm.

They had struggled up the side of the hill with the aid of one frail pony, pushing the wheels with their hands in the waning light. The sky was like bruised jade, traversed by a shoal of dense conchoidal clouds gliding smoothly just above their heads. The excavation site was a maze of rain-dimpled blocks that lay scattered in an indecipherable code.

The cart was too heavy for the pony to pull up the last stretch, so they simply tied the hastily made wooden box to its harness and dragged it along the ground. Here and there it dug itself into the soft flesh of the hillside as though resisting their efforts, and they had to stop to free it. When they finally reached the top he rigged a pulley with the scaffolding and ropes and slowly lowered the rough coffin down into the western trench, then he swung down the rope behind it. She waited on the top, with the wind tugging at her clothes. On his knees he dug away at the far wall, which had not been sealed with stone. It took the best part of the day. His body shook with cold and he could barely feel his fingers. The rain started and then stopped and then it became snow again, the downpour punctuated only by the harsh grate of rooks from the high trees that circled the lake below.

He had to crawl inside the chamber that he had cut in the shiny mud. He crawled in until his feet were inside, out of the rain. He clawed away in the narrow space with his hands, trying to reach just a little further. It felt strange in there, with the earth above him and around him. This was the place where Heinesen would rest and perhaps it was fitting that he should be buried here beneath the very monument he had dreamed up, but all Rashid wanted now was to be done with it.

He drew himself backwards out of the chamber, careful not to pull on the walls for fear of bringing them down on him. Then he was out. He had little strength left now, but began pushing and lifting, slowly edging the wooden chest into the hole. It almost fitted. The stubborn length of a handspan still protruded from the hole. He was too weak and tired to pull it out and begin again, so he bent forward and, putting his back to it, tried rocking it from side to side to ease it further in. Nothing worked. He was exhausted. His hands and fingers were shaking and he hardly had the strength to stand on his own two feet. The snowflakes landed in the damp shiny pools around his feet to melt and vanish. He glanced up towards where she stood and yelled for her to turn away. She did not seem to understand and so he shouted again, waving his hand. This time she moved, stepping back away from the rim of the trench, out of sight. Then he lifted the shovel high into the air and with a cry plunged it into the chest. There was a splintering sound. He raised it again and there was a crack. The end of the chest burst into two and out of this Heinesen's blue face thrust itself into the rain.

Throwing aside the shovel, Rashid got down and cradled the head in his hands. It was cold and frozen, like a kind of wood or stone, but harder. He tried to bend the body forwards and finally, with great difficulty, managed to force it further into the hole, bowing the neck forwards. The splinters of wood came apart in his hands and he threw them aside. He reached into his clothing and removed the brass box. He held it in his hands for a moment, and then reaching inside, he placed it beside the dead man. He began sealing the hole up; lifting handfuls of mud, he sealed up the entrance. He could see the side of the pale ivory face until the last handful coated Heinesen's left ear. Then he collected the smaller stones and built up a wall over the chamber entrance. He dragged a heavy slab along and levered it into place. The western trench would be slightly shorter than the others, but that could not be helped.

He hauled himself hand over hand up the rope at the end of the trench and together they hurried down the hill towards the house.

On the way down she collapses. Her legs give way and she folds up into a square of sodden cloth spread on the ground. He kneels without hesitating, pushes his hands under her, feeling the softness yielding to his pressure. The pain in his hands is gone. She shudders, her eyes flickering in deep troughs of dreaming. Her teeth grind lightly together. His muddy hand wipes the water from her face. This close, her eyes were like shells brushed gently by the undertow. Her lips were waves caught in the perfect expression of their motion. Slivers of light glanced off the bones of her cheeks and chin, and her hair was now free of the austere frame of her scarf. The soft hair which he had traced so many times with his eyes and now his fingers to the source where it vanished beneath the skull. This close, so much within reach, her beauty terrified him.

He rose to his feet with her wrapped to his chest and then staggered down the rest of the way to the house.

CHAPTER THIRTY-FOUR

He falls asleep by the big fire in the kitchen. She is beside him, crouched in a ball, staring at the flames. She has not moved for three days. He rises and walks again up through the silent house. He moves restlessly back and forth, trailing through the empty rooms, waiting. Outside, the huddled clouds have given way to a clear starlight. Soon, he knows, they will be coming, and this time there will be no quarter given, no mercy. They would come to cut the evil boil away from the skin of this world of theirs. For a moment he entertains the notion of staying. With her by his side, he could perhaps make a life for himself here. This was a place that was neither his nor, any longer, hers. The moment slips from his grasp.

As he turns away from the window a glint, like moonlight on metal, catches his eye; something stirs in the shadowy whispers of the gatehouse. He stands for a moment, watching but, seeing nothing else, he moves on. He walks through the great darkened gallery, feeling the volume of space looming above him. In the centre of the room is the telescope, a mound of books and manuscripts which he has collected.

Out of the darkness of his mind hands reach out for him and roughly pull him aside. He hits the wall with a thump. He is pressed into a corner of the hallway beneath the stairs. The shadows are speaking in quick, nervous voices. They smell of animal hide, tallow fat, and fear. They spit back and forth at one another in a torrent of confusion. He realizes that they are not afraid of him. That what they fear most is what they are capable of doing.

One of the faces looked familiar. The father of the boy who died. The priest is there too, Rusk, his face now subdued by shadows. There were ten, maybe more of them. He had the sense that there were others from the town outside, waiting. The priest stepped forwards, looked him in the eye for a moment and then turned away. There was a call from someone further away down the hall, close to the stairs that led to the kitchen. The others assembled quickly around him. Rashid thrust himself forwards, thinking he would delay them, long enough for her to get away. That was when he smelt the smoke.

The men became agitated. No longer worried about stealth, they shouted to one another. A large man attempted to descend the steps to the kitchen, but it was already too late. A few moments later he came staggering back up, coughing, choking. He was helped to his feet and by now the heat could be felt. Glowing embers, fragile orange stars floating in a cloud up out of the dark well below, like a long warm breath blowing into their faces. They stamped at the floor, beat at each other's coats to stamp out the light, fell over one another in their haste to get out through the front door. A tongue of flame now leaped up the stairwell.

He stood alone. How long, he could not remember. The house was moving. He could hear their hurried footsteps, urgent whispers in the corners of the rafters and walls. He thought he heard her voice, confused, tortured with guilt or pain, he was not sure, not sure that it was her and not the old dry timber yielding to the fire. The men were gone. He was

273

forgotten. Through the window he saw the large crowd gathered in the starlight, gazing up at the house. Then he was moving, back into the gallery, the smoke seeping up through the floorboards where he walked. He stumbled through the graveyard of instruments and ambition. He found a length of twine and began binding manuscripts and scrolls together, books and charts tied into tight bundles which he slung around his shoulders, knotted around his waist. The smoke made his eyes smart. He shifted the weight, distributed it around his body so as to allow him as much freedom of movement as possible. He was moving swiftly now, his eyes grazing the pages of things that had occupied him for so long. Numbers, words, figures tumbled before his eyes, trying to choose what to take and what to leave. He had learned all he could here, nothing more. He had learned that the sun was the source of the world's life and that the earth was a simple singing orb. He had peered into the well of knowledge and felt real fear.

He could think of nothing but her, that she was finally becoming that which she had always been at last, casting aside the shroud to reveal herself as incandescence, as light itself. He moved towards the doorway, cumbersome with his burdens. He paused, lifted the telescope from its case and, tucking it under his arm, stepped into the hallway without looking back. The floor was on fire; parts of the ceiling were falling around him. He felt his hands and face begin to shrivel and crack. Close by the window now, and out in the yard he saw the figures of men moving like fish submerged within the depths of oceans. Their faces aglow, they were cheering, raging, praying. This, then, was to be their sacrifice, for the dead boy, for the purity of their souls and the sanctity of their minds. He retreated, turned, found his way barred by flames, turned again and then once more until finally he reached the back wall of the house. He lifted a chair and threw it with all his might. The crystal lattice shattered and he fell through the tunnel of black stone towards the night. Then he was out, beating the flames away from his sides, the bundles of charred paper bound to his body.

He could feel the hair on his face burning, could smell the singed flesh in his nostrils. The cool air, nothing but the cool dark air. Already the flames and smoke were emerging in a thin trickle of embers into the night sky. She was rising through the night, fluttering grey ashes moving in the dark towards the precious stars. He began to climb the hill for the very last time. Coughing, perhaps weeping even, but always moving.

EPILOGUE

With this one eye, gaze out upon the world. Stretching out across the turbulent drumming of restless waves, out over the wax-green ocean towards the simple, perfect brush stroke of the horizon which remains, as ever, out of reach. Towards the very ends of the earth, and beyond. The hollow tubular instrument bringing what is distant near. A gleaming conduit that can reach out, forwards into the distance and the future, and backwards into the past.

The instrument in question is deceptively simple: a brass casing open at either end into which hard droplets of glass are squeezed. The light enters through the glass, bending as it does so – air and glass being so related – and passes, thus transformed, into the long brass tube of time. The rays are collected like so many threads and sewn together again, much like in the telling of a tale. What seems at first far thus becomes near. Time is hurled out at the void and the distant extinguished stars. The past reaches out and for a brief, fleeting moment the present is faintly illuminated.

In the distance he can hear the sound of the sea, a dull, mammalian thump across the sheet of ice. In the grey distance there is an inlet where a shaved forest of tall masts can just be glimpsed.

Paper licks and crackles about his body as he lies there in the wind, a destitute warrior of ancient times, weighed down with books and sodden parchments, useless, cumbersome instruments that might be mistaken for weapons. He is lying on a frozen stretch of unfamiliar land in territory that is alien and repelling. He has no idea of exactly where he is going; all he knows is that it has to be south.

A telescope, then.

Life swells, funnels through the brass casing. He clutches the sacred instrument in his numb fingers to stave off the ink which seeps from the clouds in the sky above him. His breath comes in short, shallow gasps that stab away at the inside of his chest. The wind huddles in the restless ditches and his turbulent dreams are invaded by the steam-breathing horses. The world has stopped moving and has drawn itself down, inwards into this singular, final twitch of mobility. He burns incandescently, briefly, like a moth flickering in the icy sheet of wind, in the flurry of snow.

His eyes are open, staring unblinkingly at the foggy bank that begins to envelop him as the words of Hermes Trimegistus come back: *'In the midst of all resides the sun, for who could place this great light in any better position in this most beautiful temple than there where it may illuminate all at once? So that it is called by some the Lamp of the World, by others the Mind, by yet others the Ruler. And Hermes Trismegistus calls it the Visible God.'*

He fumbles, raises the instrument to his eye and aims it at the thick clouds above him. Then a strange thing begins to happen. He feels himself rising upwards, up towards the viscous mass that whirls overhead. He rises through the glass, turning slowly through the grainy beams of light. Far below he sees the small, frozen figure wrapped in muddy rags, hardly recognizable as a human being, let alone as himself. The ice is an interminable sheet and the day is just a thin, pale blue rip in the grey cloud.

He finds himself floating upwards and backwards through time to where it all began.

The Scorpion has descended from the heavens and now crawls through the dry rocks above the orchard where he played as a child. He sees the green salamander clinging to the trunk of an apricot tree, hears the voice of his mother calling him.

The ice is eating its way into his body. He feels the stiffened reeds of grass crackling beneath him like fragile bones. The weight of the paper which he has carried is going to be the death of him. He reaches to his belt, draws the knife that is there and begins to saw away. The straps, belts, ropes which fixed this burden to his body give way. He sits up and lifts the telescope in his hands and looks at it. He has been chasing a sarab, a mirage – science cannot lead us anywhere, but back to ourselves. He gets to his feet and tosses the brass casing aside, hearing it strike a hollow note against the frozen surface of the world. It vanishes in the descending darkness. Across the sheet of frozen sea, in the distant twilight, he can make out the flicker of lamps being lit. His feet are wrapped in countless layers of cloth bandaging which are two numb and cumbersome blocks. He lifts one foot, and then the other. Slowly he begins, like a child learning to walk for the first time, to move.

In the quickening distance there is a nameless ship waiting for him and a passage to work his way south, back to the world he left behind, away from the dark climates. With each step, he tells himself, it will get easier.

The world tilts and he spills down the incline towards the patient, unassailable stars and the prayer on his lips is that he does not fall into the darkened gaps between the frail flickers of silent unspoken light.